I·N·T·R·O·D·U·C·I·N·G

TAIWAN
IN ENGLISH

by
Sandra S.Y. Tsai
Bruce S. Stewart
Thomas Chung
Edward C. Yulo
John C. Didier

LEARNING PUBLISHING CO., LTD.

編者的話

應邀回國演講的名作家龍應台曾指出,在國外一提起台灣,外國人一致的反應是:a very rich country,對台灣其他方面的印象則懵懵然。

由這個事實可以知道,對國際友人「**英語介紹台灣**」(*Introducing Taiwan in English*)的機會必然俯拾皆是。

—— 老中 VS. 老外必須言之有物 ——

時下台灣正向已開發國家的目標大步邁進,在這種躍昇期間,各種問題層出不窮,可以提出來討論的 **issue**(問題)也跟著比比皆是。

例如,在台北市曾出現數以千計的農民走上街頭,抗議美國農產品「入侵」台灣,影響本地農民生計,在抗議標語中,赫然出現 " *Yankee Go Home!* "(美國佬滾回家!), " *Down with American Imperialists!* "(打倒美國帝國主義者!)等第三世界國家典型的反美口號。而 *AIT* (*The American Institute in Taiwan* ,美國在台協會)對這些抗議的反應是發表了一篇聲明,聲明中辯解台灣農產品問題不應怪罪給美國:" *Instead, the problem is probably due to **inadequacies in the marketing and distribution networks, overproduction and the changes of consumers' tastes**.* "(反之,問題可能是由於**市場行銷、經銷網的不足,生產過剩及消費者口味的改變**所造成。)

這次抗議事件正是「英語介紹台灣」的一個活生生例子。

—— 用最傳神的英語‧介紹台灣此時此地 ——

又例如，現在政治翻案事件時有所聞，以 *reversion of previously held verdict* 來表示翻案並沒有錯，但是如果用 *political archaeology* 或 *dragging historical skeletons out of the closet* 則高段多了。

所謂 ➡ ➡ ➡ *A doubting Thomas hates a lot of bunk.*
（懷疑的人討厭胡扯一通。）

在向外國人介紹斯土斯民時，您必須把說話的對象都當成是 doubting Thomas，言之有物自然就不會造成 a lot of bunk。

「英語介紹台灣」這本書能告訴您如何言之有物。

本書涵括的內容應有盡有，舉凡全省各大觀光勝地、節慶、傳統藝術、民俗，以及外國人最關心的 issue 等皆詳列在內，結合**名勝、風土民情介紹與此時此地現實中的涓流點滴**。教您中國式的幽默，如何用英語表達，在編排方面，綜合了「深入淺出」、「方便記憶」的特色，讓您在 VS.老外時，英語思路靈思泉湧！

當台灣的水碧山青，透過您的介紹，「汩汩而流」地呈現在外國人面前時，別忘了讓我們分享您的驕傲與喜悅！同時，本書從最初搜集資料到編寫、定稿，每一階段均投以極大的心血，如有疏漏之處，敬祈各界先進不吝斧正為荷。

編者　謹識

本書採用米色宏康護眼印書紙，版面清晰自然，不傷眼睛。

CONTENTS

Chapter 1　環島采風篇・Tour Sites

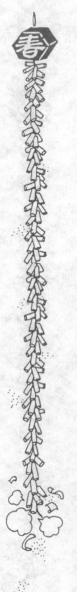

Chapter 2 台灣風情畫 A Window to Taiwan

Chapter 3 節日・Festivals

Chapter 4 文化・Culture

Chapter 5　社會・Society

Chapter 6　問題・Issues

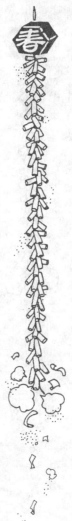

Chapter 7 接待外賓基礎會話 Basic Conversation

本書另附有高品質錄音帶四捲500元，由美籍電台播音員錄音，配合學習，效果更佳。

Chapter 1

TOUR SITES

二 環島采風篇

LUNG SHAN TEMPLE

巧奪天工‧神佛合一的寺廟

位於萬華的龍山寺是台北市**最古老的廟宇**（*the oldest temple*），至今已有二百二十餘年的歷史。清朝乾隆年間，福建省渡海來台的人士，特別由福建晉安縣海鄉龍山寺分靈建廟，寺內主祀**觀音菩薩**（*the Goddess of Mercy*），以祈求海上航行者的平安。此外，也同時奉祀**媽祖**（*Matsu, Goddess of the Sea*）、**海龍王**（*the Dragon King*）、**十八羅漢**（*the eighteen saints*）、**城隍爺**（*the City God*）、**土地公**（*the God of the Earth*）、**關聖帝王**（關羽，*Kuan Yu*）、註生娘娘等，是典型神佛合一的寺廟。

龍山寺向來以雕工考究的**寺廟建築**（*architecture*）為人所稱道，其建築工程龐大而耗時，僅大殿中的六對花崗石蟠龍大柱就花了二十幾位名匠三年的時間才雕刻完成。上面浮雕有山水花木、八仙、十八羅漢、龍鳳、水族、以及歷史故事，雕工精細而生動。寺廟內部的雕刻也相當精巧，其中以正殿內的**藻井**（*plafond*）和**神龕**（*sanctuary*）最為出色。想要欣賞到中國式寺廟建築之美，必然不能錯過龍山寺。

龍山寺的香火十分鼎盛，與北港朝天宮齊名並稱。每**年元宵節**（*the Lantern Festival*）時，寺內所舉辦的放水燈、花燈大展等活動更是人山人海，擠滿了大批前往觀賞的人潮。此外，每月初一、十五，各地的善男信女也會固定來此**朝拜**（*worship*）祈福。

近年來，龍山寺已經成為台北市內重要的觀光據點，因此寺廟的管理與發展都朝著吸引觀光客的目標，使得很多活動已不再保有濃厚的地方色彩，而逐步沾染上商業化的氣息了。

TOPIC 1

龍山寺 Lungshan Temple

📼 Introducing Taiwan

- *architectural note* : Lungshan (Dragon Mountain) Temple is regarded as the island's finest example of temple architecture. The original structure of the temple, completed in 1740, was razed by an earthquake in 1817 and later replaced by another that was destroyed in a typhoon in 1867. Since then it has undergone two more complete transformations, the first in 1926 and the second in 1959.

（建築小史：龍山寺被視爲是這個島上寺廟建築最精巧的例子。完成於一七四〇年的寺廟原始構造，在一八一七年一次地震中損毀。隨後取代的建築在一八六七年的颱風來襲中也遭毀壞。從那時起，龍山寺又歷經了兩次更完整的改建工程，一次在一九二六年，一次在一九五九年。）

- Besides Lungshan Temple is Snake Alley as it is more popularly called by foreign tourists. This place got its name for the various restaurants that have snake dishes as their specialty. The snakes are cut up alive right before your eyes. The gall bladder and the blood are drained and removed to be mixed with some wine as an elixir. The meat is then cooked in any way you like it.

（此外，龍山寺也是蛇巷所在,這是外國遊客對它愈來愈普遍的稱呼。這個地方由於有各種賣蛇肉特產的餐館而得名。蛇就在你眼前活生生的切碎。膽及血就被瀝乾，拿來和些酒混合起來當長生不老藥。然後，蛇肉可以煮成任何你喜歡的方式。）

** 蛇巷（ Snake Alley ）即指華西街。

📼 **Dialogue 1** ▶

外國人：I notice there are many temples in Taipei. Which one
would you advise me to visit?
我注意到台北有許多廟宇，你會建議我去參觀哪一座呢？

中國人：I would suggest you pay a visit to Lungshan Temple
in Wanhua. 我會建議你去看看萬華的龍山寺。

外國人：Is it an old temple or a modern *replica*?
這是一座古廟還是現代**複製品**？

中國人：The Lungshan Temple is the oldest *Buddhist* temple
in Taiwan. It was *originally* built in 1738.
龍山寺是台灣最古老的**佛教**廟宇，**最初**建於西元一七三八年。

外國人：Is it *noted for* its *architecture*?
這座廟以**建築聞名**嗎？

中國人：It has very *elaborate* roof *decorations*, large stone
columns, *woodcarvings* and gold-leafed Buddhas.
它有非常**精巧**的屋頂**裝飾**，大型石**柱**，**木雕**和金葉佛像。

外國人：Does it house many of these so-called Chinese "gods"?
裡面供奉有很多所謂的中國的「神」嗎？

中國人：The temple houses images of the Goddess of Mercy
and a number of other gods *venerated* in Chinese folk
beliefs. 廟裡供奉觀音菩薩的神像和其他一些中國民間信仰
所**崇拜**的神祇。

** replica〔'rɛplɪkə〕*n.* 複製品　elaborate〔ɪ'læbərɪt〕*adj.* 精巧的
decoration〔,dɛkə'reʃən〕*n.* 裝飾　column〔'kɑləm〕*n.* 圓柱；柱
woodcarving〔'wʊd,kɑrvɪŋ〕*n.* 木雕　venerate〔'vɛnə,ret〕*v.* 崇拜；敬奉

📼 **Dialogue 2**

外國人：Are any famous *festivals* celebrated here？
有沒有任何著名的**節日**，在這裏慶祝呢？

中國人：The festival that attracts the most people is the
Lantern Festival which *is held* at the end of the Chinese
New Year holiday. The Chinese have for a long time
celebrated the festival of Lanterns. At the temple
during the Chinese New Year you will see many Lanterns in various shapes and sizes, representing animals or other kinds of objects.
在中國新年假期最後所**舉行**的**元宵節**，吸引了最多人前往。
中國人慶祝元宵節已經有長久的一段時間了。在中國新年時，
你可以在廟宇裡見到許多大小不一、形狀各異的燈籠，代表
各種動物或其他種類的事物。

外國人：Is the temple very *crowded* during such festivals？
在這些節日裡，廟裡頭會很**擁擠**嗎？

中國人：In the evening it is absolutely *jam-packed*, but during
the day it is much easier to get around.
傍晚時分絕對是**擠得滿滿的**，但是在白天走動就容易得多
了。

外國人：Sounds like I should go there for a visit some time.
聽起來我應該找個時間到那裡參觀一下。

** festival〔'fɛstəvḷ〕*n.* 節日；慶典   *Lantern Festival* 元宵節
crowded〔'kraʊdɪd〕*adj.* 擁擠的   jam-pack〔'dʒæm'pæk〕*v.* 塞滿
get around 走動（＝ *get about*）

WANHUA

最富鄉野情趣的夜市

萬華(*Wanhua*)昔稱艋舺,是台北市開發最早的地方。清朝道光年間曾與台南、鹿港併稱「一府、二鹿、三艋舺」,一時極盡繁華。然而在時代的淘洗之下,萬華一地已不復昔日盛景,如今僅以龍山寺(*Lung-shan Temple*)古廟以及萬華夜市(*Wanhua nightmarket*)著稱。

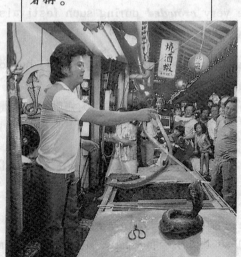

萬華夜市本身是以龍山寺為中心所興起的,許多來此朝拜(*worship*)的香客(*pilgrim*)便是基本的顧客。富於傳統風味的各種佛具用品店,以青草茶聞名的青草巷等都值得一一仔細瀏覽。

距離龍山寺不遠處是紅燈區(*red light district*)所在地華西街(*Huahsi Street*),街道兩旁以專賣補藥(*tonic*)和海鮮(*sea food*)佔多數。順著華西街走下去是一幅深具江湖鄉野情趣的畫面:光著上身在路旁打拳賣藥的年輕人不時高喝兩聲,引來不少路人駐足觀望;蛇店主人當場宰殺毒蛇,以招徠客人;野台戲在稍大一點的空地上搭起棚架,鑼鼓喧天中熱熱鬧鬧地演起一齣悲涼的傳奇故事…。這就是萬華,不時流露出台灣人民性格中粗略不拘的一面。

TOPIC 2

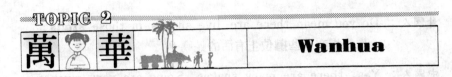

萬 華　Wanhua

[cassette icon] **Dialogue** ▶

中國人： Talking about going shopping, one place you should not miss is the area around Wanhua.
談到逛街購物，你絕對不能錯過萬華一帶。

外國人： Why's that? 為什麼？

中國人： It is a very popular place with shoppers and consists of night markets situated along a long street where there is a large variety of low-priced goods.
那是一個非常受逛街購物的人歡迎的地方，由位於沿著一條長街的夜市所組成，裏面賣有很多各式各樣低價位的東西。

外國人： What kind of goods do they sell? 他們賣哪些東西？

中國人： All kinds, but mostly those smaller *items* like *music cassettes*, cheap *casual clothing*, and things to eat.
應有盡有，但大部分是一些小**物品**像**音樂帶**、便宜的**便服**和吃的東西等。

　　　　　*　　　　　*　　　　　*

外國人： Are there any particularly special things one can eat?
可以吃到任何特別的東西嗎？

中國人： They sell quite an odd *assortment* of *delicacies*. One particular one is snake's blood. 那裏賣有相當多**各色**奇珍的**美味佳餚**。其中一項是蛇血。

外國人： Do you mean there are live snakes in those *stalls*?
你是指在那些**攤位**上有活的蛇嗎？

中國人： Yes, there are many snakes. Some are very much a-
live, while others have been killed and preserved in *jam-
jars*. 是的，有很多蛇。有些還非常活潑，其餘的則宰殺後
存放在**果醬罐**裏。

外國人： Can one see the snakes? 我們能親眼看到那些蛇嗎？

中國人： Yes. In fact, the storekeepers like to play with the
snakes. They tie them around their necks. When the
snake gets tired they kill it, *drain* its blood and then
hang the snake up in the front of the shop.
可以。事實上，那些店主人喜歡逗弄蛇玩。他們將蛇綑綁在
自己的頸項上，等蛇疲累了就殺了它，蛇血**流盡**之後再將蛇
吊掛在商店的前面。

*　　　　*　　　　*

外國人： What else is there to see in Wanhua?
萬華還有其他什麼可看的？

中國人： There is the Lungshan Temple. This is particularly
interesting to see on festivals when the crowds *throng*
to *worship*. There is also Huahsi Street, the *red
light district* where many *prostitutes* await *clients*.
那裏有龍山寺，在節慶假日時人們**蜂擁**著去**祭拜**，特別有趣，
值得一看。另外也有一條華西街，是**紅燈區**所在。有很多**妓
女**在那裏等候**顧客**上門。

HSI MEN TING

購物者的天堂

近年來西門町由於台北市不斷向東區發展，已經逐漸走上沒落之途，不復往昔盛況。然而西門町仍是台北人**逛街購物**（*shopping*）的主要休閒娛樂區，每逢假日，多少衣著光鮮、追求時髦的人士流連徘徊於西門町街頭，遲遲不歸。這裡也是青年學生們的樂園，**電影院**（*movie theater*）、**服飾店**（*boutique*）、**飲食店**（*snack bar*）、**溜冰場**（*skat-*

ing rink）或**迪斯可中心**（*Disco Center*）比比皆是。

沿著今日東門、西門、南門、北門勾畫出一條想像的連線，便是舊日西門町**城牆**（*the wall of the city*）所在，城牆之內為老台北的**市區中心**（*downtown*），即所謂的西門町鬧區。如今城牆早已拆除，餘留兩座城門佇立原地，冷眼旁觀台北的古今演變。以中華路圓環為中心向四面街區延伸，附近的區域皆涵蓋在西門町的範圍之內，包括武昌街著名的**電影街**（*Movie Street*）、成都路的商店區、重慶南路的書局、二二八紀念公園（舊台北新公園）、以及一間間金光閃閃銀樓店面的衡陽路，這些各具特色的街區經常擠滿了大批的人潮，與交相輝映的**霓虹燈**（*neon light*）構成一幅繁華昇平的市容。

TOPIC 3 西門町 **Hsimenting**

📼 **Dialogue** ▶

外國人： Which is the most crowded part of Taipei?
台北哪一地區最爲擁擠？

中國人： Do you mean in terms of **residents** or traffic?
你是指哪一方面，**居住**還是交通？

外國人： I mean the part of Taipei where you will see the most
people. 我是指在台北，哪裏你會看到人最多？

中國人： Of course, Taipei is crowded everywhere, but I think
the place where you will see the most people is **Hsimenting.** 當然，台北每個地方都很擁擠，但是我想，你會看到
最多人的地方，是在**西門町**。

外國人： What kind of people do you see there?
那裡可以見到那些類型的人們？

中國人： Mostly young people. They like to walk around the
streets, looking at the many clothes stores. Sometimes they go to see a movie.
大部分是年輕人。他們喜歡在街上到處閒逛，瀏覽許多家服
飾店。有時，他們則去看電影。

外國人： Oh! Are there **movie theaters** there? 噢!那裡有**電影院**？

中國人： Yes, several. In fact there is a street called **Movie
Street** which **is surrounded by** movie theaters. Most

** *in terms of* 以…觀點　　resident〔'rɛzədənt〕*n.* 居民

popular movies that come to Taiwan *are* first *shown* there.
有幾間。事實上有一整條街圍繞著電影院，叫做電影街。大
部分來台灣的受歡迎片子，在此首映。

外國人： Are there many places to eat or have a rest?
那裡有很多吃東西、休息的地方嗎？

中國人： There are many good restaurants in Hsimenting. The
only problem is that the traffic gets very bad in the
evenings. If you want a rest there are several small
hotels, but you must be careful as there are many
prostitutes in these *establishments* looking for customers.
西門町有許多不錯的餐館。唯一的問題是黃昏時刻交通狀況
非常差。如果你想休息，那裡有幾家小旅館。但是你必須小
心，因為有許多**妓女**在這些**建築物**裡尋找顧客。

外國人： Really? Then why don't the police do something to
stop them? 真的？那麼為何警察不設法制止他們？

中國人： They try, but *in practice* it is not so easy. Many of
these so-called prostitutes work as *hairdressers* and
masseuses and so it is hard for the police *to bring
evidence against* them. Besides, a lot of *gangsters*
are also in this *vice business* and they are not easy to stop.
他們試過了，但**實際上**並不這麼容易。很多這種所謂的妓女
以**理髮師**和**按摩女郎**為職業，所以警察很難**提出**他們**犯罪的
證據**。此外，很多**歹徒**也加入這項**罪惡的行業**之中，這些人
並不容易制止。

** *be surrounded by* 為…所圍繞   *be shown* （電影）上片
prostitute〔'prɑstə,tjut〕*n.* 娼妓   *in practice* 實際上
hairdresser〔'hɛr,drɛsə〕*n.* 理髮師；美容師   masseuse〔mæ'sɜz〕*n.* 按摩女
bring evidence againt sb. 提出某人犯罪的證據

The Shihlin Night Market

逛街休閒的最佳去處

士林夜市（*Shihlin night market*）是台北市著名的購物逛街（*shopping*）場所。整個夜市所涵蓋的範圍相當廣大，分為兩部分：一部分以慈誠宮為中心，包括對面市場內所有的小吃攤位（*snack stand*）以及市場外延伸至基河路、金雞廣場周圍地區；另一部分以陽明戲院（*Yangming Theater*）為主，向周圍擴張，包括安平街、大東路與文林路所圍成的整個弧形區域，如今這兩部分已經相互連成一片了。新近在光華戲院附近的街道也逐漸形成另一個獨立的夜市，士林夜市的規模正不斷地在擴大。

每逢傍晚時分，士林夜市便開始湧進一波又一波的人潮，吱吱喳喳的叫鬧聲響徹道旁，不時揚起一片哄笑。各式各樣的小吃（*snack*），大餅包小餅、水煎包、蚵仔煎、蜜豆冰、雪花冰、豆干等都遠近馳名，由於消費都相當低廉，很受逛街人們的歡迎。舉目所及，每個人皆手拿一袋食物，悠閒地瀏覽著一間又一間的商店。

過了晚飯時刻，逛街人潮中還有許多是家人結伴前來購買夜市裏物美價廉的日用品（*daily necessities*），或是朋友、情侶們夜晚來此逛街消遣時間。一走進夜市，街道兩旁小販（*hawker*）響亮有力的叫賣聲立刻吸引住每個人的注意力；迎面爛燦耀眼的燈光，一間間商店裏擺售著衣服（*clothes*）、家庭用品（*family appliance*）、飾物（*ornament*）、錄音帶（*tape*）、小禮物（*little gift*）和文具（*stationery*）等，滿目繁華熱鬧的景象，令人不禁感染到某種喜孜孜的感受，份外意興高昂，覺得可以和小販們好好地討價還價（*bargain*）一番了！士林夜市的魅力除了應有盡有的各項新奇物品之外，該就是這份熱熱鬧鬧的氣氛使得大家摩肩接踵地趕集去吧。

TOPIC 4

士林🏮夜市　The Shihlin Night Market

📼 **Dialogue 1** ▶

外國人： Are there any places that are good for shopping but which are also cheap?

　　　　有沒有什麼地方適於購物，而且東西也便宜的？

中國人： You should try one of the night markets. The night market in Shihlin is famous and not far from **the Grand Hotel**.

　　　　你應該到夜市看看。士林夜市很有名，而且離**圓山飯店** 不遠。

外國人： Do many people go there? 有很多人到那裏去嗎？

中國人： Yes, it is usually very crowded in the evening, making walking difficult. However, in spite of the crowds, there are many interesting things you can buy.

　　　　有，晚上通常非常擁擠，連走路都很困難。不過，雖然人很多，但是那裏有很多有趣的東西可以買。

外國人： Oh？ Like what？ 哦？像什麼呢？

中國人： For example, clothes, shoes, and **ornaments**. What are sold at street **vendors' stalls** are certainly cheaper but usually a little **inferior** in quality.

　　　　例如衣服、鞋子、**飾物**等。在**地攤**上賣的東西當然比較便宜，但通常品質稍**差**。

外國人： Are the prices written on the goods?

貨品上面有標價嗎？

中國人： Very rarely. You have to ask the price and you should try to bargain. This is *enjoyable* and is a good way to *save money*. Make sure you compare prices first and don't buy at the first stall you see.

很少。你必須問價錢，而且你得殺價看看。那很**令人愉快**，又是**省錢**的好方法。一定要先比價，不要在你看到的第一攤上就買。

〔☰☰〕 **Dialogue 2**

外國人： Can one get something to eat at the Shihlin night market? 士林夜市有得吃嗎？

中國人： Since the Chinese are very fond of eating, there are numerous food stands. You can eat all kinds of deli-cacies at very low prices. However, you should make sure you eat with *disposable bowls* and *chopsticks*.

因為中國人很喜歡吃，所以那裏有許多飲食攤。你可以用很低的價錢吃到各式各樣的美味。不過，你得確定你是用**用完可以丟棄的**（免洗）**碗**和**筷子**吃。

外國人： Is this night market open late?

這個夜市開得很晚嗎？

中國人： Yes. These "night markets" are often open well past midnight.

是的。這些「夜市」經常開到午夜過後。

外國人：Is it safe to stay at a place like that into the small hours？

在那種地方待到午夜三、四點，安全嗎？

中國人：There is little danger of being **attacked**, but you must be aware of **pickpockets** when there are many people.

很少有被**攻擊**的危險，不過人多的時候，必須要注意**扒手**。

the Grand Hotel 圓山大飯店　　　ornament〔'ɔrnəmənt〕*n*. 飾物

vendor〔'vɛndɚ〕*n*. 小販

stall〔stɔl〕*n*. 攤位　　*street vendor's stall* 地攤

inferior〔ɪn'fɪrɪɚ〕*adj*. 較差的

enjoyable〔ɪn'dʒɔɪəbl̩〕*adj*. 令人愉快的

disposable〔dɪ'spozəbl̩〕*adj*. 用後即可丟棄的　　bowl〔bol〕*n*. 碗

chopsticks〔'tʃɑp,stɪks〕*n. pl.* 筷子

small hours 午夜後的三或四個小時　　attack〔ə'tæk〕*v*. 攻擊

pickpocket〔'pɪk,pɑkɪt〕*n*. 扒手

The National Palace Museum

中國藝術的寶庫

座落台北**外雙溪**（*Wai-shuanghsi*）的故宮博物院,是全世界最豐富的**中國藝術**（*Chinese art*）寶庫。其建築仿造當年北平故宮博物院的型式,外表宏偉而壯麗,於民國五十一年起建,民國五十四年國父誕辰紀念日舉行落成儀式。整個博物院面積佔地二十甲,四周青山綠水環繞,景緻十分清幽。

博物院是一棟四層樓建築:第一層是辦公室、演講廳、**圖書館**（*library*）所在;第二層陳列**青銅器**（*bronzes*）、**瓷器**（*porcelain*）、書畫和侯家莊墓園模型;第三層展示圖書文獻、碑帖、書畫、**玉器**（*jade*）等;第四層則是專

題研究室。每次館內展覽共陳列近乎七千多件藝術作品,**每過三個月**（*every three months*）即替換一次展覽內容,令人可想見其館藏文物之浩瀚龐大。這些**無價**（*priceless*）且珍貴的中華文物,正足以代表五千年來輝煌的歷史。

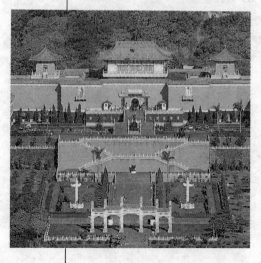

TOPIC 5

故宮博物院　The National Palace Museum

- The National Palace Museum is located in the suburbs of Taipei, in Waishuanghsi. It *houses* more than 600,000 treasures of China, including *bronzes*, *calligraphy*, paintings, *embroidery*, and jade products. These treasures were *shipped* to Taiwan from the mainland. Guided tours are available every day and English-language tours are given at 10:00 a.m. and 3:00 p.m.

（故宮博物院座落於台北市郊的外雙溪。館內**典藏**了超過六十萬件中國至寶，包括**青銅器、書法、繪畫、刺繡**、玉器等。這些寶物皆是從中國大陸**船運**來台。每天都有導引之旅，英文解說在早上十點和下午三點。）

- There is also a garden in front of the museum, called the Chi Shan Garden. Having an area of about 7,000 ping（23,100 square meters）, the garden *exhibits* the beauty of Chinese *landscape architecture*. Among the pavilions, bridges and ponds, there is "Lotus *Pavilion*", which has eight angles. Beside the pavilion is a black stone, with "Lan Ting Hsu" by Wang Hsi-chih *carved* on it. After a round of the museum, you may as well come here to enjoy the scenery.

（故宮前方有一個公園，稱爲至善園，佔地約7,000坪（23,100平方公尺），**展現**出中國庭園造景之美。在亭台樓閣、小橋池塘之間，有一座「蘭亭」，是八角形的，亭旁有一黑石，上面**刻著**王羲之的「蘭亭序」。故宮一遊後，你不妨到這兒欣賞一下此地的景緻。）

🔲 **Dialogue** ▶

外國人： I understand that Taiwan has some world-famous *museums*. Which is the most famous?

我了解台灣有一些世界聞名的**博物館**，哪一個最出名呢？

中國人： The National Palace Museum near Taipei *houses* the world's largest and most *valuable collection* of Chinese art *treasures*. It *combines* the collections of the former National Palace in Peking and the Central Museum in Nanking. 台北附近的故宮博物院**收藏**了全世界最多且最**有價值的**中國藝術**寶藏**。它**結合**了以前在北京的故宮和在南京的中央博物館的收藏。

         *   *   *

外國人： What kinds of *objets d'art* does the museum hold?

院裏有哪幾種**美術品**？

中國人： It houses more than 600,000 priceless Chinese treasures, some dating back 4,000 years. There are Tang and Sung paintings, carved *jade*, *exquisite porcelain*, *calligraphy*, *bronzes*, *cloisonné* and *lacquerware*, rare books and *documents*, *tapestries* and the *playthings* of Manchu emperors. 它收藏了六十多萬件無價的中國寶藏，有些可以上溯到四千年前。那裏有唐宋的畫、雕**玉**、**精美的瓷器**、**書法**、**青銅器**、**景泰藍**和**漆器**，珍（善）本書和**文件**，**繡帷**和清室皇帝的**玩物**。

外國人： That's really *impressive*. Can everything be seen in a day? **眞令人印象深刻**。一天內可以看完所有東西嗎？

中國人： No. You need several days. You can spend a whole day looking at one thing, for example, calligraphy.

沒辦法。需要幾天的時間。你可以花一整天看一樣東西，比如說書法。

＊　　　　　＊　　　　　＊

外國人： Do many people come here just to study, for instance, Chinese art or the history of art?

有很多人來這裏光做研究，例如，研究中國藝術或藝術史嗎?

中國人： Yes. Many Chinese and foreign students come here seeking research materials and are quick to *take advantage of* the opportunities offered at the museum.

有的。很多中國和外國學生來這裏找研究資料，而且能敏於**利用**院方提供的各種機會。

外國人： Surely a foreign student would have to be very good at Chinese before he could examine materials, etc.

當然，外國學生要很懂中文才能查資料等等。

中國人： Chinese is not that necessary. We have translated most of the *explanations* into English and we also have a *bilingual* magazine.

中文沒有那麼必要。我們已經把大部分的**說明**都翻成英文，而且我們也有本**雙語言的**雜誌。

＊　　　　　＊　　　　　＊

外國人： Can we take *photographs* inside the museum?

院內可以照**相**嗎？

中國人： No. Cameras are not allowed inside, but you can buy color *slide* reproductions of paintings and replicas of selected *masterpieces*.

不可以。照相機不准帶進去，不過你可以買到拷貝畫的彩色幻燈片和精選傑作的複製品。

museum〔mju'ziəm〕*n.* 博物館　house〔hauz〕*v.* 藏置

valuable〔'væljuəbḷ〕*adj.* 有價值的　collection〔kə'lɛkʃən〕*n.* 收集

treasure〔'trɛʒɚ〕*n.* 寶藏　objet d'art〔ɔb'ʒɛ'dɑr〕*n.* 美術品

jade〔dʒed〕*n.* 玉　exquisite〔'ɛkskwɪzɪt〕*adj.* 精美的

porcelain〔'pɔrslɪn〕*n.* 瓷器　calligraphy〔kə'lɪgrəfɪ〕*n.* 書法

bronze〔brɑnz〕*n.* 青銅器　cloisonné〔,klɔɪzə'ne〕*n.* 景泰藍

lacquerware〔'lækɚ,wɛr〕*n.* 漆器

document〔'dɑkjəmənt〕*n.* 文書，公文

tapestry〔'tæpɪstrɪ〕*n.* 繡帷　plaything〔'ple,θɪŋ〕*n.* 玩物

impressive〔ɪm'prɛsɪv〕*adj.* 留給人深刻印象的

take advantage of 利用　explanation〔,ɛksplə'neʃən〕*n.* 說明書

bilingual〔baɪ'lɪŋgwəl〕*adj.* 雙語的

photograph〔'fotə,græf〕*n.* 相片　slide〔slaɪd〕*n.* 幻燈片

masterpiece〔'mæstɚ,pis〕*n.* 傑作

石門水庫

SHI MEN RESERVOIR

水碧山青‧帆影點點

石門水庫位於**桃園縣龍潭鄉**(*Lungtan Village of Tao Yuan County*)，大漢溪中游。水庫的主要工程包括四部分：**大壩**(*dam*)、**溢洪道**(*spillway*)、**發電廠**(*electrical power generating factory*)和**環湖公路**(*round-the-lake road*)。除了具備**灌溉**(*irrigation*)、發

電(*generating electric power*)、**防洪**(*defense against flood damage*)和**公共給水**(*public water supply*)等功能之外，水庫周遭同時也是著名的渡假休閒地點所在，**亞洲樂園**(*Asia playground*)、芝蔴酒店、**仙島樂園**(*fairy island*)、童話世界、阿姆坪等，不論水上的活動或是陸上的遊樂，各種設備樣樣俱全。在歷經喧囂的都市生活之後，偶爾來此靜靜地遠眺清秀的山峰，近攬碧綠的湖水，水面上帆影點點，都足以令人心曠神怡，一解煩憂。

石門活魚(*live fish*)向來吸引著無數食客專程來訪。**銀鯉魚**(*silver carp*)、**金鯉魚**(*gold carp*)都是這裏的名海產，這些魚皆來自水庫裏清澈的湖水，絲毫不含泥濘之味，特別清新鮮美，遊玩之餘，不妨來上一道**活魚三吃**(*three flavor fish*)！

TOPIC 6

石門🐟水庫 Shihmen Reservoir

🔲 **Introducing Taiwan** ➤

- In Chinese "**Shihmen**"（石門）means stone gate. The reason it is called Shihmen is because there are two small peaks standing on both sides of the stream to form a canyon which looks like a stone gate.

（在中文裏，「石門」是指石頭做成的門。水庫之所以被稱爲石門，是因爲在溪流兩旁聳立著兩座小山峯，形成一道峽谷，看起來就像一座石門一樣。）

- Shihmen Reservoir is an excellent sightseeing spot and relaxing area and offers delicious fresh fish.

（石門水庫是一個絕佳的觀光地點和休閒地區，並且提供美味、新鮮的魚。）

- The Leofoo Safari Park is a sidetrip you can take from Shihmen Reservoir. The place boasts of the only wildlife preserve in Taiwan with animals roaming freely in its grounds. There is also a bird sanctuary within. A dip in its swimming pool can help you cast away a sizzling summer's day.

（六福村是你從石門水庫可以附帶去玩的地方。這個地方誇稱爲台灣唯一的野生動物保護區，動物可以自由地在地上漫遊。裏面也有鳥類禁獵區。在六福村游泳池中泡一下水可以幫助你拋去炎炎的夏日。）

** preserve〔prɪˈzɜv〕*n.* （魚或獸的）保護區
sanctuary〔ˈsæŋktʃʊˌɛrɪ〕*n.* （鳥類）禁獵區

📼 **Dialogue** ▶

外國人： Are there any recreational lakes in Taiwan?
台灣有任何可供遊樂的湖泊嗎？

中國人： Sure, there are quite a few. A favorite among them is Shihmen Reservoir.
當然，相當多。其中石門水庫最受人歡迎。

外國人： Where's that? 位於哪裏？

中國人： It's at Lungtan Village, 52 kilometers — 32 miles — southwest of Taipei, nestled among peaks of the Central Mountain Range.
在龍潭鄉，位於台北西南方五十二公里（即三十二英哩）的地方，環抱在中央山脈群峯之間。

外國人： Is it tourable in one day?
一天之內可以遊覽完畢嗎？

中國人： Yes, but there are also two resort hotels located only a stone's throw from the bus station at the east end of the dam. One of them is a Chinese-style building with traditional vibrant red outer walls and a green tile roof. 可以。不過，那裏也有兩間渡假旅館，離公車站只有幾步而已，在水庫的東邊盡頭。其中一間是中國式建築，有傳統喜氣洋洋的紅色外牆和綠瓦的屋頂。

** nestle〔'nɛsl̩〕v. 抱；偎依
(*within*) *a stone's throw* 很接近；一擲之遙

外國人： What is there to do there?

那裏可以從事什麼娛樂活動？

中國人： Sailing and motorboating on rented boats are popular activities, and the reservoir is open to licensed fishing as well. Perhaps the loveliest attraction of all is the round-the-lake lane, shaded by magnificent trees. Finally, there is Fairy Island, situated in the middle of the reservoir, where aborigines perform dances for visitors. Before the reservoir was completed in 1964, Fairy Island was actually a mountain peak.

租船航行和駕汽艇都是很受歡迎的娛樂。水庫同時也開放給經過許可的釣魚活動。其中最美的誘人之處，或許該算是環湖小徑，路兩旁垂蔭著高大壯麗的林木。最後，位在水庫的中央有仙島樂園，那裏有原住民為觀光客表演舞蹈。在水庫完成於一九六四年以前，仙島樂園實際上是一座山峯。

*　　　　　*　　　　　*

外國人： How long did the reservoir's construction take to complete?

水庫的興建工程花了多久的時間才完成？

中國人： Eight years, having commenced in 1956.

八年，從一九五六年開始興建。

外國人： How much did it cost to build?

建造工程花了多少錢？

中國人： US$85 million. Not cheap, huh?

八千五百萬美元。不便宜，嗯！

外國人：No... How big is the reservoir?
不便宜…水庫有多大？

中國人：8 square kilometers, or 3 square miles.
八平方公里，即三平方英哩。

外國人：Are there any other tourist attractions in its vicinity?
附近有沒有其他的觀光勝地？

中國人：Yes. There are the Window on China complex and the
Leofoo Safari Park, both within a half hour's drive
of Shihmen.
有，離石門半小時的車程以內，有小人國和六福村野生動物
園。

recreational〔,rɛkrɪ'eʃənl̩〕adj. 娛樂的；消遣的
favorite〔'fevərɪt〕adj. 最喜愛的　　n. 最受喜愛之人或物
reservoir〔'rɛzɚ,vwɔr〕n. 水庫　　kilometer〔'kɪlə,mitɚ〕n. 公里
nestle〔'nɛsl̩〕v. 擁抱　　tourable〔'tʊrəbl̩〕adj. 可遊覽的
resort〔rɪ'zɔrt〕n. 觀光勝地
within a stone's throw 近在呎尺；在投石可及的距離內（=*quite near*）
vibrant〔'vaɪbrənt〕adj. 活潑的　　tile〔taɪl〕n. 磚瓦
motorboating〔'motɚ,botɪŋ〕n. 駕汽艇之運動
license〔'laɪsn̩s〕v. 許可　　attraction〔ə'trækʃən〕n. 吸引人的事物
lane〔len〕n. 小徑　　magnificent〔mæg'nɪfəsn̩t〕adj. 壯觀的
aborigines〔,æbə'rɪdʒə,niz〕n.pl. 原始的居民；土著
construction〔kən'strʌkʃən〕n. 建築　　commence〔kə'mɛns〕v. 開始
vicinity〔və'sɪnətɪ〕n. 附近　　complex〔'kɑmplɛks〕n. 複合物

小人國

WINDOW ON CHINA

融傳統與現代於一爐

小人國位在桃園縣龍潭鄉，是台灣唯一展覽縮小模型（ *miniature* ）的遊樂場所。自從興建以來，即吸引大批好奇的民眾前往觀賞。裏面的模型係以荷蘭「小人國」的做法為藍本，以二十五分之一的比例，展現出全世界各地的建築風貌，將世界各大洲的奇景奇觀融於一園。其內部劃分包括：迷你

中國、迷你台灣、神祕東方（ *Mysterious Orient* ）、夢幻歐洲（ *Fantasy in Europe* ）、非洲歷險（ *Adventures in Africa* ）、美洲新大陸等等，並且有一座室內的遊樂園，讓大人、小孩都能玩得盡興。

目前，歐洲的德、奧、英、荷等國都有「小人國」，

其中又以荷蘭海牙的小人國最具規模，歷史最久。而日本靜岡市也有一座。看到這些縮小的建築模型與人物，令人不禁想起 **格列佛遊記**（ *Gulliver's Travels* ）裏的童話趣味，以及那份童稚時無盡的幻想！

TOPIC 7

小人國　Window on China

📼 Question ▶

What is the " Window on China "？「小人國」是什麼？

📼 Reply ▶

The "Window on China" is the world's largest exhibition of *miniature reproductions.* It's located on a 30-acre park two hours southwest of Taipei and has reproducting of modern and ancient Chinese *architecture.* *Replicas* of *the Great Wall,* *the Forbidden City,* and Chiang Kai-shek International Airport are all there. The details of the reproductions, which are 1/25 of the *original size,* are so carefully done that photographs of them cannot be distinguished from the real thing. The models are constructed with tiny bricks, stones, and roof tiles. They're painstakingly laid out piece by piece following the actual *construction plans.* The models are so flawlessly reproduced that architecture professors send their students to visit as part of their studies.

「小人國」是世界上最大的**縮小模型複製品**展覽會。它位於離台北西南方有兩小時路程的三十英畝公園裏，有現代及古代中國**建築**的複製品。萬里長城、紫禁城、中正國際機場的**複製品**都在那兒。複製品是**原來尺寸**的二十五分之一，每個小地方都做得很仔細，以致於它們的照片和真的東西使人無法分辨。模型是用極小的磚、石頭及屋瓦建造而成，照著真正的**建築設計圖**，很小心地一塊一塊設計出來的。模型複製得非常完美，所以教建築的教授都派他們的學生們來參觀，作為研究的一部分。

📼 **Dialogue 1** ▶

外國人： The details are amazing. 每個小地方都很令人驚異。

中國人： Here, use these *binoculars* to look at the *facial expressions* on the little people. Each one is *unique*.

這兒，用**望遠鏡**看小人兒們臉上的**表情**。每一個人的都很**獨特**。

外國人： *Incredible*, a lot of time must have been spent to make these. How is this whole place protected against the weather?

不可思議，一定要花很多時間來做這些。如何保護這整個地方，不被惡劣氣候侵襲？

中國人： Special building materials are used, so the models can *withstand* all kinds of weather.

我們用特別的建材，所以模型可以**經得起**各種天氣。

外國人： Besides the exhibition, are there any other things worth seeing?

除了這個展覽之外，還有其他值得看嗎？

中國人： Yes, there are performances of traditional *folk arts* every day, such as *lion-dance shows* and *stunt shows*. In addition, an indoor *amusement park* gives you both enjoyment and excitement, and the Universal Train offers free rides around the area. It's really a wonderful place to visit.

有，每天都有傳統**民俗技藝**的表演，如**舞獅**和**雜技表演**。此外，有一座室內的**遊樂區**，能給你歡樂和刺激，環球號火車免費載你遊園區。這真是一個遊玩的好地方。

▢▢ Dialogue 2

外國人： Hey look, I'm King Kong！ I'm gonna *trample* all the
little people to death.

　　　嘿，你看，我是金剛！我要把所有的小人兒都**踩死**。

中國人： Get out of there！ You'll ruin the display.

　　　走開！你會破壞這個展覽的。

外國人： I'm the King of the world！

　　　我是世界之王。

中國人： Hurry, get out before one of the guards sees you and
kicks you out.

　　　快點，在任何一個警衞看見你，把你踢出去之前趕快走開。

外國人： I'm just having a little fun.

　　　我只不過是玩玩罷了。

中國人： *Act your age*. 作些與你年紀相符的事吧。

PENGHU AND LANYU

風光旖旎的濱海島嶼

澎湖位於台灣西部台灣海峽（Taiwan Strait）海面上，為六十四個島嶼（islands）所組成的群島（archipelago），其中只有二十一個島嶼有人居住，其餘皆為無人島或礁岩。所謂的澎湖本島是指馬公、湖西、中屯、小門、漁翁、白沙等六個藉水泥大橋連接的小島。目前澎湖已是台灣省內一個獨立的縣治（county），以馬公（Makung）為中心城鎮。

一般人前往澎湖，最主要是瀏覽濱海島嶼亮麗的風光以及領略一下當地的鄉土民情，同時也順便採購澎湖著名的土產（local products），如文石、珊瑚（coral）、花生酥等。由於澎湖群島地形特殊，經年刮著強大的海風，令人望之卻步。一般說來，四月到十月之間最適宜前往澎湖旅遊，此時島上風光明媚，陽光普照，十分吸引人。

前往澎湖的交通，可以藉由搭乘輪船（steamship）或飛機（airplane）抵達；輪船以高雄為起點，往返於馬公與高雄之間；飛機方面在台北、高雄二地，遠東、復興、立榮、瑞聯等四家航空公司有往返的班機；在台中則是大華及國華二家航空公司有班次。

PENGHU AND LANYU

美麗・素樸的蘭花之島

神秘而遙遠的蘭嶼孤懸在**巴士海峽**（ *Bashi Channel* ）的北緣，距離台東四十九海里。黝黑的石礁海岸、乾燥的黃土地與鮮綠的草木，在刺目的陽光下形成一幅色彩強烈的構圖。

這裏就是**雅美族人**（ *the Yami* ）的故鄉，簡單樸素而原始，男人們下海捕魚，女人上山耕作，石牆與茅草屋頂是他們主要的住屋結構。來到蘭嶼的人一定不會錯過欣賞美麗的**木舟**（ *wooden boat* ），那些停泊在沙灘上憩息的木舟是民俗學家們研究的瑰寶，木舟的首尾翹然飛起，形狀極其優美，身身更畫上樸拙而精緻的圖案，不少人紛紛在此拍照留念。蘭嶼到處可以望見一片又一片的**水芋**（ *taro* ）田，近似於**甜馬鈴薯**（ *sweet potato* ），是雅美人的主食。

日據時代（一八九五～一九四五），**日本人**（ *the Japanese* ）曾經前往蘭嶼研究雅美族人並且將蘭嶼視為一座自然的**人類學博物館**（ *anthropological museum* ）。隨著時日推移，外來的文明力量如今已經開始襲向雅美族人，夾在舊的生活形式與新的衝擊之間而不知所措，正是目前蘭嶼的窘境。這塊美麗又陌生的**蘭花**（ *orchid* ）之島究竟該何去何從呢？值得大家來關心。

澎湖與蘭嶼

TOPIC 8

澎湖與蘭嶼 Penghu and Lanyu

🔲 **Dialogue** ▶

外國人： What is that famous *archipelago* off Taiwan's west coast？臺灣西部海岸外，那個著名的**群島**是什麼？

中國人： Penghu. It used to be called the Pescadores. 澎湖。以前被稱爲中國澎湖群島。

外國人： Is it worth going to？值得一遊嗎？

中國人： Yes, by all means. There are a lot of interesting sights. 是的，當然。有許多有趣的景色。

外國人： Can you name a few？你可以講一些嗎？

中國人： Yes. Perhaps the most *thrilling* (sight) is the Penghu Bay Bridge, which connects two of the archipelago's main islands. 好啊！最**令人震顫的**（景色）可能是澎湖跨海大橋，那連接了群島中的兩個主要島嶼。

外國人： What's so thrilling about it？那有什麼令人震顫的呢？

中國人： It's the longest inter-island bridge in Asia. 那是亞洲島與島之間最長的橋。

外國人： Yeah？How long is it？哦？有多長呢？

** archipelago〔͵ɑrkəˈpɛlə͵go〕*n.* 群島
by all means 當然；必是　　thrilling〔ˈθrɪlɪŋ〕*adj.* 令人震顫的

中國人：　Its *overall* length is 5,441 meters, or 6,060 yards, its *overwater* section extending 2,160 meters, or 2,362 yards.

全長五千四百四十一公尺，即六千零六十碼，水上部分長達兩千一百六十公尺，即兩千三百六十二碼。

外國人：　Great, but that's a long way to travel just to see a bridge!　好棒，但是那麼遠去旅行只爲了看一座橋啊！

中國人：　That's not all there is. Penghu *is dotted with* temples. There are 147 of them, and some are centuries old. The oldest one was built in 1593 to Matzu.

還有別的。澎湖到處都有寺廟。有一百四十七座寺廟；有些已經幾百年了。最早的寺廟是媽祖廟，建於一五九三年。

外國人：　Who's Matzu?　媽祖是誰？

中國人：　She's the Goddess of the Sea, and as such is every fisherman's *patron* saint. Fishermen worship her and/ or other gods before each voyage, and thank her/ or them upon every safe return.

她是海神，海神是每位漁夫的守護神。每次出航前，漁夫會拜媽祖以及／或者其他神，每次安全回來後也會感謝她／他們。

*　　　　　*　　　　　*

外國人：　Is there anything else to see there?　還有什麼東西可看嗎？

** overall 〔'ovɚ,ɔl 〕 *adj*. 自一端到另一端的
overwater 〔'ovɚ'wɑtɚ〕 *adj*. 水上的；海上的
be dotted with 星散於（地面）；點綴　　patron 〔'petrən〕 *n*. 守護神

中國人： Yes, there's also Hsitai Fort on Hsiyu Island, built
over 100 years ago.

有，西嶼島有西台古堡，一百多年前建造的。

外國人： What is there to see at that island off the coast
from Taitung?

台東海岸外的那個島嶼，有什麼東西可看的嗎？

中國人： Lanyu? The main *attraction* is the Yami, the most
primitive and smallest of Taiwan's 9 *aboriginal*
tribes. There are only 2,600 Yamis, and they all live
in 6 villages on Lanyu's coast.

蘭嶼嗎？**最吸引人的**是雅美族，那是臺灣九個**原始**部落中最
原始、人最少的一族。只有兩千六百個雅美人，全部住在蘭
嶼海岸的六個村落。

外國人： How big is Lanyu? 蘭嶼有多大？

中國人： It's 45 square kilometers — a little over 17 square
miles — in area. 四十五平方公里—— 比十七平方英里大一
點——就面積來說。

外國人： I think I'd like to go there.
我想去那裏。

** attraction 〔ə'trækʃən〕 *n.* 吸引人的東西
aboriginal 〔 ‚æbə'rɪdʒənḷ 〕 *adj.* 原始的；土著的

北部濱海公路

The North Coast Highway

浪濤拍岸的清涼去處

在台灣炎熱的夏季裏，湛藍的海水與清涼的海風是許多人消暑的好去處。北部濱海公路（the North Coast Highway）環繞在台灣北部的海岸線上，面臨台灣海峽（Taiwan Strait）與太平洋（the Pacific Ocean），從基隆（Keelung）直抵淡水（Tamsui），沿線除了野柳（Yehliu）附近遍布礁岩之外，其他各地，皆是一望無際的沙岸（sandy beach），翡翠灣（Green Bay）、金山海水浴場（Chinshan, Golden Mountain Beach）、白沙灣（Paishawan, White Sand Beach）等都是夏日弄潮的地點，適合游泳（swimming）、衝浪（surfing）、釣魚（fishing）…。

環遊北部濱海公路一週只需一天的時間，清晨自己開車到基隆沿路玩下來，黃昏時剛好抵達淡水，欣賞淡水令人嘆為觀止的夕照。如果想要好好享受一下夏日時光，也可以利用二、三天的時間，在各大海水浴場所附設的海濱別墅、旅館（hotel）過夜，聽聽靜夜裏拍岸的浪濤，也是一種難忘的經驗。🎵

TOPIC 9

北部濱海公路 The North Coast Highway

⬚ **Introducing Taiwan**

- Keelung is one of the wettest cities in the world. It rains an average of 214 days per year, mostly from October through March.
（基隆是世界上最潮濕的城市之一，平均每年有二百一十四天下雨，大部分是在十月至（次年）三月之間。）

- In 1629, the Spanish occupied Keelung and a nearby stretch of the north coast. Three years later, they extended their holdings to Tamsui where they built a hilltop castle they christened Fort San Domingo which inhabitants called Hung Mao Cheng（紅毛城）meaning "Fort of the Red Haired Barbarians."
（西元一六二九年，西班牙人佔領基隆和附近的北部海岸沿線。三年之後，並擴張他們的土地到淡水一地，建立了一座位於山頂上的城堡，命名爲聖多明哥堡，然而當地居民却稱之爲紅毛城，意指「紅髮野蠻人的堡壘」。）

- Aside from the Spaniards, Keelung has been occupied by different countries as well. The Dutch were there for 37 years after they expelled the Spaniards. Briefly, the French also occupied Keelung during the French-Chinese dispute in Yunnan-Indochina. Finally the Japanese have also, during their colonial rule on Taiwan, left their impression in Keelung.
（除了西班牙人以外，基隆也一直被許多不同的國家所佔領。荷蘭人趕走西班牙人之後，在基隆待了三十七年。法國人於中法在雲南——中印紛爭期間，也短暫的佔領過基隆。最後，日本人也在殖民統治台灣期間，在基隆留下痕跡。）

📼 **Dialogue** ▶

外國人： Are there any special attractions along the north coast?
北海岸有任何特別吸引人的地方嗎？

中國人： Yes, it′s a favorite tourist area with both foreign
tourists and R.O.C. citizens. A wonderful way to *see
the* north coast′s *sights* is to spend a day traveling
the North Coast Highway.
是的，那是外國觀光客和中華民國國民最喜愛的觀光地區。
遊覽北海岸**名勝**，有一個很棒的方法是花一天遊歷北部濱海
公路。

　　　　　＊　　　　　＊　　　　　＊

外國人： What specifically is there to see along the highway?
濱海公路沿線，有什麼特別值得看的地方？

中國人： Beginning in Keelung, one of the rainiest cities of the
world, there is the *enchanting harbor*, under the
watchful eye of a 22.5 meter-tall *statue* of Kuan Yin,
the Goddess of Mercy. The second point of interest is
Yehliu, or Wild Willow, a famous grouping of *coral
formations sculpted* by the wind and sea over perhaps
millions of years. A particularly interesting formation
is the Queen′s Head, so named because it resembles
the head of Queen Nefertiti of ancient Egypt.
從基隆，世界上最多雨的城市之一開始，有**迷人的港口**，在
二十二點五公尺高的觀音菩薩**鑄像護衛**之下。第二個有趣的
地方是野柳，有一群可能逾數百萬年以來，被風和海**雕鑿**而
成的著名**珊瑚岩層**。特別有趣的一個岩層是女王頭，因和古
埃及女王尼菲蒂蒂的頭很像而得名。

＊　　　　　＊　　　　　＊

外國人： Are there any beaches along the highway?

公路沿線有海灘嗎？

中國人： Yes. Only a short distance from Yehliu is *Green Bay*, a beach resort popular with fishermen and water sports lovers. Further along the highway is Chinshan, one of the most popular beaches in Taiwan. The highway ends in the west at Tamsui, a small town at the *confluence* of the Tamsui River and the Taiwan *Strait*. Tamsui is famous for its fresh, *succulent seafood*.

有，**翡翠灣**離野柳很近，那是很受漁夫和水上運動愛好者歡迎的海灘勝地。再沿著公路下去是金山，是台灣最受歡迎的海灘之一。濱海公路西邊的終點在淡水，那兒是個小鎮，淡水河和台灣**海峽**匯合的地方。淡水以新鮮、**多汁的海鮮**聞名。

＊　　　　　＊　　　　　＊

外國人： How long would this *excursion* take?

這個**旅行**要花多少時間？

中國人： About 7 to 8 hours, but there's an *alternative*: You could return to Taipei more quickly by turning *inland* at Chinshan.

大約七到八小時，不過有個**選擇的餘地**：在金山轉往**內陸**，可以更快回到台北。

外國人： Are there any sights to see along this route?

這條路線上有風景可看嗎？

中國人： Plenty! It's a *twisty* mountain road that leads through the Yangming mountain district of Taipei. Along the way there are *lush emerald* forests, *terraced* rice *paddies* and charming villages.

很多！那是一條**曲折的**山路，通向台北的陽明山區。沿路上有**青蔥如翡翠的**森林，**梯形的稻田**和迷人的村莊。

外國人： Can you start the trip in Tamsui and end in Keelung?

這趟旅行可以從淡水開始，到基隆結束嗎？

中國人： Sure, but most *tours* go from Keelung to Tamsui.

當然，但大部分的**旅行**是從基隆到淡水。

enchanting〔ɪn'tʃæntɪŋ〕*adj.* 迷人的   harbor〔'hɑrbɚ〕*n.* 港

statue〔'stætʃʊ〕*n.* 鑄像   mercy〔'mɝsɪ〕*n.* 慈悲

coral formations 珊瑚岩層   sculpt〔skʌlpt〕*v.* 雕刻

see the sights 遊覽名勝   bay〔be〕*n.* 海灣

confluence〔'kɑnfluəns〕*n.* 滙流處   strait〔stret〕*n.* 海峽

succulent〔'sʌkjələnt〕*adj.* 多汁液的   seafood〔'si,fud〕*n.* 海產食物

excursion〔ɪk'skɝʒən〕*n.* 遠足；旅行   alternative〔ɔl'tɝnətɪv〕*n.* 選擇餘地

inland〔'ɪn,lænd,'ɪnlənd〕*adv.* 內陸地   twisty〔'twɪstɪ〕*adj.* 曲折的

lush〔lʌʃ〕*adj.* 青蔥的；嫩綠色   emerald〔'ɛmərəld〕*adj.* 翠綠色的

terrace〔'tɛrɪs,-əs〕*v.* 使成梯形地   paddy〔'pædɪ〕*n.* 稻；稻田

tour〔tʊr〕*n.* 旅行

MT. TAIPING

古典空靈的奇景

　　太平山位於台灣東北部宜蘭縣境內，從民國三年起便開始經營林場（ *logging station* ），當時木材採伐業（ *tree-felling* ）曾盛極一時，名列台灣三大林場之一。如今由於林區逐漸縮小，台灣省林務局（ *Taiwan Forestry Bureau* ）便積極成立森林遊樂區（ *forest recreation area* ），向大眾展示充滿神秘而優美的太平山奇景。

　　太平山雖然海拔僅一九五〇公尺，一年四季却異常寒冷，整年的平均氣溫在十二度左右，一月最冷，常在零度以下。每到冬天白雪飄落山頂，一片銀色世界，引來了大批前來賞雪的人潮。往日山上運送木材所遺留下來的運材鐵路（ *logging railroad* ）、棧道（ *a log-formed road* ）、柴車、蹦蹦車、索道等，今日都成為太平山最特殊的景觀。除此之外，到過太平山的人永遠也不會忘記那片白茫茫的濃霧，經常午後便襲捲整個山頭，令人一時天地不分，眼見森林裏的林木一一幻化為空靈飄渺的景象，有時却又立即雲消霧散，令人捉摸不定。而太平山最吸引人的地方也正在於這股古典空靈，如霧一般的浪漫氣息。

TOPIC 10

太 平 山　Mt. Taiping

Dialogue 1

外國人：Are there any mountain *resorts* in northern Taiwan？
台灣北部有任何高山**勝地**嗎？

中國人：Yes, you can go to Mt. Taiping in Ilan County.
有，可以去宜蘭縣內的太平山。

外國人：Does one need a *mountain pass* to get in？
進去要**入山證**嗎？

中國人：Yes, but they are very easy to get. All you have to
do is to apply at the *Foreign Affairs Police Office* in
either Ilan City or else Taipei. You need to take
along your *passport* and two photographs.
要，不過很容易拿到。你只要向在宜蘭市或在台北的**外事**
警察局申請就可以了。要帶**護照**和兩張照片。

外國人：Do I have to apply *in advance*？
我得**事先**申請嗎？

中國人：No. In fact, you can pick one up on the very day you
go. 不必。事實上，你去的那一天就可以拿到了。

Dialogue 2

外國人：What is there to see on Mt. Taiping？
太平山有什麼好看的地方？

中國人：Mt. Taiping is basically a forest *recreation* area run by the *Taiwan Forestry Bureau*. Therefore, it has not become a typical tourist area. People go there to enjoy nature's quiet beauty.

　　　　太平山基本上是**台灣林務局**經營的森林**遊樂**區。所以，還沒有成爲典型的觀光區。人們到那裏，是爲了享受大自然寧靜的美。

外國人：Are there any *trails for hiking*？那裏有沒有**登山小徑**？

中國人：Yes, because of its natural beauty, there are many good trails for hiking. There is an old *logging* railroad which *skirts* the mountain. Several nice trails lead off it.

　　　　有，由於它的天然美景，那裏有許多很好的登山小徑。**沿著山的邊緣**，有一條舊的**運材**鐵路。有幾條很好的小徑是從這兒開始的。

🔲 **Dialogue 3** ▶

外國人：Is there any living *accommodation* there？
　　　　那裏有沒有**住的地方**？

中國人：Yes, there are several hostels in the small village at the top of the mountain, near the recreation area.
　　　　有，山頂小村莊內，靠遊樂區附近有數家招待所。

外國人：You mentioned there is a logging railroad. Is it still used to *transport timber*？
　　　　你剛才說有一條運材鐵路。現在還用來**運木材**嗎？

中國人：No, logging there ceased in 1979 after 42 years of operation.

　　沒有，那兒經過四十二年的開墾，伐木在一九七九年就停止了。

外國人：Are there any other ***attractions*** besides the nature trails and abandoned rail roads？

　　除了天然和廢棄的鐵路，還有沒有其他**誘人的地方**？

中國人：Yes, there is the ***Jentze Hot Springs*** resort near the bottom of Mt. Taiping. It is a very nice place to cool off after walking for many hours.

　　有的，靠太平山下有一個**仁澤溫泉**勝地。步行多時之後，那是一個很好的地方讓你平靜下來。

resort〔rɪˈzɔrt〕*n.* 勝地　　***mountain pass*** 入山證
Foreign Affairs Police Office 外事警察局
passport〔ˈpæs,pɔrt〕*n.* 護照　　***in advance*** 預先
recreation〔,rɛkrɪˈeʃən〕*n.* 遊樂；休閒
Taiwan Forestry Bureau 台灣省林務局　　trail〔trel〕*n.* 小徑
hike〔haɪk〕*v.* 步行　　log〔lɑg〕*v.* 伐木
skirt〔skɝt〕*v.* 沿～邊緣而行　　accommodation〔ə,kɑməˈdeʃən〕*n.* 暫時的膳宿
hostel〔ˈhɑstl̩〕*n.* 招待所；旅社　　transport〔trænsˈpɔrt〕*v.* 運輸
timber〔ˈtɪmbɚ〕*n.* 木材　　attraction〔əˈtrækʃən〕*n.* 吸引的東西
Jentze Hot Springs 仁澤溫泉　　***cool off*** 〔俗〕使冷却；平靜下來

Yangmingshan National Park

粉黛嫣紅的錦織彩繪

陽明山昔稱草山（*Grass Mountain*），政府遷台後改名陽明山，以紀念明代大儒王陽明先生。由台北市驅車沿仰德大道上山，經山仔后，首先到達陽明山的前山公園，前山公園亦稱中正公園，規模較小，公園內碧草如茵，綠樹環繞，附設有游泳池、溜冰場與籃球場，是一處天然的動態林園區。

開車繼續向前行，即抵達後山公園，此處是**陽明山國家公園**（*Yangmingshan National Park*）的精華所在，每逢二月中旬至四月初之間，園內的**櫻花**（*cherry*）、**杜鵑花**（*azalea*）、**梅花**（*plum*）、**茶花**（*camellia*）紛紛迎風怒放，一片粉黛嫣紅的熱鬧情景，與盛裝而來的遊人，交織成一幅織錦彩繪。

陽明山屬於大屯山區的一部分，大屯山區為著名的**火山群**（*volcanoes*），在此可以觀賞到火山地形的遺跡，如**噴氣口**（*fumaroles*），**火山口**（*volcanic crater*），峽谷瀑布等獨特景觀，當然陽明山著名的**溫泉**（*hot springs*）也少不了。此外，陽明山公路沿線亦有相當多的旅遊地點，觀光果園、觀光花圃、竹子湖高冷蔬菜區、夢幻湖硫磺谷、太陽谷大草原等，都能為旅途上添增不少趣味。

TOPIC 11

陽明山國家公園 Yangmingshan National Park

Introducing Taiwan

● The Yangmingshan National Park is a mountainous area in the northeastern suburbs of Taipei. The whole park covers an area of 10,000 hectares.
（陽明山國家公園是一個位於台北市東北方郊外的山區，整座公園佔地一萬公頃。）

● Driving on the road from Taipei to Yangmingshan is quite enjoyable. Being 443 meters above sea level, the weather and scenery of Yangmingshan are quite distinguishable in spring, summer, autumn and winter.
（從台北開車到陽明山的沿線路程相當令人愉快。由於位於海拔四百四十三公尺，陽明山的天氣和景色變化，春、夏、秋、多四季都可以區分得出來。）

● A night's drive to Yangmingshan is recommended for those who want to have a romantic view of the whole of Taipei. Below the mountain, you will see the whole city light up in a spectacular feast for the eyes.
（晚上開車到陽明山，是推薦給那些對整個台北想要有浪漫視野的人們。你將會看到山下整個城市的燈火，是視覺上壯觀的宴饗。）

** hectare〔'hɛktɚ〕*n.*〔法〕公頃
distinguishable〔dɪ'stɪŋgwɪʃəbḷ〕*adj.* 可區分的；可辨別的
spectacular〔spɛk'tækjələ〕*adj.* 驚人的；壯觀的

🖽 **Dialogue**

外國人： I'd like to be able to get out of Taipei for an afternoon *or so* to get some fresh air. Is there anywhere
I can go?

　　　我希望能離開台北一個下午**左右**，去呼吸點新鮮空氣。有
　　　什麼地方我可以去的？

中國人： Perhaps one of the best places you can go to is Yangmingshan *National Park* which is just to the north of
Taipei city.

　　　也許，你可以去的最好地方之一是陽明山**國家公園**，就在
　　　台北市北邊。

外國人： Surely I'd never be able to get round there in an
afternoon.

　　　當然，我沒辦法一個下午逛完。

中國人： Though the park is large, an afternoon will give you
plenty of time to walk around. It takes about an hour
by taxi from the middle of Taipei. You might want to
stop along the way. The drive is very pleasant.

　　　雖然公園很大，一個下午會給你許多時間四處走走的。從
　　　台北市中心搭計程車去，大約需要一小時。你可能想在途
　　　中停車。這趟車程是很愉快的。

外國人： Where, for instance? 比如說在哪裏停呢？

　＊＊ *or so* 大約　　　*National Park* 國家公園

中國人： About half way up you will pass the *Chinese Culture University*. There the buildings are built in the traditional Chinese style.

　　　　大約上了半路，你會經過**中國文化大學**。那裏的建築物都蓋成傳統中國式樣。

　　　　　　　*　　　　　　*　　　　　　*

外國人： What about the park itself? 公園本身如何？

中國人： Aside from a famous flower clock, there are *waterfalls* and wooded paths. Between February and April the park is full of blossoms, and it is these *cherry* trees and *azalea* trees that are the park's most famous attractions.

　　　　除了著名的花鐘，還有**瀑布**和樹木繁茂的小徑。二月和四月間，公園裏開滿了花。這些**櫻**樹和**杜鵑花**樹，就是這座公園最負盛名的迷人之處。

外國人： It's too bad that it's now July！太可惜了，現在是七月！

中國人： That doesn't matter. Yangmingshan is beautiful even without the blossoms. Besides, at this time of the year it is several degrees cooler than Taipei. That should make a *stroll* there even more pleasant.

　　　　沒關係，陽明山卽使沒有花也很美麗。而且，每年這時候，那裏比台北涼爽幾度，這使得上那兒**走走**更加愉快。

** *Chinese Culture University* 中國文化大學　　wooded〔ˈwʊdɪd〕*adj.* 樹木繁茂的
waterfall〔ˈwɔtɚˌfɔl〕*n.* 瀑布　　cherry〔ˈtʃɛrɪ〕*n.* 櫻樹
azalea〔əˈzeljə〕*n.* 杜鵑花　　stroll〔strol〕*n.* 散步；閒逛

WU LAI

山水交映的世外桃源

烏來位於台北縣（*Taipei county*）最南端，是台北地區唯一的山地鄉（*aboriginal village*），也是泰雅族（*Tai Ya tribe*）山胞最北部的據點，距離台北市僅二十五公里路程。整個烏來鄉一共包括五個村落，分別散布在廣大的山林群峰之間。

烏來的山地風光最迷人之處，便是南勢溪與桶後溪滙流的溪谷地帶，沿途走去，山水交映，直似世外桃源。經過規劃後的烏來風景區以臺車（*pushcart*）、烏來大瀑布（*waterfall*）、山地文物館、空中纜車（*cable car*）和雲仙樂園（*mountaintop amusement park*）為人所稱道。每逢假日，成群結隊的遊客便為這個寧靜的山谷帶來一串串的歡樂笑聲。「烏

來」兩個字原本是山胞稱謂「溫泉」的意思，此地的泉水清澈透明，水溫達八十度左右，水質屬於弱鹼性，除了治療皮膚病之外，還可以飲用，和陽明山、新北投並列為台北三大溫泉區。

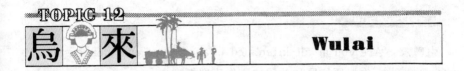

TOPIC 12

烏來　　　　　　　Wulai

Introducing Taiwan

- Wulai is an aboriginal village, famous for its waterfall and tribal dancing. A pushcart ride on the light rails from the entrance of the village to the waterfall is a thrilling and pleasant experience.

（烏來是一個山地鄉，以瀑布和山地舞蹈聞名。從入口處到瀑布，乘坐輕軌臺車，是刺激而又愉悅的經驗。）

- There is a recreation and amusement park to be found in Wulai. It'll take you the whole day to enjoy all that it has to offer. You can buy a Chinese costume or an aboriginal costume as your souvenir from Wulai. The center of attraction in the park is a water fountain that gushes up water in a wonderful display.

（在烏來可以找到一處娛樂、休閒的公園。會花你一整天的時間來享受它所提供的一切。你可以買中國或土著服飾做為你到烏來的紀念品。公園中最吸引人的中心是噴水池，神奇炫示地噴出水來。）

** **tribal dancing** 山地（部族）舞蹈
pushcart〔'puʃ, kɑrt〕 *n.* 台車；手推車　　costume〔'kɑstjum〕 *n.* 服裝
souvenir〔, suvə'nɪr〕 *n.* 紀念；紀念品（＝*keepsake, mememto*）

🔲 **Dialogue** ➤

中國人： Are you at all interested in aborigines and their customs?
你對原住民和他們的風俗感興趣嗎？

外國人： Yes, I am. Where do I have to go to see them?
是的，我很感興趣。我要到哪裏看他們？

中國人： If you really want to see some truly *primitive* aborigines, you should go to *Orchid Island* off the southeastern coast of Taiwan.
如果你想看眞正的**原始**土著，你該到台灣東南海岸外的**蘭嶼**。

外國人： Oh! That's too far. Can't I see any nearer Taipei?
哇！那太遠了。離台北近一點的，看不看得到？

中國人： Yes. You can go to Wulai about 45 minutes drive from Taipei. It is an *aboriginal village*.
有。你可以去烏來，從台北開車大約四十五分鐘到。那是一個**山地鄉**。

     *   *   *

外國人： Has the village become a modern tourist attraction?
這個山地鄉已經成爲現代的旅遊名勝了嗎？

中國人： Yes, of course. However, the people haven't entirely given up their culture. The people perform their traditional songs and dances at a mountain village not far from the main tourist spot.
是，當然。不過，人們還未完全放棄自己的文化。在離主要觀光地點不遠的山地鄉，人們表演傳統的歌舞。

** primitive〔'prɪmətɪv〕 *adj.* 原始的　　aboriginal〔͵æbə'rɪdʒənḷ〕 *adj.* 土著的

外國人： Besides the aborigines, are there any other attractions?
除了山地人之外，有沒有別的名勝？

中國人： There is a *magnificent* waterfall directly across from the village, and there is also a *cable car*, too, which takes visitors across a sharp, deep ravine and on to a *mountaintop amusement park* with a small lake. There are also plenty of good *restaurants* serving local *specialities* such as deer, wild *boar* and fresh *trout*.
有一個**壯麗的**瀑布直接穿流自這個山地鄉，也有**纜車**，載遊客穿越陡深的峽谷到有個小湖的**雲仙樂園**。還有許多很棒的**餐館**賣當地**特產**，像鹿肉、**野豬**和新鮮的**鱒魚**。

＊　　　　　＊　　　　　＊

外國人： Is there any place nearby where aborigines have *retained* more of their *original* ways of life?
附近有什麼地方，山地人**保留**較多的**原始**生活方式？

中國人： Yes, at Hsinhsien Village near Wulai. You will need to get a permit from the police station in Wulai first, but it is well worth a visit.
有的，在烏來附近的信賢村。你要先取得烏來警察局的許可，不過那裏眞的值得一遊。

外國人： That sounds very interesting. I think I'll give it a try.
聽起來很有趣。我想我會試一試。

** magnificent〔mæg'nıfəsṇt〕*adj.* 壯麗的　　ravine〔rə'vin〕*n.* 峽谷
speciality〔ˌspɛʃı'ælətı〕*n.* 特產　　boar〔bɔr〕*n.* 野豬
trout〔traʊt〕*n.* 鱒魚　　retain〔rı'ten〕*v.* 保留

The East-West Cross-Island Highway

鬼斧神工的奇麗造化

中部橫貫公路蜿蜒攀越過台灣中央山脈區（the Central Mountain Range），不但是著名的觀光地帶，劃入國家公園（National Park）的管理，同時也是連絡台灣東部與西部往來的交通大動脈，公路主線起於台中縣東勢鎮止於花蓮太魯閣（Taroko gorge），全長共一九二公里（kilometer），即一百二十英里（mile）。除了這條主線之外，還另有一條支線和供應線：支線由梨山北行，沿大甲溪上游，越過思源埡口之後，再沿濁水溪河谷下行，直抵宜蘭；供應線則由大禹嶺分叉而出，越過合歡山，前往霧社。

中橫的興建工程於西元一九六〇年完成，耗費了一萬名榮民將近四年的時間。

公路沿途的路況及景觀，真可稱上鬼斧神工的傑作，峽谷（gorge）、峭壁（cliff）、瀑布（waterfalls）、神木（Sacred Tree）等自然奇景，令人嘆為觀止。尤其是東段太魯閣到天祥間長達十九公里的路段，更是中橫的精華所在，最適宜健行，一路前去慢慢地觀賞大自然奇麗的造化。

TOPIC 13

東西橫貫公路　The East-West Cross-Island Highway

Introducing Taiwan

- The 19-kilometer stretch through Taroko Gorge is the most traveled section in the highway. The towering cliffs along the road contain billions of tons of marble deposits. About 4,700 visitors per day are attracted by the gorge, which stands as one of the great natural wonders of the world.
  （太魯閣沿路十九公里一線，是公路上最熱門的旅遊區。公路兩旁聳立的峭壁，蘊含了數十億噸的大理石礦層。每天大約有四千七百名遊客受吸引，前來觀賞這段世界上最偉大自然奇觀之一的峽谷。）

- Swallow Mouth is situated about five kilometers from Li Ning bridge. It is one of the best scenic spots of Taroko Gorge. There are steep and overhanging cliffs on both sides.
  （燕子口位於離寧橋約五公里處，是太魯閣最好的風景之一。路兩側皆是陡峭、危懸的峭壁。）

- Getting to Taroko Gorge is no problem at all. You have a choice of flying to Hualien first then taking a connecting bus to the area. A more leisurely way of doing it is by train. It'll take 4 hours to get there.
  （要到太魯閣一點也沒有問題。你可以選擇搭飛機到花蓮，然後轉搭巴士到那個地區。更悠哉的方法是搭火車。大約花四個小時到那兒。）

** deposit〔dɪˊpɑzɪt〕 *n.* 礦床；礦層
scenic spot 風景區　　steep〔stip〕 *adj.* 陡峭的；險峻的

〔➡➡➡〕 **Dialogue** ▷

外國人： What's so special about the *East-West Cross-Island Highway*?
東西橫貫公路有什麼眞的很特別的地方？

中國人： Well, first of all, it's an *incredible feat* of engineering and, secondly, a *breathtakingly* beautiful drive.
嗯，第一，那是工程上**不可思議的偉績**；第二，沿路開下去，美得**令人驚異**。

外國人： How long ago was it built? 多久以前蓋的？

中國人： It was completed in 1960 after nearly four years of *construction*. 在**蓋**了幾乎四年之後，於一九六〇年完成。

外國人： How long does it take to drive across?
開過全程要多久？

中國人： *Practically* a whole day. One must drive carefully and slowly. The main road itself is 120 miles long.
幾乎要一整天。必須小心慢慢地開。主線本身有一百二十英里長。

外國人： Are there any particularly beautiful *spots* along the *route*? 沿**路**上有任何特別漂亮的**地方**嗎？

中國人： Perhaps the best part is the 19 kilometers or so that winds itself along the Taroko Gorge near the eastern

** incredible 〔ɪn'krɛdəbl〕 *adj.* 不可思議的；難以置信的
　　feat 〔fit〕 *n.* 偉績；英勇事績
　　breathtakingly 〔'brɛθ,tekɪŋlɪ〕 *adv.* 令人驚異地

end of the highway. The Gorge is a deep, narrow *ravine* whose *cliffs* contain billions of tons of *marble*. There are 38 *tunnels* that the road passes through.

也許最好的部分是在公路東端附近，沿著太魯閣蜿蜒大約十九公里的那一段。太魯閣是一個深且窄的**峽谷**，它的**峭壁**蘊含了數十億噸的**大理石**。這條路穿過了三十八個**隧道**。

外國人： Are there any nice places where one can stay?
有任何可以逗留的好地方嗎？

中國人： If you are near the eastern end, say, you have just traveled through the Taroko Gorge, a nice place to stay is Tienhsiang. If you are a little further along, you could stay at Tayuling. There are some beautiful *sunrises* there. If you are somewhere in the middle of the highway, you could stay at Lishan which has a *splendid* view that is *reminiscent* of the Swiss Alps.

如果你在東端附近，比如說，你剛到太魯閣玩過，那麼，逗留的好地方就是天祥，如果你在遠一點，你可以在大禹嶺待一待。那裏有美麗的**日出**。如果你在公路中段某處，可以在梨山停留，那裏景色極爲**壯麗**，**令人想起**瑞士的阿爾卑斯山。

外國人： Is Lishan the highest point above *sea level* along the route? 梨山是沿途高於**海平面**的最高點嗎？

中國人： No, the highest point is at Wuling near Tayuling which has an *elevation of* 10,743 feet.
不，最高點在大禹嶺附近的武陵，**海拔**一萬零七百四十三英尺。

** ravine〔rə′vin〕*n.* 峽谷   cliff〔klɪf〕*n.* 峭壁
reminiscent〔,rɛmə′nɪsn̩t〕*adj.* 引起聯想的

墾丁與鵝鑾鼻

KENTING AND OLUANPI

景觀奇異的恆春半島

　　湛藍的海天、遼闊的視野、細緻的白沙、景觀奇異的珊瑚礁（coral reefs）岩層以及熱帶植物（tropical plants）蒲旎的風情和全年溫煦和暖的陽光，這些種種景緻使得墾丁與鵝鑾鼻所在的恆春半島（Hengchun or Eternal Spring Peninsula）成為台灣近年來最熱門的遊樂區，一年到頭皆見遊客的踪影躑躅不去。

　　如果從恆春到滿洲出風谷之間連接一線，那麼直線以南的區域就是恆春半島的觀光風景區，包括有關山的夕照、貓鼻頭（Maopitou or cat-nose-tip）的珊瑚礁海岸、南灣（Nanwan or South Bay）的金黃色沙灘、墾丁公園的熱帶原始林（tropical forest）、青蛙石（Frog Rock）和船帆石（Sail Rock）的珊瑚礁變景、號稱「東亞之光」的鵝鑾鼻、有「海神樂園」盛名的佳洛水（Chialoshui or Good-Running-Water），另外再加上恆春本地的四座古城，真是令人目不暇給，目前已規劃入國家公園（national park）的一部分。

　　除此之外，賞鳥（bird-watching）也是此處特殊的旅遊活動之一。每年雙十節前後，成千上萬的鳥類，如野鴨（ducks）、蒼鷺（herons）、千鳥（plovers）…，遠從西伯利亞（Siberia）、日本（Japan）、韓國（Korea）及中國大陸（mainland China）東北部飛往菲律賓（Philippines）避寒，中途棲息在恆春半島。這群千里迢迢而來的過客為寂靜的山巔海畔帶來一陣喧嘩繽紛的色彩，更使得遊人流連忘返，不知所歸了。

TOPIC 14

墾丁與鵝鑾鼻 Kenting and Oluanpi

Introducing Taiwan

- One of the most popular spots in Taiwan for birdwatching is Lungluan Lake（龍鑾潭）, lying about three kilometers （1.8 miles）southwest of the town of Hengchun. Fishing in Lungluan Lake is also popular. The fish in the lake are believed to be especially tasty.

（台灣最受歡迎的賞鳥地點之一是龍鑾潭，約位在恆春鎮的西南三公里（一點八英里）處。在龍鑾潭釣魚也很受歡迎，這裡的魚據信特別美味。）

- They say that on a clear day you can see the northernmost island of the Philippines on a cliff overlooking the sea in Oluanpi. If you are into scuba-diving, the coral formations off Oluanpi offer the best diving spots in the island.

（據說在晴朗的日子，你可以從鵝鑾鼻俯視海的懸崖上，看到菲律賓最北的島嶼。如果你想要潛水，鵝鑾鼻外海的珊瑚岩層，提供全台灣最好的潛水地點。）

** birdwatching〔ˈbɝdˌwɑtʃɪŋ〕n. 賞鳥；野鳥觀察
tasty〔ˈtestɪ〕adj. 美味的；好吃的
overlook〔ˌovɚˈlʊk〕v. 俯視；遠眺

〔□□〕 **Dialogue** ➤

外國人： Are there any places **worth** visiting in the southernmost part of Taiwan？

台灣的最南端有沒有任何**值得**遊賞的地方？

中國人： There are several interesting places in the southern-most part of Taiwan. Perhaps the most well-known one is **the Kenting National Scenic Area**. This is one of the loveliest regions in all Taiwan. It is **flanked** by four seas — the Taiwan Strait, the South China Sea, the Bashi **Channel**, and the Pacific Ocean.

台灣最南端有幾個有趣的地方。其中最有名的可能要算是**墾丁國家風景區**。這裡是全台灣最怡人的地區之一。**側面**包圍著四個海——台灣海峽、南中國海、巴士**海峽**和太平洋。

* * *

外國人： Kenting？ Does the word "Kenting" have any special meaning？「墾丁」？這個名字有任何特別的意義嗎？

中國人： "Kenting" means "**Plowmen**". The name **originated** with the arrival of farmers from mainland China who **settled** in the southernmost part of Taiwan.

「墾丁」意思是「**農夫**」。這個字**起源自**中國大陸的農夫抵達，並且**定居**在台灣的最南端。

** worth〔wɝθ〕 *adj.* 值得　　flank〔flæŋk〕*v.* 在…之側
channel〔'tʃænl̩〕*n.* 海峽　　plowmen〔'plaumɛn〕*n.* 農夫
originate〔ə'rɪdʒə,net〕*v.* 起源　　settle〔'sɛtl̩〕*v.* 定居

外國人：What is special about the Kenting area?

　　　　墾丁地區有什麼特別嗎？

中國人：This area contains the Kenting Forest Recreation Area,
　　　　a large **botanical** garden. There are more than 1300
　　　　different **species** of **exotic** plants from many parts of
　　　　the world there. Some of them are quite rare.

　　　　這個地區包括有墾丁森林遊樂區，一座大型的**植物**園。裡
　　　　面有一千三百多種來自世界各地不同**品種**的**外來**植物。有
　　　　些相當罕見。

外國人：Is it possible to **identify** these plants?

　　　　有沒有可能**認出**這些植物？

中國人：Yes. All the trees are identified in Chinese, English,
　　　　and Latin.

　　　　有。所有的樹都標上中文、英文和拉丁文來分辨。

　　　　　　　　＊　　　　　　＊　　　　　　＊

外國人：Are there any nice beaches nearby?

　　　　附近有沒有不錯的海灘呢？

中國人：Yes, a few kilometers from the park is Kenting beach.
　　　　This beach is famous for its clean white sand, fresh
　　　　air, sea shells and pieces of **coral**. There are also
　　　　not many people there.

　　　　有，離公園幾公里遠有墾丁海灘。這個海灘以潔淨的白沙、清新
　　　　的空氣、海貝和片片的**珊瑚**而聞名。而且那裏也沒有很多人。

**　botanical〔bo'tænɪkl〕*adj.* 植物的　　species〔'spiʃɪz〕*n. pl.* 品種
　exotic〔ɪg'zɑtɪk〕*adj.* 外來的；奇異的
　sea shell 海產軟體動物的貝殼；海貝　　coral〔'kɑrəl〕*n.* 珊瑚

外國人： Besides the park and the beach, is there anything else
I can see?

除了公園和海灘之外，其他我還能看到什麼？

中國人： There are many things you can see. For instance, a
few miles down the road, situated at the southernmost
tip of Taiwan there is the Oluanpi Lighthouse built in
1882. There is also a new hostel in Kenting which
resembles traditional Chinese **architecture**. It is truly
magnificent.

你可以看到很多事物。例如，沿路幾里遠的地方，位置在
台灣最南端的頂點上，有鵝鑾鼻燈塔，建於一八八二年。
墾丁也有一間新建的旅社，**類似**傳統的中國式**建築**，真的
很壯麗。

外國人： Is it easy to find a place to stay in or around Kenting?

在墾丁或是墾丁附近容易找到停留過夜的地方嗎？

中國人： That should be no problem. There is the first-class
Caesar Park Hotel in Kenting. If you do not want to
spend too much, there are cheaper places, too.

應該是沒問題。在墾丁有最高級的凱撒渡假飯店。如果你
不想花太多錢的話，也有比較便宜的地方。

** resemble〔rɪˈzɛmbl〕 v. 類似；相似
architecture〔ˈɑrkɪˌtɛktʃɚ〕 n. 建築

MT. ALISHAN

翁鬱秀異的山林風姿

曾經有多少人為阿里山美麗的景色而讚嘆不已，嘖嘖稱奇過，那壯麗迷濛的雲海(the Sea of Clouds)、霞光滿天的日出(sunrise)和絢爛瑰麗的晚霞(rosy clouds just before sunset)曾深深打動過多少人們的心靈！

阿里山是祝山、石水山、大小塔山等山峰的總稱，屬於玉山(Mt. Jade)的支脈，位

置在嘉義市(Chiayi)的東北七十二公里處，不但是台灣第一大林產區，同時也是馳名中外的觀光地點。林中蜿蜒爬升的高山鐵道(the Alpine Railway)小火車穿梭於翁鬱青蒼的森林叢樹之間，尤其構成一幅獨具山林趣味的景象，吸引著無數人們前往。沿著鐵道兩旁，可以觀賞到三種不同林相的樹木，從竹崎盤旋而上至獨立山一帶隸屬熱帶林，從獨立山到屏遮那是溫帶林，之後往上則屬於寒帶林，一直擴展到阿里山頂。細心的遊客可以從中領略到其間相異的山林風姿。

此外,幽雅的姊妹潭(Two Sisters Pond)，岸然挺立的神木(Sacred Tree)以及三代木(Three-Generation Tree)的奇態也是旅遊的重點所在，足可在未來的生活中留下一段難忘的經驗與回憶。

TOPIC 15

Alishan 阿里山

- The Sacred Tree is a 3,000-year-old red cypress that was struck dead by lightning in 1947. Sprouts grow on the top of the trunk which is 182 meters (60 feet) tall. The circumference is 14.6 meters (47.9 feet) and the chest-high diameter is 4.7 meters (15 feet).

（神木是一株樹齡三千年的紅檜，在一九四七年時被閃電擊中而枯死。在樹幹頂端上長出的新芽高一百八十二公尺〔即六十英尺〕。樹木本身的圓周有十四點六公尺〔即四十七點九英尺〕，而樹胸高度的直徑長則是四點七公尺〔即十五英尺〕。）

- At five o'clock in the morning, it is customary for visitors to wake up to catch the train that will lead you all the way up to view the sunrise in the mountains. During winters you can also see a bit of snow still lingering in the higher elevations of the mountains. The grandeur of the sunrise usually depends on atmospheric conditions and the time of the year.

（習慣上，在早晨五點叫醒遊客趕上火車，火車會帶你一路上去，看山上的日出。冬天時，你也可以看到在海拔更高的山上還有一點點雪殘留著。日出的壯觀通常視大氣狀況，以及是屬於該年哪一個時令而定。）

Dialogue 1

外國人：　I understand there are many mountains in Taiwan.
　　　　　Are there any that we can visit without difficulty?
　　　　　我知道台灣有很多山岳，有沒有任何山我們可以輕輕鬆鬆不
　　　　　費勁地遊賞？

中國人：　Yes, there's Alishan, which is part of the Alishan
　　　　　Forest Recreation Area, a popular tourist *attraction*
　　　　　in Central Taiwan. 有啊，阿里山就是了，它是台灣中部
　　　　　一個受歡迎觀光**勝地**，阿里山**森林遊樂區**的一部分。

外國人：　How does one get there? 怎麼到哪裏呢？

中國人：　Well, most people first of all go to Chaiyi which can
　　　　　be reached from Taipei by train or by bus. It is a
　　　　　large town in southwest Central Taiwan.
　　　　　嗯，大部分的人首先到嘉義，由台北搭火車或搭巴士就可以
　　　　　抵達。嘉義在台灣中部的西南地區是一個大城鎮。

Dialogue 2

外國人：　Is Alishan very near Chiayi? 阿里山離嘉義很近嗎？

中國人：　Not really. In fact it is 45 miles away. The reason
　　　　　why people go to Chiayi is because they can take a
　　　　　diesel-powered train on the *narrow-gauge* alpine rail-

** *Forest Recreation Area* 森林遊樂區
　　attraction〔ə'trækʃən〕*n.* 吸引人的東西；誘惑物
　　diesel〔'dizl〕*n.* 柴油引擎　　gauge〔gedʒ〕*n.* 鐵路軌道
　　alpine〔'ælpaɪn〕*adj.* 高山的

way. As I said, the railway is 45 miles long and there
are 80 bridges and 50 *tunnels*.

沒有十分近。事實上，阿里山是在四十五英里之外。人們到
嘉義的理由是因爲他們可以搭乘行走在**窄軌**高山鐵道上的**柴
油引擎**火車。正如同我所說的，鐵道有四十五英里長，而且
中間通過了八十座橋和五十個**隧道**。

外國人：　How long does the train take? 火車要搭多久呢？

中國人：　It takes three hours each way. The railway began to
be used by the Japanese in 1912 to *deliver* timber
from the forests. 每一次車程要花三個小時。日本人在一
九一二年，開始使用這條鐵路，用來**運送**森林裏的木材。

外國人：　Three hours sounds like a long time. Isn′t there a
quicker way to get there? 三小時聽起來好像很久。有沒
有快一點的方法可以到達那裏？

中國人：　Well, you can *of course* take a bus, but the train journey is much more interesting. For instance, on the
way the train will stop at a point of special interest,
the Sacred Tree, which has been there for 3000 years.
那麼，**當然**你可以搭乘巴士，但是火車的旅程要有趣多了。
例如，在途中，火車會在一個特別值得遊賞的地點——**神木**
停留。這棵神木已經在那裏活了三千年了。

** tunnel〔′tʌn̩〕*n*. 隧道　　deliver〔dɪ′lɪvɚ〕*v*. 運送
the Sacred Tree 神木

Dialogue 3

外國人：**Apart from** the train journey, what else is there to
　　　　see at Alishan?

　　　　除了火車的旅程**之外**，阿里山還有什麼可看的地方？

中國人：When you **get off** the train, you will be 2,190 meters
　　　　(7,185 feet) **above sea-level**. Near the station there
　　　　are **enchanting** beauty spots known as the Two Sisters
　　　　Pond, and the Three-Generation Tree — where trees
　　　　grow out of each other. However, one of the most
　　　　beautiful sights in Taiwan is to watch the sunrise
　　　　from a **vantage point** that is situated at an **elevation**
　　　　of 2,490 meters (8,170 feet).

　　　　當你**下火車**之後，你將在**海拔**兩千一百九十公尺（七千一百
　　　　八十五英尺）之處。火車站附近有**迷人的**美麗風景區，叫做
　　　　姊妹潭和三代木—— 樹木從彼此之間生長出來。然而，台灣
　　　　最美麗的景緻之一是在**海拔**兩千四百九十公尺（八千一百七
　　　　十英尺）的高山上，從**有利地勢**看日出。

外國人：That means I'll have to get up very early, doesn't it?

　　　　這意味著我將必須很早起床，不是嗎？

中國人：It will be well worth it. The hotel where you stay
　　　　will **see to it** that you get up early. If you are lucky,
　　　　you may see a magnificent sunrise, with the sun
　　　　emerging from a sea of clouds encircling Yushan (Mt.

＊＊　*apart from* 除了…之外　　　　sea-level *n.* 海平面
　　enchanting〔ɪnˈtʃæntɪŋ〕*adj.* 迷人的　　*vantage point* 有利地勢；地利
　　elevation〔ˌɛləˈveʃən〕*n.* 高度（尤指海拔）
　　see to it 留心；設法　　emerge〔ɪˈmɝdʒ〕*v.* 顯露

Jade), the highest *peak* in Northeast Asia.

為了觀看日出的景色絕對值得。你停留過夜的飯店，會**留心**讓你早起的。如果幸運的話，你可能會看到壯麗的日出，整個太陽從圍繞著玉出，東北亞最高**峰**，的雲海中出現。

外國人：How do I *book* a room in the hotel?
我要如何向飯店**預訂**房間？

中國人：The tour office in Taipei will *take care of* that. It will also book your train tickets, as there is a great *demand* for these.
台北的旅行社會**照應**訂房間的事情。同時也會預訂你的火車票，因為對這些服務的**需求**很大。

** peak〔pik〕*n.* 山峯　　book〔bʊk〕*v.* 預訂
tour office 旅行社　　demand〔dɪˈmænd〕*n.* 需求

SUN MOON LAKE

群山環繞的秀麗風光

　　清澈如鏡的湖水，恬淡如詩的青山，這該就是日月潭的速寫了。日月潭位在南投縣魚池鄉水社村，座落於群山環繞之間，是一個天然的內陸湖泊（ landlocked lake ），標高在海拔（ above sea level ）二千五百公尺高處。湖面寬闊，約有八百公頃之廣。

　　日月潭的日暮晨昏是許多人難以忘懷的回憶，無論是迎著清新的晨光，或是守著安詳的落日，都足以令人領受到那一份屬於山水的寧靜與詳和。文武廟（ Literature-Warrior Temple ）、慈恩塔（ Filial Devotion Pagoda）、玄奘寺（ The Hsuan Chuang Temple ）、孔雀園（ Peacocks Garden ）、德化社山地文化村（ aborigine village ）

等名勝據點圍繞在環湖的道路上，開車沿著這條長達十七公里的環湖公路兜風可以充分飽覽日月潭具有亞熱帶情調的秀麗風光。當然，搭乘小舟或汽艇等航行於碧波萬頃之上，也不失為暢快的旅遊方式。

TOPIC 16

日 月 潭 **Sun Moon Lake**

Introducing Taiwan

- There is a small island named "Kuang Hua Tao"（光華島）
  in the middle of the Sun Moon Lake. This island divides
  the lake into two parts resembling the Sun and the Moon.
  （在日月潭中間有一座小島叫「光華島」，這座小島將整個潭面劃
  分爲形似太陽和月亮的兩部份。）

- The Wen-Wu（Literature-Warrior）Temple is dedicated to
  Confucius as Master of the Pen and Kuan Ti, God of War,
  as Master of the Sword.
  （文武廟是爲文學的導師——孔子，戰爭的大將——戰神關帝而建
  造的。）

- The two-hour boat ride around Sun Moon Lake is becoming
  more and more a popular point of any tour of Taiwan. The
  man-made lake is situated 2,500 feet above sea level in
  Nantou county in the Central Mountain Ranges. This will
  be one of the more relaxing parts of your tour in Taiwan.
  （環繞日月潭兩個小時的遊湖，漸漸成爲台灣任何旅遊中，一項流
  行的重點。這個人造湖位於南投縣，中央山脈海拔二千五百英尺。
  這將會是台灣旅遊中，最令你放鬆的部分之一。）

** resemble〔rɪˈzɛmbḷ〕*v.* 類似；相似
　　dedicate〔ˈdɛdə,ket〕*v.* 奉獻給；供奉

Dialogue

外國人： Looking at my map, I notice that there is a lake
called the Sun Moon Lake in the middle of the island.
我看地圖，注意到台灣中部有一個叫日月潭的湖。

中國人： Yes. It is a *landlocked* lake above sea level in the
lofty mountains of central Taiwan. 是的。那是台灣中部
崇山峻嶺間，高於海平面的一個**內陸**湖。

外國人： Is it easy to get to? 那裏很容易到達嗎？

中國人： It's about 50 miles southeast of Taichung and the
drive is very pleasant and the area is considered one
of the loveliest *regions* in Taiwan.
它在台中東南五十英里左右，這趟車程非常愉快，這個地區
被認爲是台灣最美麗的**地方**之一。

外國人： Can one swim or go boating in the lake?
可以在湖裏游泳或划船嗎？

中國人： There are small *rowing boats* for hire. You can swim,
too, but it is best to wear a *life jacket* as the
water is very deep and some people have drowned before. 有小**划艇**可以租，也可以游泳，不過最好穿上**救生衣**，
因爲水很深，以前淹死過一些人。

　　　　　　＊　　　　　＊　　　　　＊

外國人： Are there any things worth seeing around the lake?
湖周圍有什麼值得看的？

中國人： There are some temples, the Wen-Wu or Literature —
Warrior Temple being a famous one. The two stone
lions *guarding* the temple are the biggest ones of their
kind in Taiwan. 有些廟，文武廟就是出名的一個。守廟的
兩隻石獅子是在台灣同樣種類中最大的。

外國人： I'm not too *keen* on temples, so is there anything
else? 我對廟宇不太熱衷，還有沒有別的？

中國人： There is a nine-storied Tzu En or Filial Devotion
Pagoda which is very impressive. As it stands at a
higher elevation than any other temple in Taiwan, its
top floor affords visitors *enchanting vistas* of the
beautiful surroundings.
有一座九層的慈恩塔，令人印象深刻。因為它所在的海拔高
度，比台灣其他廟宇都要來得高，遊客從頂樓可以看到周遭
美麗事物的迷人景色。

外國人： Are there any aborigines living around the Sun Moon
Lake? 日月潭四周有沒有山地人居住？

中國人： Yes, there are. There is an aborigine village on one
side of the lake. By the way, if you are interested in
peacocks, there is a garden specially created as the
home of a large *flock* of them.
有的，湖邊有個山地村。對了，如果你對孔雀有興趣，那邊
有一個園，特別設立來當一大群孔雀的棲息地。

TAI CHUNG

風和日麗的渡假都市

西元一七二一年，一條來自中國大陸(*Mainland China*)的移民船停泊在台灣中部，隨後在此地建立起一座村莊，取名為「大肚」(*Big Mound；Tatun*)。西元一八九五年，日本人在台灣展開近半世紀的殖民統治(*colonial occupation*)時，將大肚改名為台中(*Taichung*)，意指「台灣的中部地方」(*Central Taiwan*)。

今日的台中由於地理位置優越，扼台灣中部樞紐，無論是經濟(*economy*)、文化(*culture*)、交通(*communication*)各方面的發展都相當快速，目前已經成為僅次於台北市、高雄市的第三大都市。台中市位居台中盆地的中心，東邊倚靠中央山脈(*the Central Mountain Range*)地勢峻峭，西面鄰大肚山脈，坡度較為平緩。全年平均氣溫為22.4℃，風和日麗，絕少塵沙飛揚、寒風凜冽的時節，是台灣氣候最佳的地區。

台中市夙有「農村都市」、「寧靜之都」、「消費都市」等稱號，再加上溫和的氣候、淳樸的民風、濃厚的文教氣息、以及四周奇峰環繞，這些條件都使得台中市發展為優良的渡假都市，不斷地吸引著人們前往。

TOPIC 17

臺中 **Taichung**

Dialogue 1

中國人： You might be interested in visiting Taichung, the
third largest city in Taiwan after Taipei and Kaohsiung. 也許你會有興趣到台中玩一玩，台中是繼台北、高
雄之後的台灣第三大城。

外國人： Is it a very old city? 那是個非常古老的城市嗎？

中國人： Not really, but by 1895, the year in which the Japanese began their half-century *colonial occupation* of
Taiwan, it had already become one of the main cities
in Taiwan.
不盡然，不過，在一八九五年，日本人開始對台灣半個世
紀的**殖民佔據**時，它就已經成為台灣的主要城市之一了。

*　　　　　　*　　　　　　*

外國人： What *remains* of the city that existed last century?
這都市有什麼上世紀就有的**遺跡**？

中國人： The site on which the city was originally built has
evolved into the present-day Chungshan(Sun Yat-sen)
Park, a *notable* example of classical Chinese *landscape* in the center of downtown Taichung.
最初蓋起這座城市的地點，已**發展**成現在的中山（孫逸仙）
公園，位於台中市城區中心，是古典中國**山水**的**著名**例子。

Dialogue 2

外國人：What is the city special for？這個都市有什麼特別的？

中國人：It is the *principal economic*, *cultural* and *communications* center of Central Taiwan. Besides, it is also a major *political* center.

它是台灣中部**主要的經濟、文化**和**交通**中心。此外，它也是個主要的**政治**中心。

外國人：That sounds strange. I thought all the government offices were in Taipei.

這聽起來很奇怪。我以為所有的政府機關都在台北。

中國人：That's not exactly true. *Chung Hsing Village*, near Taichung, is the seat of the *Taiwan Provincial Government*. 那並不完全正確。靠近台中的**中興新村**，就是**台灣省政府**的所在地。

Dialogue 3

外國人：Does Taichung have an international *flavor* as far as business is concerned？

就商業而言，台中有國際**風味**嗎？

中國人：In recent years its international *standing* has been greatly *enhanced* with the opening in 1976 of an international *seaport* only 16 miles from the city and connected by a 10-lane highway.

近年來，隨著一九七六年國際**港**的開啓，它的國際**地位**已大大的**提高**。台中港離台中市只有十六英里，而且有一條十線道的公路相連。

外國人：Does Taichung have many temples？

　　　　台中有許多寺廟嗎？

中國人：Not as many as some places in Taiwan. However, Taichung **boasts** the tallest statue of Buddha on the island— 88 feet high, which is known as the Happy Buddha of Taichung.

　　　　不像台灣的某些地方那麼多。不過，台中**誇稱**有全島最高的佛像——八十八英尺高，就是衆所周知的台中彌勒佛。

colonial〔kə'lonɪəl〕 *adj.* 殖民地的　occupation〔ˌɑkjə'peʃən〕*n.* 佔領
remains〔rɪ'menz〕*n.* 遺跡　evolve〔ɪ'vɑlv〕*v.* 發展
notable〔'notəbl̩〕 *adj.* 著名的　landscape〔'lændskep〕*n.* 山水
principal〔'prɪnsəpl̩〕 *adj.* 主要的　economic〔ˌikə'nɑmɪk〕*adj.* 經濟的
cultural〔'kʌltʃərəl〕 *adj.* 文化的
communication〔kəˌmjunə'keʃən〕*n.* 交通
seat〔sit〕*n.* 所在地；中心；場所　　flavor〔'flevɚ〕*n.* 味道
standing〔'stændɪŋ〕*n.* 地位　enhance〔ɪn'hæns〕*v.* 提高
seaport〔'siˌpɔrt〕*n.* 海港　boast〔bost〕*v.* 自誇
Happy Buddha 彌勒佛

KAO HSIUNG

民風純樸的國際大都會

高雄市是一個新興的大都市，濱臨**台灣海峽**（*Taiwan Strait*），地居要衝，緊握台灣南部的經濟命脈，無論在軍事或經濟各方面都佔有相當的重要性。全市**人口**（*population*）已經超過一百二十八萬人，和台北市同是台灣的**特別行政區**（*special municipality*），屬於兩大**直轄市**（*the status of a province*）之一，為僅次於台北市的第二大都市。

高雄舊名**打狗**，目前雖然已躍昇為國際性的**大都會**（*metropolis*），但是仍然洋溢著舊時淳厚樸實的民風。每星期固定一次的**夜間市集**（*night market*）活動仍在高雄各地盛行著，每逢此時，人們便趿著一雙拖鞋，身著汗衫、短褲上街**購物**（*shopping*），食衣住行、吃喝玩樂各項用品一一俱全。這種熱熱鬧鬧，悠閒而不拘束的活動，很可以代表典型的台灣鄉間的夜市型態。

西子灣海水浴場（*Hsi Tzu Bay Beach*）、**萬壽山**（*Long Life Mountain*）、**愛河**（*Love River*）、**澄清湖**（*Crystal Clear Lake*）以及位於左營附近的**蓮池潭**（*Lotus Lake*）、**孔廟**（*Confucian temple*）、**春秋閣**（*Spring and Autumn Pavilions*）等都是高雄地區為人熟知的觀光勝地。

TOPIC 18

高雄　　　　Kaohsiung

▶ Introducing Taiwan

- Kaohsiung is an excellent base for visits to other points of sightseeing interest in South Taiwan, all conveniently and easily accessible. By bus or train, the historic city of Tai-nan（台南）is only a 40-minute drive from Kaohsiung. Kenting National Park and Fo Kuang Shan（Buddha Torch Mountain 佛光山） are other points of interest south of Kaohsiung.
（高雄是到南台灣其他旅遊地點的絕佳根據地，交通都很方便、快捷。古城台南，搭巴士或火車，距離高雄只有四十分鐘的車程。墾丁國家公園和佛光山，是高雄以南其他吸引人的觀光地點。）

- Kaohsiung is the fastest growing city in Taiwan next to Taipei. It is the bastion of the Taiwanese-speaking people of Taiwan. In contrast to Taipei, Mandarin becomes the second language, the primary language is "Tai-yu" or Tai-wanese.
（在台灣，高雄是除了台北之外，成長最快速的城市。它是台灣人的基地。和台北相比，國語變成次要語言，主要語言是「台語」或台灣話。）

** bastion〔'bæstʃən〕*n.* 基地；堡壘

Dialogue 1

外國人： I have heard that, besides Taipei, there is another big city in the south of Taiwan. Could you tell me more about it？

我聽說除了台北以外，在南台灣也有另一個大城市。你能告訴我一點嗎？

中國人： The second largest city in Taiwan is Kaohsiung on the southwest *coast* of Taiwan. It is the biggest international *seaport* in Taiwan and the island's biggest industrial center. It is also the largest *shipbreaking* center in the world and the world's fifth largest *container*-handling port.

台灣第二大的城市是高雄，在台灣的西南**沿岸**。它是台灣最大的**國際港**，而且是島上最大的工業**中心**。同時，它也是全世界最大的**拆船**中心和世界第五大**貨櫃**進出港。

Dialogue 2

外國人： Is it much different from Taipei？
高雄和台北有很大的不同嗎？

中國人： Though Taipei and Kaohsiung are both large cities Kaohsiung having a *population exceeding* 1.2 million, Kaohsiung appears to have a *distinctively appealing* character. It seems to combine the *serenity* of a quiet rural town with the *vibrancy* of a large *metropolis*. 雖然台北和高雄都是大城市，高雄**人口超過**一百二十萬人，但是，整個城市顯示出一種**特殊吸引人的**性格。高雄似乎融合了寧靜鄉鎮的**安詳**和**大都會的活力**。

外國人：What makes you think that？你為什麼會這樣想呢？

中國人：Well, although it is a big city like Taipei, the traffic is not so *congested* and the people appear friendlier.
嗯，雖然它像台北一樣是個大城市，交通卻沒有如此**擁擠**，人們看起來也友善多了。

外國人：What is there I can see in Kaohsiung？
在高雄我可以看到什麼？

中國人：You can go to *Long Life Mountain*. From there you can get a *panoramic view* of the city and harbor. Furthermore, don't miss *Buddha Torch Mountain*. This scenic spot, about an hour's drive from Kaohsiung, is the site of Taiwan's tallest image of Buddha and is the center of Buddhism in southern Taiwan.
你可以到**萬壽山**，從那兒你可以看到這個城市和港口的**全景**。此外，別錯過了**佛光山**，此處距高雄約一小時車程，有著全台灣最大的佛像，也是南台灣的佛教中心。

外國人：How about in the city？市區內呢？

中國人：Kaohsiung boasts excellent shopping and night life. Running through the city, there is the Love River. By the river there is a very large underground *bazaar*. Besides, there are many lakes, pagodas and pavilions near Kaohsiung.
高雄也有很棒的購物聚點和夜生活。有一條愛河流經整個高雄市，河岸邊有一座很大的地下**商場**。此外，高雄附近還有許多湖泊、寶塔，和樓閣。

Dialogue 3

外國人： Where do all the people who live in Kaohsiung go to when they want to *take a break* from city life？

住在高雄的人們想要遠離城市生活休息一下時，到哪裡去呢？

中國人： Many of them like to go to Cheng Ching（Crystal Clear）Lake which is only a 15-minute drive from the downtown district. This beautiful resort includes a beautiful *pagoda*, a *pavilion*, a long *zigzag* bridge, a lovers' bridge and an activity center. Near the lake there is also a golf course which, like all other golf courses in Taiwan, is open to visitors.

很多人喜歡到澄清湖，從市區去只要十五分鐘的路程。這個美麗的勝地包括一座很美的寶塔、一個樓閣、一座很長的曲橋、一座情人橋和一間活動中心。澄清湖附近也有一座高爾夫球場，就像台灣所有其他的高爾夫球場一樣，對遊客開放。

shipbreaking〔'ʃɪp,brekɪŋ〕 n. 拆船業　　exceed〔ɪk'sid〕 v. 超過
appealing〔ə'pilɪŋ〕 adj. 吸引人的　　serenity〔sə'rɛnətɪ〕 n. 安詳；安靜
vibrancy〔'vaɪbrənsɪ〕 n. 活力　metropolis〔mə'trɑplɪs〕 n. 大都市
congested〔kən'dʒɛstɪd〕 adj. 擁擠的
panoramic〔,pænə'ræmɪk〕 adj. 全景的
bazaar〔bə'zɑr〕 n.（城市中的）市場及商業區
pagoda〔pə'godə〕 n. 寶塔　　pavilion〔pə'vɪljən〕 n. 亭；閣
zigzag〔'zɪgzæg〕 adj. Z字形的；彎曲的

HUA LIEN

崇山與海岸交織

相傳大約在七百五十多年前（元朝中葉），馬來西亞（*Malaysia*）發生火山爆發，摧毀了當地的房舍與田產，於是民眾們競相逃難，覓尋可供移居之地。其中一位婦人名叫阿覓賜知蚋，和她弟弟隨著一葉扁舟在海上飄流一個月之後，抵達花蓮，定居於附近納納山麓，成為最早的花蓮居民，他們的後代子孫便是如今的阿美族（*Ami tribe*）人。

花蓮的原住民（*aborigines*）除了阿美族之外，尚有泰雅族、平埔族和布農族。這些部族經常發生爭鬥，甚至成為世仇，彼此之間不相往來。他們一直穴居（*live in caves*）山野，過著以漁獵為生的原始生活（*primitive life*）。清朝康熙年間，才有廣東客家人來此定居，開墾平地，隨後來此的漢人愈來愈多，花蓮也就逐漸地被開發出來。

花蓮東瀕太平洋（*the Pacific Ocean*），西臨中央山脈（*the Central Mountain Range*），境內連綿的崇山峻嶺與曲折的海岸線，構成十分迷人的景緻，令人嘆為觀止，其中尤以中部橫貫公路（*East-West Cross-Island Highway*）的太魯閣峽谷（*Taroko Gorge*）最為知名。

往昔花蓮以八景稱頌全台，此八景為：築港歸帆、能高飛瀑、紅葉尋蹊、秀姑漱玉、八螺疊翠、太魯合流、澄潭躍鯉與安通濯暖。另外神祕谷、木瓜山森林遊樂區、三棧溪谷、美崙山、砂婆噹水、慈惠宮、東淨禪寺、勝安宮等皆位於花蓮市近郊，值得一遊。而阿美文化村（*Ami Culture Village*）更是別具土著風味的觀光地點，除了欣賞山胞（*mountain people*）們表演例行的歌舞節目之外，每當豐年祭、捕魚節、成人節之時，另有特殊的民俗活動，可以深入地探討山胞們熱情洋溢的生活面。

TOPIC 19

花蓮　　　**Hualien**

📼 **Dialogue 1**

外國人：Are there any places of interest on the east coast of Taiwan? 台灣的東岸有沒有任何值得一遊的地方？

中國人：There is Hualien. It is the *capital* of Hualien *County*, the largest but *least densely populated* county on the island as it is a very mountainous region.
花蓮。它是花蓮**縣**的**縣府**，由於花蓮縣是一個非常多山的地區，雖然是島上最大的縣，却**人口最為稀少**。

外國人：Talking of mountains, are there any "mountain people" living there?
談到山地，那裡有沒有任何「山地人」居住？

中國人：About one quarter of the population are *aborigines*, most of whom belong to the *Ami tribe*.
大約四分之一的人口是**原住民**，其中大部分屬於**阿美族**。

📼 **Dialogue 2**

外國人：Is there anything to see in Hualien city itself?
花蓮市本身有沒有任何可看的？

中國人：One of Taiwan's most famous temples is situated in Hualien, the Tze Hui Tang (Temple of Motherly Devotion), a *Taoist complex* that attracts many visitors including *foreigners*. You can also visit a marble plant and *showroom* in Hualien.

台灣最著名的廟宇之一，慈惠宮，位於花蓮市。這是一座**道教的複合建築**，吸引了許多包括**外國人**在內的遊客前往。你也可以參觀花蓮的大理石工廠和**產品陳列室**。

外國人： Can I see the aborigines in Hualien?

在花蓮可以看到原住民嗎？

中國人： Of course you will see them in the street, but if you want to see them *performing* a song-and-dance *show*, you can either see this in Hualien or else go to the nearby Ami Culture Village.

當然，你在街上就會看見。不過，如果你想看他們**表演**歌舞的話，可以在花蓮看或是到附近的阿美族文化村。

🔲 **Dialogue 3**

外國人： Do many people visit Hualien? 很多人到花蓮遊覽嗎？

中國人： Since there is now a railroad through to Taipei, many people visit Hualien. However, they usually go there in order to *tour the East-West Cross-Island Highway.* The prettiest part of the highway, *the Taroko gorge*, is near Hualien and can be visited in a day. On the whole, Hualien is a nice place to relax as the *pace* of life is much slower than in Taipei.

因為目前有一條鐵路直通台北，很多人都到花蓮遊覽。不過，他們通常是為了到**東西橫貫公路旅遊**，而到花蓮的。這條公路最美麗的部分是**太魯閣**，靠近花蓮市，一天之內可以來回。大體上，由於花蓮的生活**步調**比台北慢，是個很好的遊憩地點。

TAINAN

邁向現代化的鳳凰城

古都台南舊名**赤嵌**（*Chinkan*），面積約一百七十多平方公里，南北長約二十多公里（*kilometer*），東西寬約十三多公里，市區分為東、南、西北、中、安南、安平等七區。其舊日市街和**羅馬**（*Rome*）一樣建立在七個高低不平的山丘上，多數以城牆圍繞起來。縱觀整個台南市區，到處可見古老文化的遺跡。

西元一五九〇年（明萬曆年間），福建泉州移民首

度出現此地。西元一六二四年（明天啓年間），從澎湖撤退來台的**荷蘭人**（*the Dutch*）以台南為中心，在此建築**普羅民遮城**（*Fort Providentia*，即今赤嵌樓附近），作為**指揮總部**（*headquarters*）。當時適逢明末李自成作亂，於是閩粵兩省近十幾萬名人民移居台灣，與荷蘭人共同雜居經商。從西元一六六三年**國姓爺**（*Koxinga*）鄭成功驅逐荷蘭人到清朝末年之間歷時二百多年，台南一直是本島的首府所在。

漫步於台南紅磚街道的古老巷弄之中，目睹兩旁高齡老榕與陳年舊屋，不禁令人緬懷古都舊時風情。今日的台南正逐步走向現代化的過程，道路不斷地開拓，樓房一棟棟地蓋起，就如同夏日台南街頭蓬勃怒放的**鳳凰花木**（*flaming tree*）一般，正以活潑生動的精力迎接未來的挑戰，這也許是每個古老城市所必經的變革吧！

TOPIC 20

Tainan

🔲 Introducing Taiwan ➤

- Fort Providentia, the Dutch headquarters in Taiwan, was leveled by an earthquake in 1862. Later, in 1875 the Chihkan Tower（赤嵌樓）was erected by Chinese authorities on the same spot.

（普羅民遮城，在台的荷蘭人總部，在一八六二年一次地震中夷為平地。後來在一八七五年，中國政府當局在同一地點建造赤嵌樓。）

- The Chinese authorities commissioned the French engineers to design "Eternal Castle"（Yi Tsai Castle，億載金城），and it was built in the year of 1874.

（中國政府當局委託法國工程師設計「億載金城」，並且於一八七四年建造。）

- Tainan is known as the city of temples. In total, there are two hundred and seven temples in the city and the surrounding environs. Temple-hopping is something you can do on your visit there. A trip to Tainan will make you an expert in Chinese temples.

（台南以古寺聞名。總計這個城和周圍近郊共有二百零七座廟宇。穿梭於廟宇之間，是你到台南遊覽時可以做的事情。到台南一遊會使你成為中國廟宇專家。）

** environs〔ɪnˈvaɪənz, ˈɛnvərənz〕*n. pl.* 近郊；郊外

▶ Dialogue

外國人：Which is the oldest city in Taiwan？
台灣最古老的都市是哪一個？

中國人：Tainan, in the southwest part of Taiwan not far from
Kaohsiung. In fact it was the **capital** of this island
for 222 years from 1663 to 1885, and is forever **linked**
with the memory of Cheng Cheng-Kung, better known
as **Koxinga,** one of China's greatest national heroes.
台灣西南部離高雄不遠的台南。事實上，從一六六三年到
一八八五年，二百二十二年間，它是本島的**首府**。而且永
遠使人**聯**想起鄭成功，大家都叫他**國姓爺**，中國最偉大的
民族英雄之一。

外國人：Who was he？ What did he do to be called a hero？
他是誰？他做了什麼，而被稱爲英雄？

中國人：He was a Ming dynasty **Loyalist** from the China Mainland,
who, together with 30,000 troops in war **junks**, put
an end to the 37-year Dutch colonial occupation of
Taiwan that had begun in 1624.
他是來自大陸的明朝**忠臣**。他和乘著戰**船**的三萬軍隊，結
束了自一六二四年開始，歷時三十七年的荷蘭人對台灣的
殖民佔領。

外國人：Wow！ That was some **feat.** Is there anything in Tainan
to **commemorate** him？
哇！那是一大**功績**。台南有什麼東西是**紀念**他的？

** capital〔ˈkæpətl〕n. 首都　　link〔lɪŋk〕v. 連結
loyalist〔ˈlɔɪəlɪst〕n. 忠臣；勤王者　　junk〔dʒʌŋk〕n.中國大帆船（三桅平底）

中國人： There is the **shrine** to Koxinga in Tainan which was built in 1875. It seems that it took the Ching dynasty （which followed the Ming）over two hundred years to **recognize** him as a national hero. Besides this shrine, there is the **Lu Erh Men** （Deer's Ear Gate）where Koxinga landed in Taiwan in 1661 and also the **Chihkan Tower** which was formerly the site of the Dutch-built **headquarters** in Tainan.

台南有一座一八七五年蓋的國姓爺的廟。清朝（明朝之後）似乎在兩百多年之後才肯承認他是民族英雄。除了這座廟，還有一個鹿耳門，是國姓爺一六六一年登陸台灣的地方，而赤嵌樓是以前荷蘭人蓋在台南的總部地點所在。

*   *   *

外國人： What else is Tainan famous for？台南還有別的出名的嗎？

中國人： Its temples. There are over two hundred of them. There is also the **Yi Tsai** （**Eternal** ）**Castle** built in 1874 as a **coastal defense** position. However, it does not command a view of the sea, because the **accumulation** of **silt** has extended the **coastline**.

台南的廟很出名，總共有兩百多個。還有一座一八七四年蓋的作爲海岸防衛地點的億載金城，不過，從這裏無法俯視海，因爲泥沙的淤積已經延伸到海岸線。

** shrine〔ʃraɪn〕*n.* 廟   headquarters〔'hɛd'kwɔrtɚz〕*n.* 總部
coastal〔'kostl̩〕*adj.* 海岸的   defense〔dɪ'fɛns〕*n.* 防衛
accumulation〔ə,kjumjə'leʃən〕*n.* 積聚   silt〔sɪlt〕*n.* 淤泥；淤沙

Chapter 2

A WINDOW TO TAIWAN

一

台灣風情畫

一

TOPIC 21

Hot Springs

Question

Where are Taiwan's world famous hot springs?
在台灣，全世界著名的溫泉在哪裏？

Reply

Most of the nearly one hundred sites are located in the *valleys* of the Central Mountain Range. Many of these sites have hotels that pipe the water into their own *bathtubs* and *bathing pools*. Others are *remote* and have no *facilities* at all. The best known and most widely used are located at Peitou and Yangmingshan. Also popular are hot springs located at Wulai and Chiaohsi. These sites are located in spectacular mountain *sceneries*. During chilly mornings a *mist* rises from these springs adding a *fairyland* quality to the setting. Some people like to soak in hot springs on cold days believing it'll help their *circulation*.

將近有一百處的溫泉，大部分是位於中央山脈的**山谷**裏。這些地方很多都有旅館，用管子輸送水到**浴缸**和**浴池**裏。其它的就很**遠**，而且沒有任何**設備**。最有名、利用最廣的，位於北投和陽明山。同樣受歡迎的還有位於烏來和礁溪的溫泉。這些地方都地處於蔚爲奇觀的山**景**裏。在寒冷的早晨，一陣**霧**由這些溫泉間昇起，爲這個背景增添了**仙境**之質。有些人喜歡在冷天時泡在溫泉裏，認爲這將有助於**循環**。

** spectacular〔spɛk'tækjələ〕*adj*. 蔚爲奇觀的；壯觀的
   soak〔sok〕*v*. 浸泡

Dialogue 1

外國人： Are there any hot springs near Taipei?
台北附近有任何溫泉嗎？

中國人： Yes, Peitou is only about an hour north of Taipei and it's famous for its hot springs.
有，北投在台北以北，大概只要一小時，它是以溫泉出名的。

外國人： Oh yes, I've been there. There are a lot of *Japanese-style inns* at Peitou. Why is that?
喔！對！我曾去過那裏。在北投有很多**日式酒館**。那是爲什麼呢？

中國人： Peitou was a *resort* for Japanese officers and officials when Taiwan was a Japanese colony.
在台灣是日本的殖民地時，北投是日本軍官和官員**常去之處**。

外國人： Wasn't *prostitution* a big attraction there?
那裏的**娼妓業**，是不是個很大的吸引？

中國人： Yes, it was. However, that is in the past, our government has long since cleaned it up.
是的，曾經是。然而，那是在過去，我們的政府長久以來，一直在整頓。

Dialogue 2

外國人： Wow! That's hot! Feel it for yourself.
哇！好燙！你來試試看。

中國人： Hmmm, that is hot. 嗯！很燙。

外國人：We can't go in there, we'll be *boiled* alive!
　　　　我們不能進去，會被活活**煮熟**的。

中國人：In that case, let's boil some eggs.
　　　　如果那樣的話，我們來煮些蛋吧。

外國人：You brought eggs with you？你帶了蛋了？

中國人：Yeah. 是啊。

外國人：Did you know the water was going to be this hot？
　　　　你知道水會這麼燙嗎？

中國人：Yeah. 是的。

bathing pool 浴池　　bathtub〔'bæθ,tʌb〕*n.* 浴缸；浴盆

circulation〔,sɝkjə'leʃən〕*n.* 循環（尤指血液出入心臟的運行）

dehydration〔,dihaɪ'dreʃən〕*n.* 脫水；使乾

facility〔fə'sɪlətɪ〕*n.* 設備（常用複數）

fairyland〔'fɛrɪ,lænd〕*n.* 仙境；仙國　　inn〔ɪn〕*n.* 酒館；客棧

mineral water 礦泉水（天然含有礦物質的水，尤指有醫藥價值者）

mist〔mɪst〕*n.* 霧　　potable〔'potəbl̩〕*adj.* 可以喝的（= *fit to drink*）

prostitution〔,prastə'tjuʃən〕*n.* 賣淫；娼妓業

remote〔rɪ'mot〕*adj.* 遙遠的　　resort〔rɪ'zɔrt〕*n.* 常去之處；勝地

scenery〔'sinərɪ〕*n.* 風景；景緻（例如高山、平原、谿谷、森林）

steam〔stim〕*n.* 蒸氣；水氣　　sulfur〔'sʌlfɚ〕*n.* 硫磺

sweat〔swɛt〕*n.* 汗　*v.* 出汗；使出汗　　*Turkish bath* 土耳其浴

water-logged〔'wɔtɚ,lagd〕*adj.* 吸飽水的；浸水的

TOPIC 22

臺灣野生動物 Wildlife in Taiwan

Question

What kinds of wildlife are there on Taiwan?

台灣有哪些種類的野生動物？

Reply

Our island was rich with wildlife but excessive hunting has pushed many species close to *extinction*. For example the Formosan black bear, the *leopard cat*, the spotted deer, and *civet* are all very rare. Some *species*, however, are managing to *thrive* in remote mountainous regions such as the *wild boar*, mountain hare, and Formosan Rock monkey. Our bird population is also flourishing with over 400 species. And unfortunately we also have a large variety of *poisonous* snakes. The story goes that the Japanese were *experimenting* with poisonous snakes and set them all free when they were forced to return Taiwan.

我們島上有很多的野生動物，但是過度的捕獵已使得很多種類瀕臨**絕種**。譬如台灣黑熊、**野貓**、梅花鹿、**麝貓**都是非常稀罕的。不過，像**野豬**、山兔、台灣石猴等，有些**種類**，正設法在偏遠的山區**繁殖**。我們鳥類數量同樣有四百種以上之多。很不幸地，我們也有很多各種不同的**毒蛇**。傳說，日本人以前拿毒蛇**作實驗**，當他們被迫歸還台灣時，就把這些毒蛇都釋放了。

** hare〔hɛr〕*n.* 野兔

🔲 **Dialogue 1** ▶

外國人： Let's go *hunting*. 我們去**打獵**。

中國人： Impossible, it's against the law here and anyway, *private citizens* are not allowed to have *firearms*.
不可能，在這裏打獵是違法的，而且無論如何，**平民**是不允許擁有**輕武器（槍砲）**的。

外國人： Why is that? Hunting is such a *bloody* good sport.
爲什麼？打獵是**非常**好的運動。

中國人： Our wildlife has suffered enough from *excessive* hunting in the past, so we have to protect them now.
台灣的野生動物在過去已受夠了**過度**的捕獵，所以我們現在必須保護牠們。

外國人： How about duck hunting? There's no shortage of birds here. 獵鴨怎麼樣？這裏不缺鳥類。

中國人： Yes, but it's still illegal. We can go bird watching though！對，但仍是違法的。不過，我們可以去賞鳥！

🔲 **Dialogue 2** ▶

外國人： How's the fishing here? 這裏釣魚如何？

中國人： Taiwan is the ideal place for fishing. The *warm currents* off our east coast and shallow waters off our west coast attract *abundant* varieties of fish.
台灣是釣魚的理想地方。我們東海岸外的**暖流**，和西海岸外的淺水，引來了種類**繁多的**魚。

外國人： What varieties? 有哪些種類？

中國人： There's *sailfish*, *tuna*, *bonito*, *moray eel*, and more.
有**旗魚**、**鮪魚**、**鰹魚**、**海鰻**以及更多其他的。

外國人： Do I need a fishing *license*? 我需要釣魚執照吧？

中國人： No, all you need is a *fishing rod*.
不必，你所需要的就是一支**釣魚竿**。

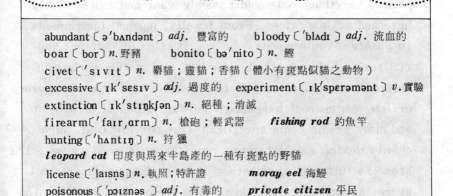

abundant〔ə'bʌndənt〕*adj*. 豐富的　　bloody〔'blʌdɪ〕*adj*. 流血的
boar〔bor〕*n*. 野豬　　bonito〔bə'nito〕*n*. 鰹
civet〔'sɪvɪt〕*n*. 麝貓；靈貓；香貓（體小有斑點似貓之動物）
excessive〔ɪk'sɛsɪv〕*adj*. 過度的　　experiment〔ɪk'spɛrəmənt〕*v*.實驗
extinction〔ɪk'stɪŋkʃən〕*n*. 絕種；消滅
firearm〔'faɪr‚ɑrm〕*n*. 槍砲；輕武器　　***fishing rod*** 釣魚竿
hunting〔'hʌntɪŋ〕*n*. 狩獵
leopard cat 印度與馬來半島產的一種有斑點的野貓
license〔'laɪsn̩s〕*n*.執照；特許證　　***moray eel*** 海鰻
poisonous〔'pɔɪznəs〕*adj*. 有毒的　　***private citizen*** 平民
sailfish〔'sel‚fɪʃ〕*n*. 旗魚　　species〔'spiʃɪz,-ʃiz〕*n*. 種；類
thrive〔θraɪv〕*v*. 繁盛；健旺　　tuna〔'tunə〕*n*. 鮪
warm currents 暖流

TOPIC 23

購物 **Shopping**

🔲 **Question** ▶

Is the shopping any good on Taiwan?

在台灣逛街有什麼好處?

🔲 **Reply** ▶

Are fishes good swimmers? Taiwan is a paradise for shoppers. Everything you could possibly want and more is sold
here and at low prices. From jewelry, musical instruments,
to *yachts* — you name it, we've got it. One of Taiwan's spe-
cialites is Chinese art, here you'll find a wide variety of
antiques, ***exquisite reproductions***, and works by ***contemporary
artists***. An unusual bargain in Taiwan is dental treatment
and many people come specifically for our low cost, high
quality ***dental care***. Whatever your taste or mood we have the
store to turn you on, whether it be a gigantic department
store, a ***cozy specialty shop***, or a lively night market. And
feel free to just ***browse*** as we don't employ ***high pressure
selling*** tactics. 魚是游泳好手嗎?台灣是購物者的天堂。每一樣東
西都是你可能會想要的,而且這裏的東西比較多,價格低廉。從珠
寶、樂器,到**遊艇**,你說的出來的,我們都有。台灣的特產之一是中國
藝術,在這裏你會發現各式各樣的**古董、精美的複製品**,以及**當代
藝術家**的作品。在台灣,牙齒的診療索價非常便宜,很多人為了我
們**看牙**的低收費、高品質而特地跑來。不論你的品味、心情怎麼樣,
我們都有使你興奮的商店,不管是超大型的百貨公司,**溫馨舒適的
小型商店**,或是熱鬧的夜市。不要拘束,**隨便看看**,因為我們不採
用**高壓的銷售**策略。

📼 **Dialogue 1**

外國人：How much is this necklace? 這條項鍊多少錢？

中國人：Five thousand dollars. 五仟元。

外國人：Why is it so expensive? 為什麼這麼貴？

中國人：This is made from the finest *pearls* available.
這是用最好的**珍珠**作的。

外國人：It's still too expensive. No thanks.
還是太貴了。不必了，謝謝。

中國人：Wait! Come back! OK, I'll let you have it for $ 4,500.
等一等！回來！好吧！四千五百元賣給你。

外國人：No, that's still too expensive. I'll give you 3000 for it.
不，還是太貴了。我出三千元。

中國人：I'll have to ask the boss, please wait a second. (*moments later*) OK, he says he'll make an *exception* this
time because he's in a good mood.
我必須問問老板，請等一下。（過一會兒之後）好吧，他說
這次是**例外**，因為他心情不錯。

外國人：Great, in that case I'll take three sets.
太棒了，那麼我買三組。

📼 **Dialogue 2**

外國人：How do you know you exist? 你怎麼知道你存在著？

中國人：I think, therefore I exist. 我思，故我在。

外國人：I've got a better reply for this ***modern age***：I shop, therefore I exist. Shopping defines people's lives now.
在這個**新潮的年代**，我有個更好的回答：我逛街，所以我存在。逛街爲現在人們的生活下了定義。

中國人：I see what you mean. If people couldn't go shopping, there would be no reason for them to work.
我知道你的意思。如果人們不能去逛街，他們就沒有理由工作。

外國人：That's right, and then society would ***fall apart***, and chaos would reign. 對，然後社會會**解體**，就會一片混亂。

中國人：Hey! I just got paid today, let's go shopping.
嘿！我今天才剛領薪水，我們去逛街吧。

外國人：OK, I need another new pair of shoes to wear on Thursday. 好啊，我需要另一雙新鞋，星期四要穿的。

antique〔æn'tik〕*n.* 古董　　bargain〔'bɑrgɪn〕*n.* 索價便宜的東西
browse〔braʊz〕*v.* 漫然地觀看店內或攤上的貨；瀏覽
cozy〔'kozɪ〕*adj.* 溫暖而舒適的　　discount〔'dɪskaʊnt〕*n.* 折扣
exquisite〔'ɛkskwɪzɪt，ɪk's-〕*adj.* 精美的
gigantic〔dʒaɪ'gæntɪk〕*adj.* 龐大的；巨大的
jewelry〔'dʒuəlrɪ〕*n.* 珠寶（集合稱）；珠寶類　***mark down*** 減價
musical instrument 樂器　peddler〔'pɛdlə〕*n.* 小販
proprietor〔prə'praɪətə〕*n.* 所有者；有專利權者
reproduction〔,riprə'dʌkʃən〕*n.* 複製品　　reign〔ren〕*v.* 盛行
specialty shop 只出售一種或數種有關貨物之小規模商店（如文具店）
yacht〔jɑt〕*n.* 遊艇；快艇
window shopping 逛街；瀏覽商店的櫥窗（不一定想買東西）

INTRODUCING TAIWAN IN ENGLISH • TOPIC 24

　　台灣的氣候有三大特徵：高溫（ *hot* ）、多雨（ *rainy* ）、多颱風（ *typhoon* ）。一年四季裡均相當溫暖，除了山地之外，每年四月至十月，月均溫都在攝氏（ *Centigrade* ）二十度以上；冬季時偶有低到十度以下的寒天，則是因為大陸冷氣團（ *air mass* ）南下的結果。一般説來，台灣地區雨量由於受地形影響，高山多於平地，東岸多於西岸。季風（ *monsoon* ）是構成雨量分配的主要因素，夏天西南季風（ *south-west monsoon* ）從海上帶來暖濕的西南氣流，西南部各地水量充沛，佔全年降雨量的百分之八十以上。冬天時，東北季風（ *northeast monsoon* ）盛行，造成台灣東北部一帶冬雨連綿，極為惱人。夏秋之際是台灣著名的颱風季節，颱風屬於熱帶氣旋（ *tropical cyclone* ），不但風力強勁，而且水氣沛然，經常狂風挾持暴雨掠過，帶給島上極大的威脅。平均每年均有三點五次的颱風來襲，尤以八月份最多，七月九月份次之。

《 Terms and Phrases 》

* atmosphere〔ˋætməsˌfɪr〕 *n.* 大氣　　***cold air mass*** 冷氣團
* ***cold front*** 冷鋒　　Fahrenheit〔ˋfærənˌhaɪt〕 *n.* 華氏溫度
* ***weather forecasting*** 天氣預報　　cloudy〔ˋklaʊdɪ〕 *adj.* 多雲的
* overcast〔ˋovɚˌkæst〕 *adj.* 陰的　　drizzle〔ˋdrɪzḷ〕 *n.* 毛毛雨
* shower〔ˋʃaʊɚ〕 *n.* 陣雨　　***thunder shower*** 雷陣雨
* ***meteorological satellite*** 氣象衛星　　***weather report*** 氣象報告
* ***damp spring weather*** 黃梅天氣　　downpour〔ˋdaʊnˌpor〕 *n.* 滂沱大雨
* ***heat wave*** 熱浪　　（ ***dense; thin*** ） ***fog*** （濃；薄）霧
* frost〔frɔst〕 *n.* 霜　　***wind direction*** 風向
* ***trade wind*** 信風；貿易風（由東南或東北方向赤道吹襲的強風）
* hurricane〔ˋhɝɪˌken〕 *n.* 颶風　　breeze〔briz〕 *n.* 微風

TOPIC 24

天氣　Climate

▭▭ Dialogue 1 ▶

中國人： Who can tell me something about Taiwan's weather？
誰能告訴我有關臺灣的氣候呢？

外國人： It rains a lot. 常下雨。

中國人： Right, but there's more to it than that. Taiwan's people are fond of saying, "Taiwan's weather is as **unpredictable** as a woman's mood." It really is unpredictable. One minute you're enjoying the beautiful
afternoon sun, and the next (minute) you're running
for cover from the **torrential rain**！ What I want to
point out to you is that while we're in Northern Taiwan, you don't want to leave your umbrella at the hotel.
對了，可是還不止這樣。台灣人喜歡說，「臺灣天氣像女
人情緒一樣**難測**。」眞的是不可測。前一分鐘你才享受午
後美好的陽光，下一分鐘你會爲了找一個躲**傾盆大雨**的地
方而奔跑！我要**指出**的是：當我們在台灣北部的時候，不
要把雨傘放在旅館。

外國人： Why do you say " in Northern Taiwan"？ Is the weather
in Southern Taiwan different？
你爲什麼說「臺灣北部」呢？台灣南部天氣不一樣嗎？

中國人： Yes. In winter and spring, Northern Taiwan is cool
and rainy, but the south is warm and sunny. Then,

in summer and fall, the North is hot and less rainy, but the South gets **drenched**. Anyway, this is the middle of May now, one of the most unpredictable times of the year throughout the island.

是啊。冬天和春天時,臺灣北部天氣冷、常下雨,南部則溫暖、陽光充足。夏天和秋天時,北部天氣熱、較少下雨,而南部非常**潮濕**。不管怎麼說,現在是五月中旬,是全島一年當中,天氣最難預料的時候之一。

Dialogue 2

外國人: Why is there such a large difference between the North and South? 南部和北部氣候為什麼有這麼大的不同呢?

中國人: It's because there are two annual **monsoons**: the northeast **monsoon** during the winter and the southwest **monsoon** during the summer.

因為每年有兩個**季風**:冬天有東北**季風**,夏天有西南**季風**。

外國人: Is there any east-west difference in weather? 東部和西部天氣有什麼不同嗎?

中國人: Yes. The central west coast gets much less rain than do other areas. The east coast weather follows the north-south pattern. 是的,中西海岸雨量比其他地區少得多。東部海岸天氣與前述北部──南部型態一樣。

外國人: When do the typhoons come? 颱風什麼時候來呢?

中國人: Any time between mid-June and mid-October. Don't worry, you'll miss them **completely**.

六月中到十月中任何時候。別擔心,你們**絕對**會躲過的。

INTRODUCING TAIWAN IN ENGLISH • TOPIC 25

台灣省(*Taiwan Province*)是中國最小的省份,在地理上包括台灣本島(*Taiwan proper*)和其餘大大小小的附屬島嶼共七十七個,散布在中國大陸(*Chinese mainland*)東南方的海面之上。一般人對台灣的印象以台灣本島為主,台灣本島東濱太平洋(*the Pacific Ocean*),南臨巴士海峽(*the Bashi Channel*),西隔台灣海峽(*Taiwan Strait*)與大陸遙遙相望,中間僅距一百多公里。島上的地形以山地最為顯著,佔全島面積百分之六十以上,其中中央山脈(*the Central Mountain Range*)盤據台灣中部,阻絕東部與西部的交通往來。其他散布在四週海面上的附屬島嶼很多僅是狹小的珊瑚礁岩,一無人煙;擁有居民的島嶼是面積較大的金門(*Chinmen*)、馬祖(*Matzu*)、蘭嶼(*Orchid island*)、綠島(*Green island*)和澎湖(*Penghu*)等。

《 Terms and Phrases 》

- ***mountain range*** 山脈   ***foot of the mountain*** 山麓(= *piedmont*)
- foothill〔ˈfʊtˌhɪl〕*n.* 山麓丘陵   basin〔ˈbesn̩〕*n.* 盆地
- archipelago〔ˌɑrkəˈpɛləˌgo〕*n.* 群島   peninsula〔pəˈnɪnsələ〕*n.* 半島
- plateau〔plæˈto〕*n.* 高原;臺地   ***coastal plain*** 海岸平原
- coastline〔ˈkostˌlaɪn〕*n.* 海岸線   gulf〔gʌlf〕*n.* 海灣
- ***sunken reef*** 暗礁(= *submerged reef*)   ***coral reef*** 珊瑚礁
- continent〔ˈkɑntənənt〕*n.* 大陸;洲   watershed〔ˈwɔtɚˌʃɛd〕*n.* 分水嶺
- ***terrace tablelands*** 梯形臺地   ***volcanic rocks*** 火山岩
- area〔ˈærɪə〕*n.* 地區;面積

TOPIC 25

   **Geography**

📼 **Dialogue 1** ▶

外國人： How many islands *comprise* Taiwan *Province*?
台灣**省包括**多少個島？

中國人： There are 77 in all. 總共有七十七個。

外國人： I never imagined there were so many.
我從來沒想過有這麼多。

中國人： Still, many of them are only small *islets*. Most of them,
64 to be exact, are part of the Penghu *Archipelago*,
also called the Pescadores, and lie to the west of
Taiwan *proper*.
還有，其中有很多祇是**小島**。而且大部分，正確的數字是六
十四個，屬於澎湖群島，澎湖**群島**又稱中國澎湖群島，位於
台灣**本島**的西方。

外國人： Are there any other fairly large islands?
有其他比較大的島嗎？

中國人： No, but Green and Orchid islands to the east, and
Matzu and Chinmen islands, within sight — and *firing
range* — of mainland China, are worthy of mention.
沒有，不過東方有綠島和蘭嶼以及在中國大陸視界——**射程**
——內的馬祖和金門，值得一提。

外國人： What's the total land area of Taiwan？
臺灣的土地總面積是多少？

中國人： The areas of all 77 islands combined *add up to* 35,981 square *kilometers*, or 13,850 square miles, about the same as Holland. Taiwan is the smallest Chinese province. 七十七個島合起來，面積**總共**是三萬五千九百八十一**平方公里**，或一萬三千八百五十平方英里，大約和荷蘭一樣大。台灣是中國最小的省。

🔲 **Dialogue 2**

外國人： Tell me something about Taiwan proper.
告訴我有關台灣本島的事情吧。

中國人： Well, its length is 394 kilometers and *breadth* is 144 kilometers at the widest point. Roughly two thirds of the island is *mountainous* or *hilly*, which theoretically leaves us with over 10,000 square kilometers of *arable land*, but not all of that is actually *farmed*.
嗯，它的長度是三百九十四公里，最寬的地方**寬**一百四十四公里。島上大約三分之二的地方**多山**，這樣一來，理論上我們剩下一萬多平方公里的**可耕地**，但實際上並沒有全被**耕種**。

外國人： Why not？ 為什麼不？

中國人： For one thing cities, towns and factories take up a lot of space, and further, some flatland areas simply have poor soil. 一則是城市、鄉鎮和工廠占去了許多空間，而且有些平地根本是土壤貧瘠的。

外國人：　Taiwan's mountains appear to be fairly tall. How tall
　　　　　are they？台灣的山好像相當高。有多高呢？

中國人：　There are 62 peaks over 3,000 meters tall. At 3,997
　　　　　meters, *Jade Mountain* is the tallest.
　　　　　有六十二座山峯超過三千公尺。**玉山**最高，有三千九百九十
　　　　　七公尺。

外國人：　Do any of the mountains ever get snow？
　　　　　有任何一座山上下過雪嗎？

中國人：　Sure. There's even a ski resort at Hohuan Mountain,
　　　　　if you can believe that！
　　　　　當然。如果你相信的話，合歡山上甚至有個滑雪勝地！

comprise〔kəm'praɪz〕*v.* 包括；由～組成
province〔'pravɪns〕*n.* 省　　islet〔'aɪlɪt〕*n.* 小島
archipelago〔ɑrkə'pɛlə,go〕*n.* 群島
Pescadores〔,pɛska'dɔrɪz〕*n.pl.* 中國澎湖群島（中譯爲 *Penghu*）
Taiwan Proper 台灣本島（proper 用於此義時，接在所修飾的名詞後面）
firing range 射程　　*add up to* 總計達～
kilometer〔'kɪlə,mitɚ〕*n.* 公里　　breadth〔brɛdθ〕*n.* 寬度
mountainous〔'mauntnəs〕*adj.* 多山的
hilly〔'hɪlɪ〕*adj.* 多小山的　　arable〔'ærəbl〕*adj.* 適於耕種的
farm〔farm〕*v.* 耕（田）　　*Jade Mountain* 玉山

中國人最早發現台灣，大致上是西元三世紀以後的事。秦漢之時，台灣尚被稱作**夷洲**（*Yi-chow*），意指「**未開化的洲**」（*barbarian state*），由此可想像當時島上一片蠻荒的景象。之後，隋煬帝曾一度派人來台訪俗。而一直要到宋元兩代之際，中國人民才開始陸續渡海**定居**（*settlement*）。

元朝**蒙古人**（*the Mongolian*）主政，台灣歸入了中國的**版圖**（*territory*）。明代鄭成功之父鄭芝龍所領導的反政府武裝交易集團曾經開拓台灣本島西南部的北港一帶，揭開了開發台灣的序幕。但是在西元一六二四年，**荷蘭人**（*the Dutch*）登陸台灣，以台南為中心開始了三十八年的殖民統治。**西班牙人**（*the Spanish*）雖然也曾據有北部的**雞籠**（現今基隆）、淡水等地十六年之久，但旋即為荷人所驅逐。

台灣正式掌握在漢人政權的直接統治之下是在西元一六六一年。這一年，由大陸退據金門的**國姓爺**（*Koxinga*）鄭成功打敗了荷蘭人，以台灣作為反清復明的根據地。不少明朝遺老知識份子由於不甘異族統治，也同時移往台灣，一時引起漢人前往台灣開墾的熱潮，這些移民「篳路藍縷，以啓山林」，充滿了**開拓者的精神**（*frontier spirit*）。

鄭氏三代統治的時期結束後，清朝接手治理台灣大約二百年，在此段時間當中，台灣人口由十二萬人激增為二百五十五萬人，並且在一八八七年躍進為一個獨立的**行省**（*province*）。可惜滿清末年腐敗無能，西元一八九五年且將台灣割據給日本，一直到民國三十四年（一九四五）**二次世界大戰**（*World War II*）結束，日本宣佈無條件投降，台灣才又重歸中國版圖。

TOPIC 26

History

Dialogue 1

外國人：Has Taiwan always been a Chinese *province*?
臺灣一直是中國的一省嗎？

中國人：No, it was first a *protectorate*, beginning in 1206, and then a *prefecture* of Fukien province for about 200 years until in 1887 the Manchu Ching Dynasty government made it a province.
不是，在一二〇六年，剛開始是一個**保護領地**，後來有大約兩百年的時間是福建省的**轄區**，直到一八八七年滿清政府才讓它成為一個省。

外國人：Wasn't there a Japanese government at one time?
不是有一段時間有日本政府嗎？

中國人：The Japanese occupied Taiwan from 1895 to 1945.
日本從一八九五年到一九四五年佔領過臺灣。

外國人：Have there ever been any other foreign *occupations* of Taiwan? 還有沒有其他外國**統治**過臺灣？

中國人：Yes. The Dutch occupied Taiwan from 1624 to 1661.
有的。荷蘭人從一六二四年到一六六一年佔據臺灣。

** province〔ˈprɑvɪns〕n. 省份
protectorate〔prəˈtɛktərɪt〕n. 保護國（受他國保護的國家）；保護領地
prefecture〔ˈprifɛktʃɚ〕n. 轄區　　occupation〔ˌɑkjəˈpeʃən〕n. 佔據

外國人： What happened in 1661？ 一六六一年發生了什麼事呢？

中國人： The Ming Dynasty loyalist general Cheng Cheng-Kung
（Koxinga） *subjugated* them in that year. He is a local
hero. 那年明朝忠臣鄭成功將軍（國姓爺）**征服**荷蘭人。他
是位地方英雄。

🔲 **Dialogue 2** ▶

外國人： Why are there two names for Taiwan？
臺灣為什麼有兩個名字呢？

中國人： You mean, why is it also called *Formosa*？ That is the
name by which the Portuguese—and later most westerners
—called Taiwan. The word is Portuguese for "beautiful(
island)." This name should no longer be used.
你是說為什麼它也稱作**福爾摩沙**嗎？那是葡萄牙人——以及後
來大多數西方人—— 稱呼台灣的名字。這個字是葡萄牙文，意
思是「美麗（島）」。這個字不應再使用了。

外國人： How long have Chinese people lived on Taiwan？
中國人在臺灣住多久了？

外國人： The earliest Chinese *settlers* arrived here from Fukien
Province in the Second and Third Centuries A.D., but
began coming in numbers only during the Fifteenth
Century. 西元二、三世紀時，早期中國**移民者**首先從福建省
來到此地，但是只有在十五世紀時才開始大量前來。

** subjugate〔ˈsʌbdʒə‚get〕*v.* 征服
Formosa〔fɔrˈmosə〕*n.* 福爾摩沙（即台灣，正式名稱為 *Taiwan*）
settler〔ˈsɛtlə〕*n.* 定居者；居留者

外國人： Did the mainland Chinese governments ever *explore*
Taiwan？中國政府曾經**踏勘**過臺灣嗎？

中國人： Yes. The first attempted Chinese exploration of yichow,
as Taiwan was then known to them, came in 239 A.D.
Yichow means " *barbarian* state."
是的。那時臺灣叫做夷洲，中國第一次踏勘夷洲是在西元二
三九年時。夷洲的意思是「**未開化的**洲」。

外國人： When did the R.O.C. establish its capital in Taipei ?
中華民國是在什麼時候建都於臺北呢？

中國人： That was in 1949, after it removed from the mainland.
Taipei is the *temporary* capital of the republic.
是在一九四九年，從大陸遷離時。台北是中華民國**暫時的**
首都。

** explore〔ɪkˈsplɔr〕 *v.* 探測；踏勘
barbarian〔bɑrˈbɛrɪən〕 *adj.* 野蠻的；未開化的
temporary〔ˈtɛmpəˌrɛrɪ〕 *adj.* 暫時的；臨時的

中國南方一帶，每年5月至7月之間是最多雨的時期，俗稱梅雨（*plum rains*）季節，此時正逢梅子成熟期，故名之。但有時亦被戲稱「霉雨」（*mold rains*），因為一旦下起梅雨，往往竟日雨絲綿延不止，難見天日，常引起潮濕發霉的現象。我國江淮一帶經常大鬧水災，多半係由梅雨所引起。台灣每年五月、六月之間也有段梅雨季節，以北部台灣最為顯著，住在台北、基隆、宜蘭一帶的居民，此時外出必然不忘隨身攜帶一把雨傘（*umbrella*），否則便有淪為街頭落湯雞之險。引起梅雨的原因，主要來自於長江（*Yangtze river*）一帶有準滯留鋒，產生一連串氣旋（*cyclone*，中間平靜四周強烈的風），使得高空西風移往喜馬拉雅山（*Himalaya mountains*）以北，而帶進來暖濕的西南氣流之故。

TOPIC 27

Plum Rains

Dialogue

外國人： I heard that it rains a lot in Taiwan. An umbrella is an absolute ***necessity***！
聽說台灣常下雨。雨傘絕對是**必需品**！

中國人： I think the problem is that you can never predict how the weather is going to ***turn out*** and so one should always carry an umbrella.
我想，問題在於你永遠無法預測天氣怎麼**變**，所以只得一直帶把傘。

外國人： When it rains, is the rain always heavy like during a ***typhoon***？下雨的時候，雨老是下得跟**颱風**時一樣大嗎？

中國人： Not necessarily. Sometimes the rain just falls lightly, a little like a ***tap dripping***.
不一定。有時雨就是下得很小，有點像**水龍頭**在**滴水**。

外國人： Is there a particular time of the year when it rains like that？每年有特定的時候，是下那樣的雨嗎？

中國人： Usually around May. In fact, we call this kind of rain "***plum rains***."
通常在五月左右。事實上，我們稱這種雨叫「**梅雨**」。

** necessity〔nəˈsɛsətɪ〕*n.* 必需品　　***turn out*** 變成
typhoon〔taɪˈfun〕*n.* 颱風　　tap〔tæp〕*n.* 龍頭
drip〔drɪp〕*v.* 滴落　　***plum rains*** 梅雨

外國人：Why's that? 怎麼說？

中國人：The term was originally **coined** in Mainland China. The people in Kiangnan said that these rains caused the plums to **swell** and **ripen**. 這名詞最早是在中國大陸**取**的。江南的人說，這些雨使梅子**變大成熟**。

外國人：Well, at least they had a **favorable** reaction to the rain. Most of us always **moan** when it rains.
嗯，至少他們對這種雨的反應還**不錯**嘛。每當下雨，我們大多數人總是**怨嘆**。

中國人：Rain is **unpleasant** when you live in a city, but to farmers in Taiwan it is very important. Besides, in Taiwan the weather in summer is much cooler when it rains. When it is dry, the weather is often **extremely hot**. 你住在都市裏，雨當然**令人討厭**，但對台灣的農民來說，雨卻很重要。而且，台灣的夏天，下雨的時候會比較涼快點。如果不下雨，天氣就經常會**極度地熱**。

外國人：Are these plums a **delicacy** in Taiwan？
在台灣梅子是**美味**嗎？

中國人：Yes. The Chinese like to eat them, but not necessarily fresh. They like to **preserve** them and make **sour** drinks out of them. 是的。中國人喜歡吃梅子，但不一定吃鮮的。他們喜歡把梅子**貯存**起來，再拿來做**酸酸的**飲料。

＊＊ coin〔kɔɪn〕v. 造（字） ripen〔ˋraɪpən〕v. 成熟
moan〔mon〕v. 呻吟；怨嘆 extremely〔ɪkˋstrimlɪ〕adv. 極度地
delicacy〔ˋdɛləkəsɪ〕n. 佳餚
preserve〔prɪˋzɜv〕v. （藉醃漬，製成果醬等而）保藏；貯存

INTRODUCING　TAIWAN IN ENGLISH · TOPIC 28

　　台灣的**人行道**（*sidewalk*）上到處可見擺地攤的景象，尤其在台北市，凡是人群聚集的場所便有**小販**（*hawker*）夾雜其間，高聲叫賣著各種物品。對許多台北人而言，三兩好友邀約逛夜市，買地攤貨已成為休閒生活中的一部分。地攤貨種類繁多，應有盡有，不但**水果**（*fruit*）、**書籍**（*books*）、**飾物**（*jewels or ornaments*）、**衣物**（*clothing*）等琳瑯滿目，而且貨色物美價廉，極受一般大眾歡迎，因此有些學生甚至利用寒暑假擺擺地攤，賺取一筆為數不小的費用。然而攤販叢集街頭卻同時造成**交通阻礙**（*traffic congestion*）與環境髒亂等問題，影響市容的整潔與觀瞻，尤其是路邊任意擺設的飲食攤，由於衛生條件不足，更易引起細菌傳染，危害民眾健康。近幾年來，日漸富裕的經濟狀況使得人民開始關注到生活環境的品質，因而地攤的髒與亂也更為人所垢病，也許有朝一日在大家共同的自覺努力之下，攤販佔據街頭的景像能從台北市消踪匿跡！

TOPIC 28

跳蚤市場　**Flea Market**

> **Dialogue**

外國人： I noticed as I arrived at the Hilton that there were many people selling *goods* like belts, clothing and apples on the *sidewalks*. Is this common in Taiwan?

　　我到達希爾頓飯店的時候，注意到**人行道**上有許多人在賣**東西**，像皮帶、衣服和蘋果等。這種情形在台灣很普遍嗎？

中國人： Yes, very common, particularly in certain parts of Taipei. Some streets are very crowded with these *hawkers* as well as the *customers* they attract.

　　是的，很普遍，尤其在台北的某些地方。有些街道全擠滿了這些**小販**和他們引來的**顧客**。

外國人： What kinds of things do they sell? 他們賣些什麼？

中國人： All sorts of things. Of course, it depends on where you are. If you are, for instance, near a university there will be several people selling *stationery* and books. If you are near a big hotel, they may try to sell *fashionable* clothing to the visitors. Then, in almost every place you will see them selling fruit. 什麼都賣。當然，要看地方。譬如說，如果你是在大學附近，就有幾個人賣**文具**和書籍。如果在大飯店附近，他們可能就賣些**流行的**服飾給觀光客。而幾乎在每個地方，你都會看到他們在賣水果。

** sidewalk〔ˋsaɪdˏwɔk〕*n.* 人行道　　　hawker〔ˋhɔkɚ〕*n.* 小販
stationery〔ˋsteʃənˏɛrɪ〕*n.* 文具　　　fashionable〔ˋfæʃənəbl〕*adj.* 流行的

外國人： If there are so many of these hawkers in a small area, won't they cause traffic ***congestion*** and make a general ***nuisance*** of themselves？ 這麼多小販擠在一個小地方，不會造成交通**阻塞**，令大家**討厭**嗎？

中國人： Yes. They frequently disrupt the traffic as they ***use up*** a large part of the road. They also make a lot of noise late into the night which disturbs ***residents***.
因爲他們**佔掉**一大部分的路，經常使交通中斷。他們也製造大量的噪音直到夜裏，擾亂**居民**。

外國人： Why don't the police stop them？ 警察爲什麼不阻止他們？

中國人： The police often do stop them. However, as soon as the police walk away they start selling again. If a hawker sees a policeman ***approaching***, he will warn the other hawkers and they quickly stop selling. One big problem is that people in general like to buy things on the street as prices are lower, and this only encourages the hawkers. 警察是經常阻止他們。不過，警察一走開，他們又開始賣了。一個小販看到警察**來了**，會警告其他的小販，他們就很快停止販賣。一個很大的問題是，一般的人民因爲價錢比較便宜，都喜歡在街上買東西，這只有助長這些小販。

外國人： Perhaps I should try and buy something, too！
也許我也該去買點東西！

** congestion〔kən'dʒɛstʃən〕*n*. 擁塞
nuisance〔'njusns〕*n*. 討厭的人（事物、行爲等）
use up 用盡　　resident〔'rɛzədənt〕*n*. 居民
approach〔ə'protʃ〕*v*. 行近

TOPIC 29

建 設 | **Construction**

As a result of the rapid growth of Taiwan's economy, **bottlenecks** are occuring in transportation, and shortages in raw materials. In early 1980, the government **embarked upon** fourteen new projects in order to prepare the nation for new economic challenges. These include the around-the-island railroad, nuclear power plants, and even cultural centers. In this modern day and age it is important to rejuvenate our people's spiritual lives, by promoting traditional Chinese culture. One significant project is *the Mass Rapid Transit System* (MRT) which was began in 1988. It **boasts** six lines totalling 88 kilometers, and costs an estimated US $17.1 billion. One line is already in service. The MRT did not go as well as had hoped, but hopefully things will improve in the future. The MRT should be totally completed by the year 2000.

由於台灣經濟的快速成長，造成交通上的**瓶頸**及原料的短缺。在一九八○年初，政府開始**著手從事**新的十四項建設，以為國家將來的經濟挑戰作準備，這其中包括了環島鐵路、核能發電廠，甚至還有文化中心。在現代生活裏，藉著提倡傳統中國文化，來使我們人民的精神生活恢復活力，這是很重要的。有一項重要計劃，就是一九八八年開始的**大眾捷運系統**，整個系統以包含六條路線，總長八十八公里而**自豪**，且耗資估計約一百七十一億美金。其中一條路線已開始營運，但不如所希望的好，但如果順利的話，未來的情形應會改善的，捷運系統應該會在西元二千年前全部完成。

🔊 **Dialogue 1**

外國人：What do you think Taiwan will look like in ten years?
你想台灣在十年內會像什麼樣子？

中國人：Most of the changes are *concentrated* in the cities. As you can tell just by walking around Taipei, new buildings are going up everywhere. Back in 1972 the Taipei Hilton Hotel was the tallest building in town, *looming* like a *lighthouse* in a sea of one or two story houses. Today you can barely notice it in the mist of new high rises. Taipei has been called the *ugly duckling* that grew up. In ten more years it'll be even more beautiful.

大部分的改變都**集中**在城市中。就像你只要在台北四處走走，就可以預知，到處都在蓋新的建築。在一九七二年時台北希爾頓大飯店是市區中最高的建築。在一望無際的一、兩層樓房子裏，像是海中**隱約可見的燈塔**。今天，在霧一般的新建多層建築中，你幾乎不會注意到它。台北被稱爲長大了的**醜小鴨**，再過十年，它將會更漂亮。

外國人：Are the rural areas also being developed?
鄉下地方同樣也發展起來了嗎？

中國人：Yes, and the first step is improving transportation. Roads which connect these areas to major cities are being built and improved. The government is also helping farmers to *mechanize*. Rural areas are losing labor to the cities every year and there are no longer enough workers to do all the work. 是的，而且第一步就是改善交通。聯接這些地區到主要城市的道路，都興建而且改善了。政府同時幫助農民**耕作機械化**。鄉下地方每年都有勞工跑到都市中，不再有足夠的工人做所有的工作。

Dialogue 2

外國人： The around-the-island railroad sounds neat.
環島鐵路聽起來很棒！

中國人： Yes, it has been a big *tourist attraction* since it's completed in 1992. The entire trip will take about a day.
是的，自從環島鐵路在一九九二年完成以來，就**吸引很多遊客**。整個環島旅程大概只要一天。

外國人： Oh I love choo-choos, I've ridden on trains all over the world. 喔！我愛火車，你知道我在全世界都搭火車。

中國人： Really？Which is your favorite？
眞的？你最喜歡哪條鐵路？

外國人： I remember once while riding the Trans-Siberian Railway through a vast *evergreen forest*. It was way past midnight and all the other passengers were asleep. A fresh *blanket of snow* covered the scene, the sky was clear, full of stars, and the moon *illuminated* the whole *spectacle*. I opened the window a crack and filled my *compartment* with the cold *pine-scented* night air. Ah, I felt like I was *reborn*. It was really beautiful.
我記得有一次搭橫越西伯利亞的大鐵路，穿過一片廣袤的**常綠林**。已經過了午夜，所有其他的乘客都睡著了。**如氈的新雪**厚厚地蓋著這個景致，天空澄明，星群密布，月亮**照明**整幅**景象**。我把窗子開了一個小縫，使**小房間**中充滿了冷冽**松香**的夜晚氣息。啊！我覺得像是**重生**了。眞是美極了。

** chou-chou〔ˈtʃʊˌtʃʊ〕*n.*〔兒語〕火車

中國人：Where is the Trans-Siberian Railway？
　　　　告訴我橫越西伯利亞的大鐵路在哪兒？

外國人：It runs through Siberia, from Europe to China.
　　　　它從歐洲到中國大陸，穿越了西伯利亞。

blanket of snow 如氈之雪　　bottleneck〔'batḷ,nεk〕*n.* 瓶頸
compartment〔kəm'partmənt〕*n.* 火車中的小房間
concentrated〔'kansṇ,tretɪd, -sεn-〕*adj.* 擁擠在一起
embark〔ɪm'bark〕*v.* 著手；開始；從事
evergreen forest 常綠樹林　　illuminate〔ɪ'lumə,net, ɪ'lju-〕*v.* 照亮
labor〔'lebɚ〕*n.* 勞工　　lighthouse〔'laɪt,haʊs〕*n.* 燈塔
loom〔lum〕*v.* 隱約可見　　mechanize〔'mεkə,naɪz〕*v.* 使機械化
nuclear power plant 核能發電廠　　*petrochemical complex* 石油化工廠
pine-scented 松香味的　　*raw material* 原料
reborn〔ri'bɔrn〕*adj.* 再生的　　Siberia〔saɪ'bɪrɪə〕*n.* 西伯利亞
spectacle〔'spεktəkḷ〕*n.* 奇觀；景象
tourist attraction 吸引遊客的東西
transportation〔,trænspɚ'teʃən〕*n.* 交通業；運輸
ugly duckling 醜小鴨　　weird〔wɪrd〕*adj.* 奇怪的

TOPIC 30

現代中國婦女 — Modern Chinese Women

📼 **Question**

What is the *status* of women in Taiwan?

台灣女性的**地位**怎麼樣？

📼 **Reply**

In traditional Chinese culture, women are *subordinate* to men, but as in other *developed countries*, this is changing in Taiwan, and modern Chinese women are becoming very *aggressive* in demanding equal rights and opportunities. But Chinese women still have a way to go compared with women in western countries. For instance, Taiwan's *marriage* and *divorce* laws clearly favor the husband. The laws *entrust* the children of a divorced couple to the father—unless they are under seven and need *maternal care*. Nonetheless, Chinese women's increasing access to higher education can only mean more changes toward equal rights and opportunities.

中國傳統文化裏，女性**附屬於**男姓，但正如其它**已開發國家**，這在台灣已經在改變中。現代的中國婦女在要求權利與機會平等上，變得非常**積極**。不過，中國婦女跟西方國家婦女比較起來，仍然有一段路要走。比如說，台灣的**婚姻**法與**離婚**法顯然對丈夫有利。法律把一對離婚夫妻的孩子**交託**與父親——除非他們在七歲以下，需要**母親的**照顧。雖然如此，中國婦女有更多的機會接受更高的教育，祇能表示權利和機會平等，會有更大的變遷。

** compare〔kəm'pɛr〕v. 比較　　favor〔'fevɚ〕v. 對～有利
access〔'æksɛs〕n. 接近

🔳 **Dialogue 1** ▶

外國人： Why is the status of Chinese women changing?
為什麼中國婦女的地位會改變？

中國人： It's because in Taiwan, as in other developed countries, brains, not muscle, determines success. Women are not *handicapped* in *mental* capabilities as they are in *physical* capabilities.
因為在台灣，就和在其它已開發國家一樣，頭腦而不是體力決定成功與否。婦女在**智力**方面並不像在**體力**上那樣遭受到**阻礙**。

外國人： Are there many successful women in Taiwan?
台灣有很多成功的女姓嗎？

中國人： Yes there are. And they even have a *nickname*, "Nue Chao Ren" which means "superwomen." Many head their own companies.
是的，有，而且她們甚至有「女強人」的**綽號**，表示「女超人」。很多擁有自己的公司。

外國人： But don't their families suffer? I mean who takes care of the kids?
但是，她們的家庭不是遭殃了？我是說誰來照顧孩子？

中國人： Yes, of course, there's a *dark side* to every success story. Many of these women choose not to marry or *postpone* marriage in order to *concentrate* on their careers. However some are able to maintain a *balance*

between family and career. Also husbands are taking
a more active role in raising the kids.

當然，每個成功的故事後面都有它**黑暗的一面**。很多這樣的
女姓選擇單身或**遲婚**，以**專心致力**於自己的事業。不過，有
些還是可以保持家庭及事業之間的**平衡**。同時，丈夫在養育
孩子方面，也擔負比較積極的角色。

Dialogue 2

外國人：Do Chinese women still practice foot binding?
中國婦女仍然實行纏足嗎？

中國人：Oh no, " lily feet " have long gone *out of style*.
喔，沒有了。「三寸金蓮」很早就**不盛行**。

外國人：Why did they do it before? 她們以前為什麼要纏足呢？

中國人：The lily-footed *maiden* was considered the *ideal* in
China. Women with lily feet walked with very short
steps and *swayed* in a manner considered very attractive. The wealthy bound their daughters' feet to demon-
strate their *high class*, and the poor did it to give
their girls a chance to rise.
三寸金蓮的**閨女**在中國被認為是**完美的**。三寸金蓮的女子走
起路來那種用小碎步而且有點**搖擺**的樣子，被認為是很迷人
的，有錢人家纏他們女兒的腳，來證明他們**階層高**，窮人家
如此作是讓他們的女孩有出頭的機會。

外國人：Did the process hurt? 纏足的過程痛不痛？

中國人：Oh you better believe it did. "Every pair of small feet costs a bath of tears," goes a Chinese saying. The process begins when a girl is as young as four. The *bandages* are tightened every week until the growth process stops. The *aim* was to *retard* the growth of the foot, not to make it smaller.

　　喔，你最好相信那眞的很痛。中國諺語說「一雙小腳，一盆淚水」。這個過程打從女孩子四歲那麼小的時候，就開始了。每個星期上繃帶都要變得更緊，直到腳變大的過程停止。目的在於阻礙腳變大，而不是使它變得更小。

aggressive〔əˈgrɛsɪv〕*adj.* 積極的　　balance〔ˈbæləns〕*n.* 平衡
concentrate〔ˈkɑnsn̩ˌtret〕*v.* 專心
dark / light side 黑暗面／光明面　　entrust〔ɪnˈtrʌst〕*v.* 交託
handicapped〔ˈhændɪˌkæpt〕*adj.* 受到妨礙的
maternal〔məˈtɝnl̩〕*adj.* 母親的（相反詞爲 *paternal* "父親的"）
maiden〔ˈmedn̩〕*n.* 少女　　nickname〔ˈnɪkˌnem〕*n.* 綽號
postpone〔postˈpon〕*v.* 延緩　　retard〔rɪˈtard〕*v.* 阻礙
status〔ˈstetəs〕*n.* 身分；地位
subordinate〔səˈbɔrdn̩ɪt〕*adj.* 附屬的　　sway〔swe〕*v.* 搖擺；擺動
wedding dowry 嫁粧

✦ Chitou / 溪頭

Q : I've read somewhere that there is a ***bamboo forest***
here in Taiwan. I've never seen a bamboo forest.
Can you tell me where it is？

我曾在某處讀到臺灣有**竹林**。我從來沒看過竹林，您可
以告訴我它位在哪裏嗎？

A : The bamboo forest you are talking about is in Chitou
in Central Taiwan. It is a favorite destination for
campers and hikers. Once a year, during the summer, bamboo sprouts shoot up from the ground
right before your eyes. This happens right after a
rain. The oldest tree in Taiwan is also found in
this place. It is now hollow. Being inside is like
being inside a cathedral. The wooden walls deaden
all noise and the streaming sunlight from above
gives it a very solemn atmosphere.

您所提到的竹林，是位在台灣中部的溪頭。那是一個最
受露營和健行者喜愛的地方。每年夏天時一年一度，竹
子會從您眼前的土地上冒出新芽，這都是發生在下雨過
後。台灣樹齡最老的樹也可以在這個地方發現到。這棵
樹現在是中空的。待在裏面就像待在大教堂內部一樣。
木造牆壁阻隔了一切的吵雜聲，而從上頭射下的陽光則
造成非常莊嚴的氣氛。

Chapter 3

FESTIVALS

一節日一

中國傳統**節慶**（ *festivals* ）的形成，主要有兩個來源：一是配合**古代農業社會**（ *ancient agrarian society* ）的生活**節令**（ *times or seasons* ），二是來自與鬼神有關的**傳說**（ *legends* ）。有時一個節日不但包含有節令的意義，同時亦添加上鬼神傳說的附和。一般說來，傳統節慶多半具有祈福、消災、團圓聚會、天人合一等特質。

中國人不但認為山川大地皆具神性，而且相信人死後善者升天成神、惡者入地獄為鬼這種靈魂不滅的現象。於是對於**祖先**（ *ancestors* ）的崇敬祭拜等儀式當然不會輕忽，因為祖先的神靈長存，時時注視護佑著後代子孫。除了過年過節不忘祭拜祖先之外，**清明節**（ *Ching-ming* ）更是一個緬懷先人的節日。這一天全家大小前往祖墳清掃整理，供奉**三牲**（ *three sacrificial offerings— ox, sheep and hog* ）、清酒與糕點，因此清明節又稱**掃墓節**（ *Tomb Sweeping Day* ）。魏晉以來清明節一直定為農曆三月三日，時值**梅雨季節**（ *plum rains* ）。近年來政府特定國曆四月五日為清明節，與農曆三月三日時序相當接近。古時清明亦為出外踏青的日子，民間有放風箏、射箭、打秋千等習俗，不過如今皆已相繼失傳了。

《 Terms and Phrases 》

- immensely〔ɪˈmɛnslɪ〕*adv.* 極度地；非常地　　manifest〔ˈmænəˌfɛst〕*v.* 證明
- cremate〔ˈkrimet〕*v.* 火葬　　cremation〔krɪˈmeʃən〕*n.* 火葬
- urn〔ɝn〕*n.* 骨灰缸　　incense〔ˈɪnsɛns〕*n.* 供神所焚燒的香
- **_paper money_** 冥紙　　reminisce〔ˌrɛməˈnɪs〕*v.* 回憶
- imitation〔ˌɪməˈteʃən〕*n.* 仿造物；模擬之物
- canonize〔ˈkænənˌaɪz〕*v.* 永久認可　　agrarian〔əˈgrɛrɪən〕*adj.* 農地的

TOPIC 31

 **Tomb Sweeping Day**

Dialogue 1

外國人：Will I get to see any festivals while I'm here?
　　　　我在此地時，會看得到什麼節日呢？

中國人：When do you leave? 你什麼時候走？

外國人：On April 12. 四月十二日。

中國人：Then you'll be able to see the Ching-ming, or Tomb
　　　　Sweeping Day. It's on April 5.
　　　　那你就能看到清明（掃墓）節。是四月五日那天。

＊　　　　　＊　　　　　＊

外國人：Is it an important holiday? 那是一個重要的節日嗎？

中國人：Very important. Chinese people *immensely* respect
　　　　their ancestors, and this holiday, set according to
　　　　the solar calendar, *manifests* this. On a spiritual
　　　　level, this is perhaps the most important festival.
　　　　非常重要。中國人**非常**尊敬祖先，根據陽曆所定的這個節
　　　　日，就可以**證明**這件事。就精神層面而言，這可能是最重
　　　　要的節日。

外國人：Then does everyone go out and sweep his or her an-
　　　　cestors' tombs?
　　　　那麼每個人都會出去掃祖先的墳墓嗎？

中國人：No, not everyone, because as with many of our other traditions, the younger people are participating less and less as time goes on.

不是的，並非每個人都去，正如我們其他許多傳統一樣，時間一久，年輕人越來越少參與了。

外國人：What do you do if your ancestors were *cremated* ?

如果祖先是**火葬**的，那怎麼辦？

中國人：Then you still go to where the *urn* that holds his or her ashes is kept, possibly to burn *incense* and/or *paper money* and pray, or perhaps to *reminisce* and keep in touch with your roots. However, cremations in China are still uncommon.

那麼，你還是要去放祖先骨灰**甕**的地方，可能去燒**香**，以及/或者燒**紙錢**、祈求，也可能去**緬懷**祖先，和自己的根保持連繫。不過在中國，火葬還不太普遍。

📼 **Dialogue 2**

外國人：Are there any other activities usually scheduled for that day ?

通常那天還安排有什麼其他的活動嗎？

中國人：Yes. Depending on the weather, we like to take advantage of the opportunity to have a picnic in the countryside.

有的。視天氣而定，我們喜歡利用這個機會到鄉間野餐。

外國人：What do you actually do when you go to sweep a tomb?
掃墓時，你們實際上都做些什麼事？

中國人：We repair it and clear away overgrown grass and
bushes. Buddhists and Taoists never fail to set out
feasts for their ancestors' spirits, and burn *imitation*
paper money, all to comfort and assist them in their
spiritual world.
我們修補墳墓、清除長滿的草和灌木。佛教徒和道教徒總
會爲祖先上天之靈供上盛宴，燒**仿造**的紙錢，這都是爲了
安慰和幫助在陰間的他們。

外國人：Why do the Chinese respect their elders so?
爲什麼中國人那麼尊重長輩呢？

中國人：It was an ancient tradition which Confucius *canonized*
nearly 2,500 years ago. It's essentially a *holdover*
tradition from China's ancient *agrarian* society.
那是將近兩千五百年前孔夫子所**認可**的古老傳統。基本上
是一種從中國古代**農地**社會**延續**下來的傳統。

INTRODUCING TAIWAN IN ENGLISH • TOPIC 32

端午節

每年農曆五月五日為**端午節**（ *the dragon boat festival* ），相傳這一天即是大**詩人**（ *poet* ）屈原感時憂國，投入汨羅江以死諫君的日子，因此為了追懷詩人偉大的情操，端午節也同時訂作「**詩人節**」（ *Poet's Day* ），此時各地紛紛舉辦詩人聯吟大會。據說屈原死後，人民為了尋找屈原的屍體便相繼組成船隊，這就是今日**龍舟競賽**（ *dragon boat races* ）的來源。另外，人民不忍屈原的屍體在水中為魚蝦吞噬，並且包裹**粽子**（ *Chung-tze* ）投入水中餵飽魚蝦。早在南北朝時期，划龍舟與包粽子已普遍成為一項民間習俗流傳各地。

除了屈原的傳說之外，端午節在古代一直是個消毒避邪的節日，民間俗忌五月為「**毒月**」（ *Evil Month* ）或「**惡月**」，因為當此之時氣候濕熱，百病易生，而五月五日尤列九毒日之首，家家戶戶均在門口懸插**艾草**（ *moxa* ）、**菖蒲**（ *calamus* ），婦女鬢邊須插戴**榴花**（ *pomegranate flower* ），男人飲**雄黃酒**（ *realgar* ），小孩身配**香包**（ *fragrant sacks or sachet* ），無非是藉此避邪，消除毒蟲毒物，保障身體安泰。中國古代又將五月五日出生的嬰兒視為不祥之物，任其棄斃荒野，今日觀之當然純屬無稽之談，然而由此也可見不當的迷信貽害人民良深。

≪ Introducing Taiwan ≫

- The Dragon Boat Festival is one of the three greatest annual festivals celebrated in Taiwan. The greatest festival of them all is the Lunar New Year. The other one is the Mid-Autumn or Moon Festival. 端午節是台灣一年當中慶祝的三大節日之一，其中最盛大的節日要屬農曆新年，另外一個節日則是中秋節。

TOPIC 32

The Dragon
Boat Festival

Dialogue 1

外國人：When is the Dragon Boat Festival?
端午節在什麼時候呢？

中國人：It's on the fifth day of the fifth lunar month. And in memory of Chu Yuan, we also call it Poet's Day. This year it fell on June 20 of the *Solar Calendar*.
農曆五月五日。而爲了紀念屈原，我們也稱它爲詩人節。今年是在**陽曆**六月二十日。

外國人：Is it a major festival? 端午節是一個主要的節日嗎？

中國人：Yes. It's one of the three major Chinese lunar year festivals. 是的。那是中國陰曆三大主要節日之一。

外國人：What do you do on the Dragon Boat Festival?
你們端午節時做些什麼呢？

中國人：*Among other things*, we have dragon boat races and eat *Chung-tze*. **其中**，我們有龍舟競賽和吃粽子。

外國人：What's a dragon boat?
龍舟又是什麼呢？

中國人：It's a boat carved to resemble a dragon, the dragon's head at the bow and its tail at the *stern*, of course. Twenty-two *oarsmen* row the boat while a *helmsman*

steers, a drummer beats out the pace, and a bow
sitter *snatches* the flag at the finish line.
那是把船雕刻成像龍的樣子，當然龍頭在**船首**，龍尾在**船
尾**。二十二個**划手**划船，而一位**舵手**掌舵，一位鼓手敲出
速度，還有一個人坐在船頭，到了終點線時**伸手拿**旗子。

🔲 **Dialogue 2** ▶

外國人：What was that you said you eat during the festival？
你說你們端午節時吃什麼？

中國人：*Chung-tze*. They're rice dumplings wrapped in bamboo
leaves. Haven't you ever eaten one？ They're available
all the year-round. 粽子。那是用竹葉包起來的米糰。你沒
有吃過嗎？一年到頭都買得到。

外國人：No. Why do you eat them especially during the Dragon
Boat Festival？沒吃過。你們為什麼特別在端午節的時候吃呢？

中國人：This has to do with the festival's origins. As *legend*
has it, during the Fourth Century B.C., Chu Yuan, a
senior government official, *committed suicide* on the
fifth day of the fifth lunar month by throwing himself into the Milo River in Hunan Province. He did
so to *protest* the king's *corrupt practices*, hoping that
by dying he could cause the king to come to his senses
and return to honest and upright practices.
那跟節日的來源有關。有個**傳說**是，西元前第四世紀時，
有位政府的高級官員名叫屈原，農曆五月五日投到湖南省
汨羅江**自殺**。他這麼做是要**抗議**國王**舞弊**，希望他的死能
使國王醒悟，恢復誠實正直的行為。

Dialogue 3

外國人：What does that have to do with dragon boats and rice dumplings？龍舟、粽子和這個有什麼關係呢？

中國人：The people of the nearby village rushed out in fishing boats to save him, because they knew he was a good, honest man. When they failed to find him — or his body —, they threw cooked rice into the river.
附近村莊的人，都連忙趕出去划著漁船要救他，因為他們知道屈原是誠實的好人。他們沒有找到他——或他的屍體後，就把煮好的米丟到河裏。

外國人：What for？為什麼呢？

中國人：One *version* of the legend has it that they did this to keep the fish from eating Chu Yuan's body. According to the other version, the rice was meant to feed Chu Yuan's soul.
有一種**説法**是，這麼做是讓魚不要吃屈原的屍體。根據另一種說法，則是米是用來給屈原的靈魂吃的。

Dialogue 4

外國人：Then how did *Chung-tze* come about？
那麼，**粽子**是怎麼來的呢？

中國人：Chu Yuan's spirit is said to have appeared to the villagers. He told them that a *monster* had intercepted the gifts of rice, and further described to them how they should wrap the rice so the *demon*

wouldn't recognize it and would therefore let it pass.
What Chu Yuan's spirit described was a *Chung-tze*.

據說屈原向村民顯靈。屈原告訴他們，有個**怪物**攔截米的
贈與，還向他們描述怎麼把米包起來，**惡魔**才不會認出來，
就會讓米通過。屈原描述的就是**粽子**。

🔲 Dialogue 5

外國人：How interesting! But where do dragons fit into all of
this? 真有趣！不過，龍跟這些是怎麼湊起來的？

中國人：Chinese people have believed since the earliest times
that dragon gods control the waters, including seas,
lakes, rivers, and even rain. In southern China, where
rivers *abound*, fishermen and farmers alike believed
they needed the *assistance* of river dragon gods in the
spring to help them reap their harvests : the farmers
wanted rain, of course, and fishermen fish. In order
to get what they needed, they had to *bribe* the dragon
gods. They used rice and later *Chung-tze* as their
" payment. "

古早以來，中國人就相信龍神掌管水，包括海水、湖水、
河水，甚至雨水。中國南方**有許多**河川，漁夫和農夫都相
信春天時他們需要掌管河水的龍神**幫助**，才會有收穫：因
此農夫想要雨水，當然漁夫也想要魚。為了得到他們所需
要的，必須向龍神**賄賂**。他們用米，後來用粽子當作「報酬」。

外國人：But didn't you just say that this tradition *stemmed
from* Chu Yuan's suicide？

但是你不是說這個傳統**源自**屈原自殺嗎？

中國人：That's the popular legend, but the festival, falling near the summer *solstice*, most certainly was agricultural in origin. The story of Chu Yuan, though probably at least partly true, was fitted to the festival date later on. We Chinese like to justify our festivals with legends. 那是一般的傳說，但是這個節日接近夏**至**，起源一定跟農業有關。不過，屈原的故事可能至少有部分真實性，後來才和這個節日湊合起來。我們中國人喜歡用傳說來作爲節日的理由。

外國人：What else do people do during the Dragon Boat Festival? 人們在端午節還做些什麼事呢？

中國人：Some people wear *hsiang-bao*, or "fragrant sacks" around their necks. 有些人在脖子上戴**香包**，或稱爲「香袋」。

　　　　　＊　　　　　＊　　　　　＊

外國人：What are they? 那是什麼？

中國人：They're little sacks filled with medical *herbs* and *spices*, in the past worn — like *garlic* in the West to ward off misfortunes — during Evil Month. Nowadays they're given as symbols of affection.

過去那些小袋子裝有**藥草**和**香料**，在毒月佩戴——就像西方用**大蒜**去霉運。現在用作**贈**送，表示（親）愛。

外國人：What's Evil Month? 「毒月」是什麼月份？

中國人：The fifth lunar month, so called because it's the time when, along with high temperatures, insects and bacteria come to life and spread diseases and *infections*.

是農曆五月。之所以這樣叫它，是因爲這段時間氣溫很高，昆蟲、細菌甦醒，傳佈疾病和**傳染病**。

INTRODUCING TAIWAN IN ENGLISH · TOPIC 23

農曆七月在台灣民間相傳是「鬼月」（*Ghost month*），七月初一開始打開**鬼門**（ *the gate of hell* ），直到七月三十才關閉鬼門。因此，這段時間內**陰間**（ *hell* ; *Hades* ）的孤魂野鬼皆爭先恐後地跑到人間來逍遙，尋找吃喝。

這個月份裡，台灣各地均紛紛舉行「普渡」的祭儀，以超渡那些無祀的孤魂野鬼。「中元普渡」其實沿襲於**佛教**（*Buddhism*）的「盂蘭盆法會」，在七月十五「盂蘭盆節」這一天，佛教徒必須奉請**僧伽**（ *the Buddhist priests*）舉行盂蘭盆法會，一方面為現生父母植福，同時也為過去的七世父母超渡。

在鬼月裡經常盛傳著各種鬼怪神奇的事件，免不了有人要譏之為無稽之談，然而信仰四方神明向來是中國人生活中的一部分，數千年來的代代傳承使得這種信仰已經不是**迷信**（ *superstition* ）與否的問題，而演變成屬於民間鄉野文化的內涵，所以不論往後人類科學文明將如何引導我們逼視各項**真象**（ *truth* ），幽靈鬼神帶給中國人的幻想空間將永遠也不會消失。

《 Terms and Phrases 》

- superstitious〔ˌsupəˈstɪʃəs〕 *adj.* 迷信的
- ***close down*** （指工廠、公司行號等）關門；停業　　　fall〔fɔl〕*v.* 來臨
- run〔rʌn〕*v.* 經營　　***paper money*** 冥紙
- sacrifice〔ˈsækrəˌfaɪs〕*n.* 祭品　　appease〔əˈpiz〕*v.* 安撫
- spirit〔ˈspɪrɪt〕*n.* 幽靈；鬼　　***go on*** 渡過
- plunge〔plʌndʒ〕*v.* 跳入　　coincidence〔koˈɪnsədəns〕*n.* 巧合
- glutinous〔ˈglutɪnəs〕*adj.* 黏的　　***glutinous rice*** 糯米
- mushroom〔ˈmʌʃrum〕*n.* 蘑菇　　wrap〔ræp〕*v.* 包
- bamboo〔bæmˈbu〕*n.* 竹　　pyramid〔ˈpɪrəmɪd〕*n.* 金字塔

TOPIC 33

農 曆 七 月　The Seventh Lunar Month

Dialogue 1

外國人：Are the Chinese very *superstitious* people？
中國人是非常**迷信**的民族嗎？

中國人：Very much so. In fact during the seventh lunar month,
the "*ghost*" month, people very rarely *move house*, or
get married, because they believe they will experience
bad luck. Some businessmen even *close down* during
the month. 非常迷信。事實上在農曆七月，「**鬼**」月裏頭，
人們很少**搬家**，或**結婚**，因為他們相信會觸到霉頭。有些
商人在這個月甚至就暫時**停業**。

外國人：When is the seventh lunar month？
農曆七月在什麼時候？

中國人：It usually *falls* in August or September or both.
通常在（陽曆）八月或九月**來臨**，或者兩個月之間。

外國人：Besides ceasing to *run* their businesses, is there anything else that people do？
除了停止**經營**生意之外，人們還做些什麼別的？

中國人：You will notice that people burn a great deal of *paper
money* during this month, more than at other times.
Burning paper money is a kind of *sacrifice* to *appease*
the *spirits* of the dead. 你會注意到，這個月大家**紙錢**燒
得比其他時候多。燒紙錢算是一種**祭品**，用來**安撫亡魂**。

🔲 **Dialogue 2** ➤

外國人： Are people afraid of **going on** holiday during this month?
這個月人們會怕**度**假嗎？

中國人： A lot of people stay at home to avoid bad luck. In fact there was once a sightseeing bus **plunging** down a cliff on Yangmingshan during " ghost " month, killing over twenty passengers and injuring the rest. Is that a pure **coincidence**?
很多人留在家裏以免倒楣。事實上，就曾經有一部遊覽車在「鬼」月**翻落**陽明山的懸崖，死了二十多名遊客，其餘全部受傷。這純粹是**巧合**嗎？

外國人： I now see what you mean. Perhaps I had better not travel either during that month！ By the way, as the Chinese are very fond of eating, do they eat anything special during ghost month？
我現在懂你的意思了。也許我在那個月最好也不要旅行！對了，中國人是很好吃的，他們在這個月吃些什麼特別的嗎？

中國人： You will see many women preparing **glutinous rice** dumplings. These consist of rice and red beans or peanuts and **mushrooms wrapped** up in **bamboo** leaves in the shape of a **pyramid**.
你會看到許多婦女在準備**糯米**粽子。粽子是由米和紅豆或花生，還有**香菇**組成，**包**在**竹**葉裏，像一個**金字塔**的形狀。

INTRODUCING TAIWAN IN ENGLISH · TOPIC 34

農曆八月十五日**中秋節**(*the Moon Festival*)是個屬於月亮的節日,在中國人的心目中,月亮不僅僅是天空上運行的星球而已,所謂「月宮娘娘」、「月姑」、「月光菩薩」、「太陰星主」等稱謂均可表達出中國人對月亮的浪漫懷想。一般中國的傳說中,掌理月亮的**女神**(*Goddess*)即是指稱奔月的**嫦娥**(*Chang-O*),「嫦娥應悔偷靈藥,碧海青天夜夜心」,嫦娥奔月的故事深入人心已久,即使今日科學事實證明月球表面並無任何生命跡象,但是中秋夜裡清亮而圓滿的月亮所帶給人們那份「月圓人常好」的溫馨,依舊不失其浪漫與優美。

中秋節當天月出之前,家家戶戶皆在庭院裡對月擺設**香案**(*incense table*),供奉瓜果、**月餅**(*moon cake*)、清香等,燒香遙拜月娘,此即民間的「祭月之禮」。當天晚上,在皎皎月光之下,一家子便集聚月下酌酒,吃中秋月餅歡渡佳節。中秋月餅均製成圓形,象徵**團圓**(*reunion*),表出「月圓人團圓」的吉祥佳意。在台灣過中秋,並準備有**柚子**(*pomelo*)佐食月餅,是比較獨特的應節水果,其他省份並無此項習俗。

《 Terms and Phrases 》

- **moon cakes** 月餅 **Christian era** 耶穌紀元;西曆紀元
- yolk〔jok〕*n.* 蛋黃 patriot〔'petrɪət〕*n.* 愛國者
- conceal〔kən'sil〕*v.* 隱藏 folklore〔'fok,lor,-,lɔr〕*n.* 民間傳說
- supreme〔sə'prim〕*adj.* 至高的 matchmaker〔'mætʃ,mekɚ〕*n.* 媒人
- despotic〔dɪ'spɑtɪk〕*adj.* 專制的
- elixir〔ɪ'lɪksɚ〕*n.* 長生不老藥(= *elixir of life, elixir vitae*)
- immortality〔,ɪmɔr'tælətɪ〕*n.* 不死;不朽 eternity〔ɪ'tɜnətɪ〕*n.* 永恆
- predominantly〔prɪ'dɑmənəntlɪ〕*adv.* 主要地
- yin〔jɪn〕*n.* 陰(陽之對) yang〔jæŋ〕*n.* 陽(陰之對)

The Moon Festival

🈯 **Dialogue** ➤

外國人：When is the Moon Festival？中秋節在什麼時候？

中國人：It's on the 15th of the 8th lunar month. It's also called the Mid-autumn Festival.
農曆八月十五日。也叫做中秋節。

外國人：Is it a harvest festival？是一個收成的節日嗎？

中國人：It originally was. Now, as most people live in the cities and are far removed from food production, it's really become a festival for viewing the moon.
原先是。現在，因為大部分人都住在城市裡，遠離了糧食生產，事實上已經變成賞月的節日了。

*　　　　　*　　　　　*

外國人：How do you celebrate it？你們怎麼慶祝？

中國人：Farmers for the most part still worship the Earth God on this day, in thanks for his generosity in the form of the year's harvest. However, most others enjoy eating **moon cakes** and viewing the moon from a quiet, unlit place. This practice dates back to the pre-Christian era. We Chinese say that the moon on this day is at its fullest and brightest.

這一天，農人大都還祭拜土地公，以感謝他用年收成的方式慷慨的賜予。然而，其他大部分的人喜歡吃吃**月餅**，並在一個寧靜、沒有燈光的地方賞月。這個習慣始於耶穌紀元以前。我們中國人說月亮在這一天最圓最亮。

外國人：What are moon cakes？什麼是月餅？

中國人：They're cakes round and yellow-white like the moon.
They're filled with egg *yolk*, beanpaste, nuts, meat,
etc. The legend of their origin is interesting：
During the Mongol Yuan Dynasty, Chinese *patriots*
passed secret messages by *concealing* them in festival
cakes. Exchanging the cakes became a tradition that
remains today.

月餅是像月亮般，圓圓的、黃白色的餅。裡面包**蛋黃、豆沙、核桃、肉**等等。月餅起源的傳說很有趣：在由蒙古人所統治的元朝期間，中國的**愛國志士**把消息**藏**在月餅裡面，傳遞秘密訊息。交換月餅成為流傳至今的傳統。

*　　　　　*　　　　　*

外國人：Is there an Old Man on the Moon in Chinese *folklore*？
在中國**民間傳說**裡，月亮上有一位老人嗎？

中國人：Yes. Tradition has it that he's the *supreme match-maker*, tying young couples together on the night
of the Moon Festival with invisible red silk thread.
是的。傳說中他是個**大媒人**，在中秋節晚上用隱形的紅絲線，把年輕的情侶繫在一起。

外國人： Isn't there also some story about a woman？
不是也有某個故事是關於一個女人的嗎？

中國人： Yes, that's Chang O. She was the wife of Hou Yi,
a *despotic* ruler of ancient China. Chang O stole and
drank her husband's *elixir* of *immortality*, and then
flew to the moon. Her punishment is to remain there
for *eternity*.
是的，那是嫦娥。她是后羿的妻子，后羿是中國古代**專制**
的君主。嫦娥偷了丈夫**追求不朽的長生不老藥,** 並把它喝
了，然後飛到月亮上。她被處罰**永遠**留在那裡。

外國人： Why is the moon festival considered a woman's festi-
val？ 為什麼有人認為中秋節是女人的節日？

中國人： That's because women, like the moon, are *predomi-*
nantly yin. Yang, on the other hand, is *ascendant* in
the sun and men. Yin and yang are the two major
divisions of the universe, according to the *I Ching*,
the 3,000-year-old Bible of Chinese thought.
那是因為女人，像月亮，**主陰**。另一方面，**陽則主**太陽和
男人。根據中國三千年前的思想經典——**易經**，陰陽是宇
宙的兩大分野。

　　每逢年節來臨，必然備有一些應節的食物是中國人相傳以久的習俗（ custom ）。新年（ New Year ）有年糕、年粿；元宵節（ Lantern Festival ）吃元宵；端午節（ Dragon Boat Festival ）包粽子；中秋節（ Moon Festival ）備月餅；冬至（ Winter Solstice）搓湯圓；年末吃尾牙、潤餅等，名目極為繁多。由於中國農村向以稻糧為主食（ staple ），年節食物自然幾以米食製品為主。在中國人心目中，這些食物不僅代表口腹之慾而已，更具有宗教上的意義，用來表達敬天禮神的心意與誠敬，所以通常都必須拜拜（ worshipping festival）之後，人們才可以開始品嚐享用。以往的應節食物多由家中製作，例如冬至一到，全家人便圍桌搓湯圓，邊聊天，手邊順手便揉出一粒粒圓滑的湯圓仔來，那份感覺格外溫馨。如今年節食物到處皆有售賣，人們也鮮少自行麻煩去動手，那些情景也只有往回憶中去追懷了。

《 Terms and Phrases 》

- *new year cake* 年糕　　*glutinous rice dumpling* 粽子
- *longevity nuts* 長生果　　*rice-cake* 米糕
- *glutinous rice congee* 糯米粥
- *full-moon dumpling; glutinous rice-ball* 元宵
- *fried rice noodle* 炒米粉　　*egg yolk mooncake* 蛋黃月餅
- *ham-stuffed mooncake* 火腿月餅
- *scalded glutinous rice cake* 湯年糕　　*candied lotus seed* 糖蓮子
- *spring roll* 春捲　　*steamed cake* 蒸糕

TOPIC 35

應節 食物　Festival Foods

Dialogue

外國人： There is no need for me to ask you whether the Chinese are fond of eating. However, do they eat certain meals on special days just as we eat Christmas *pudding* in the U.S.?

　　　 我不必問你中國人好不好吃了。不過，他們在特殊的日子吃些特別的食物嗎，就像我們在美國吃聖誕節**布丁**一樣？

中國人： Yes. The Chinese are very fond of celebrating certain festivals by eating special kinds of food.

　　　 有啊。中國人很喜歡吃些特別的食物來慶祝某些節日。

外國人： Tell me about one of them. 舉個例子告訴我吧。

中國人： On the eighth day of the twelfth lunar month, Chinese people usually eat a special delicacy called *La Pa Chow.*

　　　 在陰曆十二月八號，中國人通常吃一種叫**臘八粥**的特別佳餚。

外國人： Why is this？爲什麼？

中國人： *Buddhists* believe that **celebrating** this festival in this way will bring them happiness and *fortune*.

　　　 佛教徒認爲，用這種方式來慶祝這個節日,會帶來快樂和**財富**。

** pudding〔'pʊdɪŋ〕*n.* 布丁　　 La Pa Chow 臘八粥
　 Buddhist〔'bʊdɪst〕*n.* 佛教徒　　 fortune〔'fɔrtʃən〕*n.* 財富

外國人：How is La Pa Chow made? 臘八粥怎麼做？

中國人：Well, it consists of a kind of sweet rice *gruel*.
嗯，它是用一種甜米**粥**做成的。

外國人：That sounds very nice. Tell me about another such dish.
聽起來很不錯。告訴我另外一種食物吧。

中國人：On the fifth day of the fifth month, there is the Dragon Boat Festival. The food consists of *glutinous rice dumplings* boiled in bamboo leaves to which are added meat, peanuts and mushrooms or red beans.
五月五日是端午節。食物是包在竹葉裏羹的**粽子**，裏面加些肉、花生，以及香菇或紅豆。

外國人：That sounds a lot more *nourishing*! 聽起來很有**營養**多了！

中國人：Oh yes! And talking about something *heavy* like Christmas pudding, on the fifteenth day of the eighth month the Chinese celebrate the Moon Festival by eating *moon cakes*. These are small round *pies* which are as heavy as western fruitcake. There are many different kinds of *fillings*, such as nuts, fruits, *spices*, eggs, *preserves* and lotus seeds, etc.
哦，對了。說到像聖誕節布丁一樣**膩而消化的**，我們中國人在八月十五的時候吃**月餅**慶祝中秋節。月餅是圓圓小小的**派**，跟西方的水果蛋糕一樣膩而難消化。**餡**有很多種，像核桃、水果、**香料**、蛋、**蜜餞**和蓮子等。

外國人：That certainly sounds delicious! 無疑地聽起來很好吃！

中國人：And I haven′t mentioned the *sesame* balls in red-bean soup you get on another festival！
我還沒提另一個節日吃的芝麻湯圓紅豆湯吧！

✦ Tamsui / 淡水

Q : Tamsui used to be a very ***important place*** in Taiwan, wasn't it?

淡水曾經是台灣一個非常**重要的地方**，是嗎？

A : Yes. Tamsui is the focal point of Taiwan's colonial past. It has been a colonial outpost for *the Spanish, Dutch, English, French and the Japanese.* You can rent a bike in Tamsui and ride through the surrounding countryside. It is also home to a well-known university, the Tamkang University. The place is known for its seafood. People also go there to view the sunset on the banks of the Tamsui river.

是的。淡水是往昔台灣殖民時的焦點所在。曾爲西班牙人、荷蘭人、英國人、法國人和日本人用作殖民地的前哨站。你可以在淡水租輛脚踏車，騎遍近郊。它也是一所著名大學，淡江大學的所在地。淡水以海產聞名。人們也到那兒去觀賞淡水河岸的落日。

** *focal point* 焦點；集中點
colonial 〔 kə'lonɪəl 〕 *adj.* 殖民地的
outpost 〔 'aut,post 〕 *n.* 前哨站

Chapter 4

CULTURE

文化

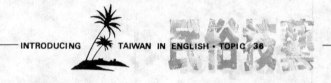

INTRODUCING TAIWAN IN ENGLISH · TOPIC 36

民俗技藝

　　台灣的民俗藝術綿延已久，長久以來，隨著歷代先民流傳下來，不僅別具民族特色，也凝聚了豐富的民族情感，充分反映出台灣人民的民俗文化面貌。在手工藝品（*handicrafts*）方面，木雕（*wood carving*）、編造竹製器具（*bamboo utensils*）、篆刻（*seal carving*）、糊紙藝術（*paper pasting techinique*）、剪紙（*paper cutting*）等皆有相當的歷史，講究精巧細膩，頗具耐人尋思的古味。戲曲方面，皮影戲（*shadow play*）、布袋戲（*Taiwanese puppet show*）、歌仔戲（*Taiwanese opera*）等是台灣獨特的民間戲劇，內容多半講述日常熟悉的忠孝節義故事掌故，唱曲通俗易懂，老少咸宜；每當迎神賽會慶典之時，各地廟口皆有上演。這些民俗藝術代表著台灣先民寶貴的精神遺產，不論時代如何變遷，永遠無法減損其光彩。

《 Terms and Phrases 》

- ***silk screening*** 絹印　　lantern〔ˈlæntən〕*n*. 燈籠
- shuttlecock〔ˈʃʌtḷ͵kɑk〕*n*. 鍵子　　kite-flying〔ˈkaɪt͵flaɪɪŋ〕*n*. 放風箏
- ***molding pastry figuriness*** 捏麵人（= *flour figuriness*）
- ***chuangyuan cake*** 狀元糕　　***Chinese knotting*** 中國結
- sachet〔sæˈʃe〕*n*. 香包　　***theatrical performance*** 戲劇表演
- backdrop〔ˈbæk͵drɑp〕*n*. 背景幕　　sculpt〔skʌlpt〕*v*. 雕刻
- sculpture〔ˈskʌlptʃɚ〕*n*. 雕刻　　***folk songs*** 民謠
- statue〔ˈstætʃʊ〕*n*. 雕像　　puppet〔ˈpʌpɪt〕*n*. 木偶

TOPIC 36

民俗技藝 Folk Arts and Skills

Dialogue

外國人：Are folk arts strongly rooted in Taiwan, or is the *contemporary* Chinese art we see in Taiwan simply *copied* from the mainland?

民俗藝術在台灣很根深蒂固嗎？還是，我們在台灣看到的**當代**中國藝術都只是**摹仿**自大陸的？

中國人：Although the artistic value of most *handicrafts* made in Taiwan is not necessarily very high when compared to some of the priceless *antiques* from Mainland China, it is quite clear that these items reflect the native *lifestyle* as *interpreted* by local artists.

雖然跟中國大陸的一些無價的**古董**比起來，大部份台灣做的**手工藝品**的藝術價值不一定很高，但無疑的，這些藝品反映了本地藝術家所**詮釋**的台灣的**生活方式**。

外國人：What kind of things are regarded as art works in Taiwan? 在台灣，什麼樣的東西被認為是藝術品？

中國人：These include *ceramics*, wood *sculpture*, *glassware*, *metal-smithing* artifacts, furniture, *knitting*, stone sculpture, bamboo and *rattan* ware, and dolls.

這包括了**陶器**、**木雕**、**玻璃器皿**、**金屬鍛冶**的藝品、傢俱、**針織**、石雕、竹器和藤器，還有玩偶。

** handicraft〔ˈhændɪˌkræft〕*n.* 手工藝品　　ceramics〔səˈræmɪks〕*n.* 陶器

外國人： Wow！ That seems to cover a lot. I guess I'll have to go to a craft *exhibition* to see some of these things.
哇！似乎包羅很廣。我想，我該去手工藝品展看看這些東西。

中國人： There are several such exhibitions, but you need not necessarily go to one of them. For instance, as you walk around the streets you may pass a *workshop* in which a man is *carving* a wooden idol. That requires real skill.
是有幾個這樣的展覽，不過你倒不一定要去。比方說，你在街上隨便走走時，可能經過一家工廠，裏頭就有人在雕一尊木偶。那需要眞功夫。

外國人： Are the Taiwanese famous for dancing or acting？
台灣人以舞蹈或者演戲聞名嗎？

中國人： There is the "Ke Tsai Hsi" or *Taiwanese opera* which is very popular in Taiwan. The performers travel around Taiwan and *literally* perform anywhere—anywhere where they can *prop* up a stage. They usually *act out* traditional Chinese stories. Some of the actors and actresses have become very famous and are *frequently* seen performing on TV. However, I feel it is better to watch a show " *Live*."
有所謂「歌仔戲」，在台灣很流行的。歌仔戲演員在台灣四處旅行，而且實際地在任何地方都表演——任何他們可以搭起一座台子的地方。他們經常演出傳統的中國故事。有些男女演員成了大名，還時常在電視上演出。不過，我覺得，還是看「現場」表演比較好。

INTRODUCING TAIWAN IN ENGLISH・TOPIC 37

中國的印章（*chops or seals*）起源甚早，商代已有製作，當時稱作「鉨」，到了周代，人民開始普遍使用印章，而在秦朝時更將天子所用的玉印特別專稱為璽（*hsi*），代表權威的象徵，是皇帝獨有的信物，以別於民間與士大夫階層所使用的印章。宋、元兩朝之後，各種印章開始應用在書畫旁的題辭落款上，極受文人重視，至此，印章的**篆刻**（*carving or engraving*）才具有獨立性，成為一種欣賞的藝術。

一位**印章篆刻家**（*seal engraving artist*）必須同時具備金石方面的**知識**（*the knowledge of stone and metals*）和熟習**書法**（*calligraphy*）的摹寫。書法是中國特有的文字藝術，**楷書**（*standard script*）、**行書**（*running script*）、**草書**（*cursive script*）固然皆應學習，而**篆書**（*clerical script*）尤為重要，一旦篆書有了基礎，冶印時自然可以筆到意來，韻緻全出。這種書法與雕刻的結合，為中國文字提供了另一種圖案性與美術性的表達方式，除了實用的價值之外，更在方寸之間，呈現出中國文字不同的意境與風韻！

《 Terms and Phrases 》

- *official seal* 官印   *personal seal* 私印
- script〔skrɪpt〕*n*. 手跡；筆跡   *red ink* 紅印泥
- *the carving techniques* 雕刻技巧   *the vermilion impression* 朱紅色印記
- *hard stone* 硬石   *soft stone* 軟石   craftsman〔'kræftsmən〕*n*. 雕刻師
- rubbing〔'rʌbɪŋ〕*n*. 研磨；石版刻印   *rubber stamp* 橡皮圖章
- intaglio〔ɪn'tæljo〕*n*. 凹刻   *artist's pseudonym* 藝術家的筆名
- *calligraphy and painting* 字畫
- *authenticate an artist's work* 辨識藝術家原跡作品

TOPIC 37

Chops

The Chinese don't use *signatures*? 中國人不用**簽名**嗎?

No, one old Chinese tradition that has held *steadfast* in Taiwan is personal seals, we all have at least one. We use them for *certifying* checks, contracts, and other important documents. There are professional seal *engravers* in Taiwan who do nothing else but make seals. Seals range from plain old everyday wooden ones to elaborate imperial seals carved from jade. Among all imperial seals, the most famous is the *legendary* state seal of the Chin Dynasty. Its characters *proclaimed*: "Long lived and Prosperous." The *grip* of this state seal is in the shape of a magnificent coiling *dragon*. As a matter of fact, the grip of some seals are so beautifully carved that they are sometimes worn as jewelry.

不,在台灣所**堅守**的一項古老中國傳統就是私章。我們都至少有一個。我們用印章來**證明**支票、契約,以及其它重要的文件。台灣有專業的**刻印師**,專門刻印章,而不做其它的。印章從普通古老日常木製的,到玉雕成的精巧皇璽。在所有的皇璽中最有名的是**傳說**中秦朝的國印。上面有文字**顯示**著:「萬壽無疆」。這個國印的**柄**是以華麗的盤**龍**爲造型。事實上,有些印章的柄雕琢的太美麗了,以致於有時候會像珠寶一樣被戴著。

** elaborate〔ɪˈlæbəˌret〕*adj*. 精巧的;複雜的

外國人：What are these "chop" things I see everyone using?

我看到每個人都在用的這些「印章」是什麼東西？

中國人：A chop is the Chinese *version* of the *signature*. We rely on a person's chop to *verify* his or her *identity*.

印章是中國式的**簽名**。我們靠印章來**查對**一個人的**身分**。

外國人：Then if you lose it you must have to go through a lot of *hassles*. 那麼如果你的印章丟了，勢必要經過一番**爭吵**。

中國人：Right. It's very troublesome. 是啊。很麻煩。

外國人：Couldn't someone make a *phony* chop with your name on it and, for instance, withdraw money from your *savings account*?

不會有人用刻上你的名字**假的**印章，然後，**譬如說**，取走你**儲蓄帳戶裏的錢**？

中國人：That would be difficult unless the person were able to secure an *imprint* of my chop.

那很難，除非這個人能獲得我的印章的**印跡**。

** version〔'vɜʒən〕 *n.* 某種特別的式樣　　verify〔'vɛrə,faɪ〕 *v.* 鑑定；查對
signature〔'sɪgnətʃə〕 *n.* 簽字　　identity〔aɪ'dɛntətɪ〕 *n.* 本人；本身
hassel〔'hæsl〕 *n.* 爭吵；困難（= *hassle*）
phony〔'fonɪ〕 *adj.* 假的；僞造的
savings account 儲蓄存款帳戶　　imprint〔'ɪmprɪnt〕 *n.* 印跡

外國人： Why？為什麼？

中國人： Each *engraver* has his or her own style. Without looking at the characters as they are *carved* on my chop,
another person could not possibly *come close to* making
a good copy.

每一個**雕刻師**都有自己的風格。如果沒有看我印章上**刻**的字，
另一個人不太可能**很精確地**複製一個印章。

外國人： But even with a bad *fake*, couldn't a person at least
temporarily use your chop without being discovered？

但是即使是不正確的**偽造品**，不會有人至少暫時使用你的印
章而不被發現嗎？

中國人： Maybe for *inconsequential* matters, yes；but at a bank
or post office, for instance, the clerk *processing* the
transaction checks your chop imprint. Banks and post
offices keep records of all their customers' chop
imprints.

也許可以用在**無關緊要的**事情；但是**譬**如說在銀行或者郵局，
處理這項事務的職員會核對你的印跡。銀行和郵局有所有顧
客印跡的記錄。

外國人： That seems like a good system. How did the use of
chops begin？那似乎是個好制度。怎麼開始使用印章的？

** engraver〔ɪnˋgrevɚ〕*n.* 雕刻師　carve〔kɑrv〕*v.* 雕刻
transaction〔trænsˋækʃən〕*n.* 事務　　fake〔fek〕*n.* 偽造品
inconsequential〔͵ɪnkɑnsəˋkwɛnʃəl〕*adj.* 不重要的
process〔ˋprɑsɛs〕*v.* 處理

中國人： The exact origins are unclear, but it's probable that they derived from decorative and artistic *seals*. For some time chops were also symbols of political power. Then by the *Warring States Period* , many individuals and businesses were already using them for *certification*.

　　確實的起源不清楚了，但有可能是起源於裝飾性、藝術性的**圖章**。有一段時間，**印章**也是政治勢力的象徵。之後，在**戰國時代**，許多人和許多行業就已經拿印章作**證明**之用了。

外國人： Do businesses still use them today?

　　現在各行業依然使用印章嗎？

中國人： Yes, even foreign businesses have to use them in their official *dealings*.

　　是的，即使外國企業也必須在正式的**來往**上使用印章。

外國人： So do foreigners that do business here all have chops?

　　所以所有在這裡做生意的外國人都有印章嗎？

中國人： Most do, and all should.

　　大部分都有，而且每個人都應該有。

** seal〔sil〕*n.* 印章　　*the Warring States Period* 戰國時代

certification〔ˌsətɪfəˈkeʃən〕*n.* 證明　　dealing〔ˈdilɪŋ〕*n.* (*pl.*) 來往

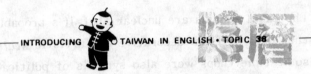

INTRODUCING TAIWAN IN ENGLISH · TOPIC 38

　　遠在西元前二千年前，中國人已開始以陰曆（the Lunar Calendar，或稱農曆）作為計算時序循環的依據。中國人民使用陰曆最主要是運用在農業耕作方面，所謂春耕、夏耘、秋收、冬藏便是依此而行；而且一般傳統民俗節慶的日期也是以陰曆為準。

　　「陰」代表月亮（the Moon），陰曆即是古人觀察月亮消長變化的現象所得到的結果。一個陰曆月（a lunar month）有二十九天十二小時又四十四分，一般俗指四個星期；而一個陰曆年（a lunar year）共約有三百六十五天又8小時。反之，現在世界上通用的陽曆（the Solar Calendar）則是依據地球環繞太陽一週所需時間製定的，陽曆一年為三百六十五天五小時又四十八分四十六秒，目前大家皆理所當然地將一年視為三百六十五天了。一般而言，陽曆較能準確地預測季節的更替，陰曆則較能掌握月亮陰晴圓缺的變化。往日中國農業社會（agrarian society）在陰曆時序下規律而單純地運作，歲歲年年，春去秋來，多少歲月便如此渡過，這種與大自然脈動相應和的生活節奏該是較適於人們的吧！

《 Terms and Phrases 》

- **common year** 平年　　intercalation〔ɪn,tɚkəˈleʃən〕 n. 置閏
- **leap year** 閏年　　**lunar cycle** 太陰周
- 24 **Solar terms** 二十四節氣　　**vernal equinox** 春分
- **autumnal equinox** 秋分　　**summer solstice** 夏至
- **winter solstice** 冬至　　**intercalary month** 閏月
- **celestial stems** (or **ten stems**) 十天干
- **terrestrial branches** (or **twelve branches**) 十二地支
- **sexagenary cycle** (**sixty-term cycle**) 甲子周期，六十年為一周

TOPIC 38

The Lunar Calendar

Dialogue

外國人： I notice that you Chinese *celebrate* your new year in
Late January or February and you do not even have a
set date. Why is this?

我注意到你們中國人在一月下旬或二月的時候慶祝你們的新年，
而且連個**固定的日子**也沒有，爲什麼？

中國人： We do have a set date, but the difference is that
we use a different calendar.

我們確實有一個固定的日子，差別在於我們用的是不同的日
曆。

　　　　　　　　＊　　　　＊　　　　＊

外國人： If your calendar and our one are different, which one
is correct?

如果你們的日曆和我們的不一樣，哪一個才是正確的？

中國人： It is very difficult to say which one is right. Even
astronomers cannot agree. The Chinese calendar,
besides helping an *agrarian* people determine the different times of the year, also has a *religious* function.
That is why religious festivals are always held on set
days in the lunar calendar.

** celebrate〔ˈsɛləˌbret〕*v.* 慶祝　　*set date* 固定的日期
agrarian〔əˈgrɛrɪən〕*adj.* 農地的　　religious〔rɪˈlɪdʒəs〕*adj.* 宗教的

很難說哪一個是對的。即使天文學家意見也不一致。中國的
日曆除了幫助農人決定一年中不同的時期，同時也有**宗教**的
功能。這是爲什麼宗教節日總是在農曆的固定日子舉行。

外國人：Does Chinese life then *revolve* around this Lunar
calendar？那麼，中國人的生活就根據這個農曆**運作**了？

中國人：Perhaps it does not nowadays as much as it did in the
past, but the Chinese are still a very superstitious
people.
也許現在不像過去那樣了，不過中國人仍然是一個非常迷信
的民族。

* * *

外國人：Which is the most *unusual* month in the Lunar Calen-
dar？農曆當中，哪一個月份最**不尋常**？

中國人：The seventh month. This is the so-called "ghost"
month, during which the spirits leave *Hades* and *roam*
around on the earth before returning to hell at the end
of the month.
七月。就是所謂的「鬼」月，這時候，鬼魂都離開**陰曹地府**，
在陽間四處**漫遊**，直到月底才回到冥府去。

外國人：Are people very *frightened* during this month？
這個月裏人人都很**害怕**嗎？

** revolve〔rɪ'vɑlv〕v. 旋轉；環繞　unusual〔ʌn'juʒʊəl〕adj. 不平常的
Hades〔'hediz〕n.〔希臘〕黃泉；冥府　roam〔rom〕v. 閒逛
frighten〔'fraɪtṇ〕v. 使害怕

中國人： Not *visibly* so. However few people get married, do
　　　　business or go on vacation during this month.

　　　　看不太**出來**。不過在這個月份裏,很少人結婚、作生意,或渡
　　　　假。

外國人： Surely there are happier times than this?

　　　　一定有比這個月快樂的時光吧？

中國人： Yes. The Lunar New Year is regarded as the most
　　　　important Chinese festival and is celebrated with the
　　　　utmost enthusiasm.

　　　　有的。農曆新年被視爲最重要的中國節日,中國人都以**最熱
　　　　烈的心情**慶祝。

** visibly〔'vɪzəblɪ〕*adv.* 明顯地　　utmost〔'ʌt,most〕*adj.* 極度的
enthusiasm〔ɪn'θjuzɪ,æzəm〕*n.* 熱心

麻將又稱麻雀，也叫方城之戰（ mah - jong ），是中國人最獨特的發明。相傳明朝年間就有宮女和太監在宮中以打麻將作消遣，爾後傳入官宦世家之中，到了明末時期，民間已經有公開的流傳。清朝道光年間洪秀全帶領**太平天國起義**（ the Taiping Rebellion ），在他的太平軍當中即有不少人是玩麻雀牌的個中好手。麻將是一種機智靈活的**博戲**（ gambling ），可以訓練組織與判斷能力，綜合西方**橋牌**（ bridge ）和**撲克**（ poker ）優點，不但中國人好此不疲，今日在世界各地也極為風行。日本東京一地設有公開的麻將館，除了禁止公務人員參加之外，人人皆可前往，館內服務人員還兼負責拉角；香港政府視麻將為一種技術競賽，不但成立有麻將學校，政府同時也抽取麻將稅；在澳門麻將則成為賭博的一種方式，設有**公開賭場**（ gambling house ）；此外，泰國、菲律賓皆准許打麻將。但是在一些嚴禁賭博的國家，如台灣、韓國等，便不准公然打麻將。有些人認為麻將當中富有許多人生哲理，不可純然以賭博論之，除了滿足人類爭強奪勝的心理之外，還可從中學習許多人生世故，養成審慎、忍耐的涵養工夫。然而即令如此，很多人打麻將却是特意注重在金錢的輸贏計較，終日沉迷其間不可自拔，喪失了原有的機智趣味，如此**麻將牌**（ Mah-Jong pieces ）僅徒流於賭博的代用工具罷了。

《 Terms and Phrases 》

- winter〔ˈwɪntɚ〕n. 冬　　**blank** (extra) **dragon tile** 白板
- bamboo〔bæmˈbu〕n. 竹　　summer〔ˈsʌmɚ〕n. 夏
- chrysanthemum〔krɪsˈænθəməm〕n. 菊　orchid〔ˈɔrkɪd〕n. 蘭
- plum〔plʌm〕n. 梅　　spring〔sprɪŋ〕n. 春　　autumn〔ˈɔtəm〕n. 秋
- **red dragon tile** 紅中　　**bamboo suit** 索；條子
- **tile of circle** (dot suit) 筒　　**green** (dragon) **tile** 發財
- **mah-jong**〔mɑˈdʒɔŋ〕n. 麻將 (= mah-jongg)

TOPIC 39

Mah-jong

Dialogue

外國人： In the United States it appears that mah-jong is a very popular game among the Chinese *community*. Is it popular in Taiwan?

在美國，麻將在華人**社區**好像是一個很流行的遊戲。在台灣也普遍嗎？

中國人： Mah-jong is *banned* in Taiwan as it is regarded as a form of *gambling*. That is why you seldom see it being played here.

麻將在台灣是**禁止**的，因爲它被認爲是**賭博**的一種形式。這就是爲什麼你很少看到這裏有人玩麻將。

外國人： Do you mean it still *exists* here?

你是說，它在這裏還**存在**著？

中國人： Yes. At night it is often possible to hear the sound of *tiles clacking* coming from a neighbor's window.

對。晚上常常可以聽到從隔壁窗戶傳來**瓷塊**的**碰撞聲**。

外國人： How it mah-jong played？ 麻將怎麼玩？

中國人： That's rather hard to explain. Basically it is a little like playing *bridge* but with *dominoes* instead of cards. I might perhaps add that it is a little more *lively* than bridge, maybe a little like *poker*. Both skill and *daring* are required.

很難說明白。基本上有點像打**橋牌**，不過是用**骨牌**而不是卡片，我也許可以補充說，它比橋牌更**靈活**點，大概有點像**撲克**。技巧和**勇氣**都要有。

外國人： I saw a store down the road selling mah-jong sets. What exactly do they consist of？

　　　　我看到沿這條路下去，有家商店在賣整套麻將。麻將到底是由什麼組成的？

中國人： There are something like 156 plastic tiles（ *ivory* is now very expensive ）which are *engraved* with Chinese *characters* and symbols. They are really very attractive.

　　　　有一百五十六塊像塑膠磚塊的東西（**象牙**現在太貴了），上面**刻**有中國**文字**和符號。真的很吸引人。

外國人： Do they have numbers？上面有數字嗎？

中國人： Like dominoes, Chinese mah-jong tiles have no *Arabic numerals*, but they are engraved with *elaborate portraits* of *mythical heroes* and *historic warriors*, flowers and *shrubs*.

　　　　和骨牌一樣，中國的麻將牌上沒有**阿拉伯數字**，但是刻有**神話英雄、歷史戰士、花和灌木**的**精巧畫像**。

外國人： Is mah-jong easy to learn？麻將容易學嗎？

外國人： I think you would be better off learning to play Chinese chess. 我看你還是學下象棋，會覺得快樂些。

**＊＊ *Arabic numerals* 阿拉伯數字　　 elaborate〔ɪˈlæbə͵ret〕*adj.* 精巧的
portrait〔ˈpɔrtrɪt〕*n.* 畫像　　 warrior〔ˈwɔrɪə〕*n.* 戰士
shrub〔ʃrʌb〕*n.* 灌木　　 *be better off* 景況更佳；更快樂；更舒服

TOPIC 40

Five Elements

▷ We Chinese have a great *affection* for the number five.
　我們中國人非常**喜歡**五這個數字。

▷ The Five Elements represent the essences whose nature is
　best defined by Metal, Wood, Water, Fire and Earth.
　五行代表本質上，以金、木、水、火、土最能詳細說明的要素。

✕　　　　　✕　　　　　✕

▷ The Five Elements are also identified with five planets, Mer-
　cury corresponding to Water, Venus to Metal, Mars to Fire,
　Jupiter to Wood, and Saturn to Earth.
　五行也被視為跟五個行星是相同之物。水星相當於水，金星相當於
　金屬，火星相當於火，木星相當於木，土星相當於土。

▷ According to celestial conditions, a sign corresponding to one
　of the Five Elements is assigned to each person on birth.
　根據天空的情況，每個人出生時都會被分到相當於五行之一的一個
　星座。

** Mercury 〔ˈmɝkjərɪ〕 *n.* 水星
corresponding 〔ˌkɔrəˈspɑndɪŋ〕 *adj.* 相當於　Venus〔ˈvinəs〕 *n.* 金星
Mars〔mɑrz〕 *n.* 火星　　Jupiter〔ˈdʒupətɚ〕 *n.* 木星
Saturn〔ˈsætɚn〕 *n.* 土星　celestial〔səˈlɛstʃəl〕 *adj.* 天空的

▷ These signs are taken into consideration in determining marriage, for instance a " Fire " girl will consume a " Wood " husband, whereas one born under the " Water " sign will *nourish* her mate.

這些星座在決定婚事時會被列入考慮。例如一個帶「火」的女孩子會毀滅一個帶「木」的丈夫，但是出生帶有「水」的星座，會有助於她的配偶。

▷ Water produces Wood, but *extinguishes* Fire ; Fire produces Earth, but melts Metal ; Wood *kindles* Fire, but destroys Earth ; Metal is friendly to Water, but harmful to Wood ; and Earth produces Metal, but soaks up Water.

水生木，但滅火；火生土，但溶金；木燃火，但滅土；金親水，但尅木；土生金，但吸水。

✘   ✘   ✘

▷ The Five Elements have given rise to the five grains, five atmospheric conditions, five colors, and five tastes.

由五行產生了五穀、五種大氣的情況、五色、五味。

▷ There are even five points on the Chinese compass with the addition of a center point. 中國羅盤甚至有五點，另外有一個中心點。

▷ Five is the number of the classic Chinese family, three boys and two girls to ensure the *predominance* of the Yang over the Yin.

五是傳統中國家庭的數字，三個男孩和兩個女孩保證陽支配陰。

** *soak up* 吸收   atmospheric〔‚ætməs'fɛrɪk〕*adj.* 大氣的

📼 **Dialogue**

外國人：What are the *five blessings*？什麼是**五福**？

中國人：They are old age, wealth, health, love of *virtue*, and a natural death. 就是長壽、財富、健康、愛德、壽終正寢。

外國人：Why a natural death? In ancient *classical Greece*, the birthplace of Western culture, the glorious, *honorable* death occurs on the *battlefield* in *defense* of your state. 爲什麼是壽終正寢？在**古希臘**，西方文化的發源地，**光榮可佩**的死亡，是發生在爲了**防禦國家的戰場**上。

中國人：Warfare was never *glorified* in China. The soldier never enjoyed a high *reputation* here. We traditionally preferred *compromise* to *bloodshed*, and a face-saving *line of retreat* was *invariably* left open to an adversary. 戰爭在中國從沒有被**頌揚**過。這裏的士兵，從沒有享過很高的**聲譽**。我們傳統上喜歡**和解勝於流血**，而且**一定會**爲敵手留下保留面子的**撤退線**。

外國人：I guess that kind of thinking changed, when the Western powers and Japan, with their superior military techniques, carved up China in 1900. 我想，在西方超級强國和日本，以其優越的軍事技術，在一九〇〇年瓜分中國時，這種想法已經改變了。

中國人：Yes, that was a *humiliating* period in China's history. The status of soldiers is still not high but we've come to recognize the importance of a strong, *up-to-date* military. 是的，那是中國史上的**屈辱**時期。士兵的地位**仍然**不高，不過，我們已承認强大、**新式**軍隊的重要性。

INTRODUCING TAIWAN IN ENGLISH · TOPIC 41

梅花是我國國花(*national flower*)，花色淡潔，共五瓣(*five petals*)，在嚴冬時節萬物靜息之際綻放，別具有一番不畏霜寒的氣勢，最能象徵中國堅忍不拔(*resilience*)的民族精神。在中國歷史上，梅花一直是文人畫家競相推崇描摹的對象，不僅是因其美好的豐姿，更由於那股傲然挺立於惡劣之中的氣魄，很能傳達出中國知識份子清高持平的態度。梅屬薔薇科(*Rosaceae*)，先開花後長綠葉，花開期在十二月到二月之間，花色有純白和淡紅兩種。四月中旬至五月上旬結實長果，未成熟的果實可以燻製烏梅，成熟的果子可生食或製成蜜餞(*preserves*)，如酸梅(*dried plum*)、話梅(*prune; dried plum*)等，極具酸味。梅原產在大陸中部及南部一帶，台灣自從早期大陸人民移入後，就開始從事梅的栽培，目前以南投縣、台中縣和彰化縣最盛。

≪ **Terms and Phrases** ≫

- peony〔'piənɪ〕*n.* 牡丹花　　orchid〔'ɔrkɪd〕*n.* 蘭花
- lotus〔'lotəs〕*n.* 荷花　　plum〔plʌm〕*n.* 梅樹
- resilience〔rɪ'zɪlɪəns〕*n.* 堅忍　　adversity〔əd'vɝsətɪ〕*n.* 逆境
- survive〔sə'vaɪv〕*v.* 存活　　tourist〔'tʊrɪst〕*n.* 遊客
- characterize〔'kærɪktə,raɪz〕*v.* 顯示～的特徵
- frugality〔fru'gælətɪ〕*n.* 節儉　　promote〔prə'mot〕*v.* 提倡
- petal〔'pɛtl̩〕*n.* 花瓣　　lavish〔'lævɪʃ〕*adj.* 浪費的；過度的

TOPIC 41

The Plum Blossom

Dialogue

外國人：Which is the most famous flower in China?
中國最有名的花是哪一種？

中國人：There have of course been very famous flowers in China such as the *peony*, the *orchid*, the *lotus*, and so on. However, only one has become our national flower, and that is the *plum blossom*.
中國當然一直有很出名的花，像**牡丹**、**蘭花**、**荷花**等等。不過，成爲我們的國花的，只有一種，那就是**梅花**。

外國人：Why is it so famous? 爲什麼它那麼有名？

中國人：Well, besides being beautiful, it is also known for its *resilience* in the face of *adversity*, a true characteristic of the Chinese people.
嗯，除了很美之外，它也以面對**逆境**而能**堅忍不拔**知名，那是中國人的標準特質。

外國人：How's that? 怎麼說？

中國人：Well, it blossoms in winter when the weather is very cold and there is a strong icy wind. Most other flowers and blossoms cannot *survive* in such conditions.
嗯，在天氣非常寒冷而且吹寒風的冬天，它照常開花。
在這種情況下，大多數其他的花就無法**生存**。

外國人： Can the plum blossom be seen in Taiwan?

台灣看得到梅花嗎？

中國人： Yes. It can be seen on Yangmingshan just north of Taipei in the national park. If you are traveling in Taiwan on the East-West Cross-Island Highway, you can see it at Lishan where *tourists* usually stop for a rest.

可以。在台北北部陽明山國家公園裏可以看得到。如果你在台灣旅行，走東西橫貫公路，你可以在梨山看到梅花。那裏經常是**遊客**歇脚的地方。

外國人： Besides being resilient, is the plum blossom *characterized* as being anything else?

除了堅忍不拔之外，梅花還有什麼別的**特點**？

中國人： The plum blossom also speaks of *frugality*. This is one of the traditional virtues of the Chinese people. The government has once *promoted* the plum blossom meal, a simple five course meal, each course being represented by one of the five *petals* on a plum blossom. Government officials are encouraged to avoid wasting public money on *lavish* forms of entertainment.

梅花也象徵**節儉**。這是中國人傳統的美德之一。政府曾經**提倡**過梅花餐，就是五道菜組成的簡餐，每道菜就以梅花五**瓣**中的一瓣來代表。政府官員被鼓勵避免把公帑浪費在**奢侈的**娛樂形式上。

** *speak of* 象徵；表示；代表

INTRODUCING TAIWAN IN ENGLISH · TOPIC 42

　　象棋是一項中國古老的**遊藝**（*intellectual pastime*），由於古代的**棋子**（*chessman*）多以象牙為飾，故稱之為**象棋**（*Chinese chess; elephant chess*）。追溯象棋的源流可以直通夏商周三代之時，然而究竟起於何人、何時、何地如今已難以考查。確定的是唐代已有傳入西域，輾轉至歐洲，演變為今日的萬國象棋。在宋朝年間，象棋已經成為大眾化的娛樂，南宋時所下的棋法，與現代幾乎無多大的差別了。人說下棋如用兵，其間寓涵存亡進退之理，經世用兵之道，在觀敵度己之餘，可以啓發智慧，陶冶性情，培養個人獨立的思考能力，聰敏如蘇東坡者，尚自嘆不如人。雖則如此，象棋自古以來一直被視為游藝性質，不入正典之門，直至今日列為**國粹**（*unique cultural features of the nation*）之一，才得到光榮的肯定與地位。近年來，高信疆先生更力倡造形象棋，將象棋的造型設計結合藝術創作，重新賦予了象棋另一番形式之美，是三百年來重大的革新之一，當有助於提昇象棋的藝術欣賞價值，打開國際上的知名度。

⟪ Terms and Phrases ⟫

- marshal〔ˈmɑrʃəl〕*n.* 帥（紅）　　councilor〔ˈkaunslə〕*n.* 相（紅）
- ***red scholar*** 仕（紅）　　***red cavalry***（*horse*）傌（紅）
- ***red chariot*** 俥（紅）　　***red cannon***（*artillery*）砲（紅）
- soldier〔ˈsoldʒə〕*n.* 兵（紅）　　***army general*** 將（黑）
- ***black scholar*** 士（黑）　　elephant〔ˈɛləfənt〕*n.* 象（黑）
- ***black chariot*** 車（黑）　　***black cavalry***（*horse*）馬（黑）
- ***black cannon***（*artillery*）包（黑）　　pawn〔pɔn〕*n.* 卒（黑）

TOPIC 42

Chinese Chess

🔲 **Introducing Taiwan** ▶

▷ Chiness Chess is called " hsiang-chi. "
中國棋叫做象棋。

▷ Chinese Chess or " hsiang-chi " was invented two thousand
years ago by the King of Jiangnan.
「象棋」是在兩千年前由江南王所發明的。

▷ During a long winter *siege* in the Chiangshi province, the King
devised the game to *amuse* his soldiers.
在江西省冬季長期圍困時，這位君王發明這個遊戲，**娛樂**他的士兵。

☒   ☒   ☒

▷ The game *mimics* warfare with generals, *secretaries*, elephants,
horses, chariots, cannons, and soldiers.
這個遊戲用將、**士**、象、馬、車、砲、兵來**模擬**戰爭。

▷ Hsiang-chi is played on a board that is divided by a " river "
into two parts which are ruled into eight columns and four
rows giving thirty-two squares each.
象棋是在一塊木板上玩的，木板被一條「河」分成被線隔成八欄四
行的兩個部分，每部分有三十二個方格。

▷ The pieces move along the lines of the squares and not in
the squares.
象棋的棋子是沿著方格的線移動，而不是在方格中移動。

▷ The movements of the general and his two secretaries are *confined* to the edges of four squares.

將和他的兩個士的移動**限定**於四個方格的邊 。

▷ The object of the game is to trap the general.

這個遊戲的目標就是要抓住將 。

▷ Hsiang-chi is more popular among the *educated* than the common people.

象棋在**受過教育的**人中受歡迎的程度 ， 甚過於在一般人中 。

𝒳   𝒳   𝒳

▷ Hsiang-chi requires good *concentration* and strong *analytical abilities*.

象棋必須要非常**專心**以及很強的**分析能力** 。

▷ European chess is very *similar* to hsiang-chi.

西洋棋和象棋很**類似** 。

🔲 **Dialogue** ➤

外國人 : I understand that the Chinese play a kind of chess game which is *slightly* different from the one we play in the West.

聽說中國人玩一種棋，跟我們在西方玩的**有點**不太一樣。

中國人 : Yes. In fact, although a Chinese chess *set* contains the same number of pieces as *European chess*, the pieces are quite different.

對。事實上，雖然**一副**象棋和**西洋棋**包含一樣的棋數，但棋子是相當不同的。

外國人 : Does it have a king and queen? 象棋有國王和皇后嗎？

中國人 : There is a king, but instead of the queen, there is a pair of *mandarins*, or *counselors*.

有一個「王」，不過沒有皇后，有一對**士**。

外國人 : Well, I guess they don't have *bishops*.

哦，我想也沒有**主教**吧。

中國人 : That's right. Instead they have two *mighty* war elephants. Furthermore, the Chinese only have five *pawns*, to the European eight, but they do have a pair of *cannon* in their *artillery*.

對的。沒有主教，而有兩個**強大有力**的戰象。而且，象棋又有五個**卒**，不像西洋棋有八個，但在象棋的**砲兵**裏還有兩隻**大砲**。

外國人：That doesn't surprise me since the Chinese invented
　　　　gunpowder！ By the way, is the *board* the same as ours?
　　　　這並不令我驚訝，因爲中國人發明了**火藥**。對了，**棋盤**跟我
　　　　們的一樣嗎？

中國人：It has 64 *squares*, but there the *similarity* ceases.
　　　　The great *Yellow River* of China divides the board into
　　　　two kingdoms eight squares wide by four squares long.
　　　　Not all the pieces can cross this river, and those that
　　　　do not, stay behind to *defend* the king.
　　　　象棋也有六十四**格**，但其他的就**不一樣**了。中國的偉大的**黃
　　　　河**把棋盤分成兩個國家，各八格寬，四格長。並非所有的棋
　　　　子都能過河，那些不能過河的，留在後面**保衞**他們的君王。

外國人：Do the pieces move about in the same way as those in
　　　　European chess? 象棋和西洋棋一樣的走法嗎？

中國人：To put it simply, no. Chinese *chessmen* travel along
　　　　the lines instead of in the squares.
　　　　簡單說吧，不一樣。象棋**棋子**沿著線走，而不在格子裏跳。

外國人：Do many people play chess in Taiwan today？
　　　　現在，台灣有很多人下象棋嗎？

中國人：As you walk around Taipei you will sometimes see some
　　　　old men playing a game. However, young people have
　　　　too many lessons to prepare for school.
　　　　你在台北走一走，有時可以看到一些老人在下棋。不過，年
　　　　輕人則有太多學校功課要準備。

** board〔bord, bɔrd〕*n.* 棋盤　　square〔skwɛr〕*n.* 正方形；格
similarity〔͵sımə'lærətı〕*n.* 相似之點　　chessmen〔'tʃɛsmən〕*n.* 棋子

TOPIC 43

圍棋   **Weichi**

Introducing Taiwan

▷ Weichi, also commonly known as "Go" was invented over two thousand years ago in China.

圍棋，也就是一般人熟知的「Go」，是兩千年多年前在中國發明的。

▷ The *playing pieces* consist of 180 white and 180 black *buttons*, the *playing board* is divided by 19 *horizontal* and *vertical* lines, creating 361 points of *intersection*.

玩的子是由一百八十枚白色和一百八十枚黑色鈕扣形的東西所組成，棋盤被十九條橫線和直線分開，造出了三百六十一個交叉點。

⋇ ⋇ ⋇

▷ The game is played by two players who take turns placing a button on any unoccupied intersection.

這個遊戲是兩個人玩的，他們輪流把子擺在任何未被佔放的交叉點上。

▷ Buttons which are surrounded by opposing buttons are *captured* and removed.

被對方的子包圍的子就被擄獲，而且拿走。

▷ The object of the game is to control more *territory* than the other player.

遊戲的目標在於，比另一個玩的人控制更多的領土。

▷ Weichi was a favorite game in the ***imperial courts*** and is mentioned in numerous old books and depicted in paintings.

圍棋是**宮庭**裏最受喜愛的遊戲，而且在很多的古書中被提及，也在畫中被描繪。

▷ Weichi players are ranked according to nine levels.

下圍棋的人，根據九個等級來分類。

▷ The Japanese have adopted weichi with great ***enthusiasm***.

日本人以極高的**熱誠**來**接受**圍棋。

⚹   ⚹   ⚹

▷ It's been said that only the wise are able to play weichi well: by ***defending*** with ***benevolence***, moving with justice, arranging with ***courtesy***, and understanding with ***wisdom***.

曾經有人說，只有聰明的人才能下好圍棋：憑慈悲的**防禦**，公正的移動，**禮貌**的佈局，並以**智慧**了悟。

▷ Weichi should not be considered a trivial pastime.

圍棋不該被看成一種瑣碎的消遣。

▣▣ Dialogue ➤

外國人： Why do so many of Taiwan's top "go" players move to Japan? 爲什麼台灣很多頂尖的「圍棋」好手都到日本去了？

中國人： There are more opportunities to play and improve in Japan. The Japanese organize more tournaments than we do and they frequently sponsor international competitions. 在日本有更多下圍棋和改進的機會。日本人比我們籌辦了更多的比賽，而且他們經常贊助國際性的比賽。

外國人： What's the name of that young man from Taiwan who captured Japan's *top prize*, and held it for many years? 從台灣去贏得日本**首獎**的年輕人叫什麼名字，蟬聯了多少年？

中國人： His name is Lin Hai Feng. We've bestowed the title of "National Representative" upon him. We're very proud of him. 他叫林海峯。我們給予他「國手」的頭衛。我們非常以他爲榮。

外國人： Taiwan has been producing quite a few top "go" players recently. Why doesn't your government encourage the game by sponsoring international competitions? It's also a nice way to promote friendly relations with foreign countries. 台灣最近產生了相當多的頂尖「圍棋」手。爲什麼貴國政府不藉著贊助國際性的比賽來鼓勵這個比賽？它同時也是提昇和外國友好關係的一個好方法。

中國人： We've been doing just that in the last few years. . 最近這幾年，我們就是一直在做這件事。

** *top prize* 首獎　　bestow〔bɪˈsto〕 *v.* 贈；給予

TOPIC 44

中國文藝復興　Chinese Cultural Renaissance

📼 **Question**

How are people's *mentality* in Taiwan *adjusting* to the rapid economic change？在台灣，人們的**心態**如何**適應**快速的經濟變遷？

📼 **Reply**

Frankly, economic change is happening faster than we are adjusting to it. Our economic growth has been described as *miraculous*. Over the past three decades, Taiwan has gone from a war-wrecked island to become one of the so-called "Newly Industrialized Countries." We went *from rags to riches* in less than half a person's lifetime. But our mentality is not adjusting in pace with our economic changes. Consequently, our overnight success is creating social problems. People are tending to seek wealth and spending it in improper ways. Robberies, *extortions*, *kidnappings*, and gambling all have become increasingly common. Fortunately, our government recognizes the root of these problems and is taking steps to correct it by encouraging and emphasizing traditional Chinese culture.

坦白說，經濟變遷發生得比我們適應它還快。我們的經濟成長被形容爲**奇蹟**。過去三十多年裏，台灣從一個戰爭破壞過的島，變成了所謂「新興工業國」之一。我們在短於一個人半輩子的時間中**從赤貧而暴富**。但是我們的心態在適應上並未跟上經濟變遷的脚步。結果，我們短時內的成功製造了社會問題。人們有賺錢，並且把錢花在不正當方面的傾向。搶刼、**勒索**、**綁架**、賭博都變得愈來愈普遍。幸好我們的政府認清這些問題的根源，並藉著鼓勵和強調中國傳統文化，採取步驟加以矯正。

〔⊡⊡〕 **Dialogue** ▶

外國人 ： What is the government doing to promote traditional culture？ 政府做了什麼來提昇傳統文化？

中國人 ： The government has set up a Council for Cultural Planning and Development with the purpose of planning national cultural development, expanding Chinese cultural development, expanding Chinese cultural *awareness*, and *enhancing* the general cultural life of all citizens.

政府已設立了文化建設發展委員會（文建會），目的是計劃全國性的文化發展，拓展中華文化**意識**，並**提高**所有國民的一般文化生活。

* * *

外國人 ： What is an example of something the Council has done？ 那麼，文建會做了什麼事，可以作爲例子？

中國人 ： To prevent the loss of *folk crafts and artistry*, the Council has promoted the demonstration and sale of folk *handicrafts* during major festivals, such as during the Dragon Boat Festival when the art of making perfumed *sachets* is featured.

爲了防止**民俗技藝**失傳，文建會在許多主要節日，推展民俗手工藝的展覽和出售，像是端午節時，以作香**包**的藝術爲號召。

Chapter 5
SOCIETY

一社會一

棒球是台灣最受歡迎的**運動**（*sport*），因為台灣氣候暖和，南部雨季少，非常適合推展棒球。

自從民國五十七年**紅葉少棒**（*little league*）掀起熱潮之後，棒球已經成為我國歷史最輝煌的運動項目。民國五十八年金龍少棒首度代表參加美國威廉波特（*Williamsport*）**世界少棒賽**（*World Little League Championships*）一舉榮獲冠軍。接著**青少棒**（*junior league*）在民國六十一年第一次參加美國蓋瑞的世界青少棒賽，勇奪冠軍寶座；**青棒**（*senior league*）也於美國勞德岱堡傳回冠軍的佳音。此後一連數年，台灣連獲三級棒球賽的「三冠王」。每逢世界性的棒球比賽期間，各家電視臺均紛紛以最快的速度利用**衛星轉播**（*satellite transmission*）傳達比

賽實況，街頭巷尾到處都在議論棒球。

三冠王的狂熱後，取而代之的是對職棒的熱情。目前職棒球隊共有六隊：味全龍、三商虎、統一獅、兄弟象、時報鷹，和興農牛。每年球季，平均都有一百多萬球迷（*fan*）到場觀賞，為他

們支持的球隊加油吶喊，而在家收看或收聽廣播者，更是不計其數，足見台灣職棒的蓬勃發展。

TOPIC 45

Baseball

📼 **Introducing Taiwan**

- Who's playing who? （那兩隊在比賽？）
- Who is on the mound for the Giants? （巨人隊誰主投？）
- Both the R.O.C. and Korea seem to be in fine shape.
  （中華民國隊和韓國隊似乎勢均力敵，不相上下。）
- Today, the R.O.C. has beaten the Americans by two runs.
  （今日，中華民國隊以二分之差贏了美國隊。）
- Now it's the second half of the seventh inning, with two
  down and bases full. （目前是七局後半，二死滿壘。）
- They went to the Taipei Ball Park to see a night game
  between the U.S.A. and Japan.
  （他們到台北市立棒球場觀看美國隊和日本隊的夜間比賽。）

pitcher〔'pɪtʃɚ〕 *n.* 投手　　catcher〔'kætʃɚ〕 *n.* 捕手
first (second, third, …) baseman 一 (二 , 三 …) 壘手
home base 本壘　　umpire〔'ʌmpaɪr〕 *n.* 裁判
out field 外野　　*right fielder* 右外野手　　*center fielder* 中堅手
shortstop〔'ʃɔrt,stɑp〕*n.* 游擊手　　score〔skɔr〕*v.* 得分　　inning〔'ɪnɪŋ〕*n.* 局
foul〔faʊl〕*n.* 界外球　　steal〔stil〕*v.* 盜壘　　*sacrifice hit* 犧牲打
hit〔hɪt〕*n.* 安打　　*single hit* 單打　　*fan out* 三振
heavy batter 強打者 (*or slugger*)　　*pinch hitter* 代打者
national staff 國手　　*be forced out* 封殺　　error〔'ɛrɚ〕*n.* 失誤

📼 **Dialogue**

外國人：What is the most popular sport in Taiwan?

在台灣最受歡迎的運動是什麼？

中國人：It *definitely* has to be baseball, although basketball is also very popular.

肯定是棒球，不過籃球也很受歡迎。

外國人：Is there a professional *league* for baseball?

你們有職業的**棒球聯盟**嗎？

中國人：Yes, the CPBL(*Chinese Professional Baseball League*) has been established for several years. There are six teams in all.

有，**中華職棒聯盟**已成立數年，目前共有六支參賽隊伍。

外國人：How did the teams come about? Are they *representative* of different cities, like in *Major League*?

這些隊伍是如何產生的？是不是像美國的**大聯盟**一樣，**代表**不同的城市呢？

中國人：No, actually the teams are named according to their *sponsors*.

不是，事實上，這些隊伍是根據他們的**贊助廠商**而命名的。

** definitely〔'dɛfənɪtlɪ〕*adv*. 一定地　　league〔lig〕*n.* 聯盟
in all 總共　　**come about** 發生；產生
representative〔ˌrɛprɪ'zɛntətɪv〕*adj.* 代表的
sponsor〔'spɑnsɚ〕*n.* 贊助廠商

外國人：That's interesting. So all the team names are company names?

眞有趣，所以所有的隊伍名稱都是公司名稱囉？

中國人：Right. For example, *the China Times Eagles*, or *the Wei-chuan Foods Dragons*.

是的。例如**時報鷹**、**味全龍**等。

外國人：How big is the *following* here in Taiwan?

台灣此地的**球迷**很多嗎？

中國人：The *fans* are really into the game. In 1993 alone there was a record following of some 1.6 million fans.

球迷們眞是**熱中**於比賽。光是一九九三年一年，就創下了一百六十萬名球迷觀衆的記錄。

外國人：Are there foreign players in the CPBL?

中華職棒聯盟有外籍球員嗎？

中國人：Of course. In fact some of the best players in the league are foreigners.

當然有。事實上，聯盟中某些最佳球員正是外籍球員。

** following〔ˈfɑləwɪŋ〕*n.* 迷；支持者　　fan〔fæn〕*n.* 迷
into〔ˈɪntu〕*adj.* 熱中的

近年來由於經濟的發展與生活水準的提高，國內高爾夫球場地與**球友**（ *player* ）人數日益增加，目前共有四十座**球場**（ *golf course* ）與十萬打球人口，然而高爾夫在台灣仍未相當普遍。早期台灣高爾夫球運動，是發源於縣**淡水球場**（ *Tamsui Country Club* ），成立於民國八年，日據時代日本人在此打球，台灣光復後，才漸有國人參與其間，我國多位高球名將都曾在淡水球場充當過**球僮**（ *caddie* ）的工作。高爾夫球是種考驗體力、耐力與腦力的運動，據研究，常打高爾夫可促進血液循環，加速新陳代謝，治療高血壓、關節炎、神經痛、糖尿病等慢性疾病。尤其是徜徉在球場寬闊整潔的綠野當中，藍天、青草、樹蔭等自然美景更可使人忘却生活所帶來的壓力與煩憂，對於身心兩方面的發展皆相當有所助益。

《 Terms and Phrases 》

- tournament〔'tɝnəmənt〕 *n.* 錦標賽；競賽
- *professional tournament* 職業錦標賽
- circuit〔'sɝkɪt〕 *n.* 巡迴賽　　**be held** 舉行
- championship〔'tʃæmpɪən,ʃɪp〕 *n.* 優勝；冠軍；冠軍賽
- *the world championship of golf* 世界高爾夫球冠軍賽
- *golf club* 高爾夫球桿　　*a set of golf clubs* 一套高爾夫球用具
- *golf ball* 高爾夫球　　stroke〔strok〕 *n.* 擊球
- *stroke play* 桿數賽（按擊出桿數少者排列名次的比賽）
- golfer〔'gɑlfɚ〕 *n.* 打高爾夫球的人
- *the teeing ground* 高爾夫開球區域　　tee〔ti〕 *v.* 將球擱在球座上
- bunker〔'bʌŋkɚ〕 *v.* 球擊入坑窪之中；〔喻〕陷入窮境
- *amateur tour tournament* 業餘巡迴錦標賽

TOPIC 46

高爾夫球　　　　　　　**Golf**

Dialogue

外國人： Is golf a *popular* sport in Taiwan?

高爾夫球在台灣是一種很**普遍的**運動嗎？

中國人： We have several golf *courses* here and a number of *good players*, but nothing like in the United States.

我們這裏有幾個高爾夫**球場**，一些打高爾夫球的**好手**，不過不像美國那樣。

外國人： Does Taiwan do well in golf on an international level？

台灣人打高爾夫球的表現很好，已有國際水準了嗎？

中國人： The *peak* years were definitely the 1980s. In 1984 the Taiwan team was ranked second in *the World Cup* and *International Trophy Championship*. Although recent performance has not been as good, Taiwan hosts many tournaments each year, including *ROC PGA Championship* which is one of Asia's major tournaments.

高峰時期顯然是在一九八○年代。一九八四年台灣隊伍在**世界盃**和**國際錦標冠軍爭奪賽**中名列第二。雖然近年來的表現不如從前，台灣每年仍然主辦許多活動，包括**中華民國職業高爾夫冠軍賽**，是亞洲主要的錦標賽之一。

＊　　　　　＊　　　　　＊

外國人： Does Taiwan hold any major *championships* ?

台灣有舉辦較大型的**錦標賽**嗎？

中國人： Well, we do not hold any competition which can compare with *the U.S. Masters* or *the British Open*, but
we have attracted some *star players* in recent years.

嗯，我們並沒有舉辦任何可以跟**美國名人賽**，或**英國公開賽**
相提並論的比賽。不過近年來，我們吸引了一些**明星球員**。

外國人： I understand you have one or two of your own star
players. 我知道你們有自己的一兩個明星球員。

中國人： Yes, the Chen brothers are very famous now, one in
the U.S. in particular. He was very successful last
year.

是的。陳氏兄弟現在很有名了，尤其一個還在美國呢。他去
年非常成功。

外國人： How did they *take up* golf?

他們是怎麼**開始**打高爾夫的？

中國人： They started as *caddies* and soon *got hooked on* the
game. When the local *professional* saw their potential,
they were encouraged to take up the game seriously.
The same *applies* to Miss Tu, Taiwan's leading fe-
male player.

他們開始先當**球僮**，很快就**迷上**這項運動。地方上的**職業球
員**看出他們的潛力，就鼓勵他們認真打。涂（阿玉）小姐，
台灣最重要的女性球員，**也是**同樣的情形。

外國人：　I'm a little surprised by their success. After all, Americans are generally taller and far stronger than their Chinese counterparts, and therefore can hit the ball further.

我對他們的成功有點驚訝。畢竟，美國人比起他們的中國對手來，通常都比較高又比較壯，所以可以把球打得更遠。

中國人：　The long-hitters like Nicklaus and Ballasteros of Spain are also more likely to hit the ball off course; golf requires *accuracy* and *consistency* and not just *brute* force.

尼可勞斯和西班牙的保烈士特羅斯的長打，也很可能把球打出球場；打高爾夫球需要的是**準確性**和**耐力**，而不是光靠**蠻力**就成的。

course〔kɔrs〕*n.* 球場　　*a number of* 一些（＝ *some* ）

peak〔pik〕*adj.* 最高峯的　　*the World Cup* 世界盃

trophy〔'trofɪ〕*n.* 優勝杯〔旗〕

PGA 職業高爾夫協會（ professional golfers' association ）

compared with 比起…　　championships〔'tʃæmpɪən,ʃɪps〕*n.* 錦標賽

competition〔,kɑmpə'tɪʃən〕*n.* 比賽　　*the U.S. Masters* 美國名人賽

the British Open 英國公開賽　　*star player* 名將；明星球員

take up 開始；從事　　caddie〔'kædɪ〕*n.* 球僮

get hooked on 迷上　　professional〔prə'fɛʃənl〕*n.* 職業球員

apply to 適用於　　accuracy〔'ækjərəsɪ〕*n.* 準確性

consistency〔kən'sɪstənsɪ〕*n.* 一致　　brute〔brut〕*adj.* 粗野的

TOPIC 47

Basketball

🔲 **Introducing Taiwan** ➤

Basketball is one of the most common sports in Taiwan. It is played mainly in the playgrounds of schools and is enjoyed by both boys and girls. The first Jones Cup *Tournament* was played in Taipei on July 13, 1977, and since then has become an *annual event*. The Jones Cup was named after Dr. William Jones, the first secretary general of the International *Amateur* Basketball Federation, and it was established for the purpose of promoting basketball, the *Olympic* spirit, and international *goodwill*. The CBA (*Chinese Basketball Association*) was *inaugurated* in November 1994, and there are currently four teams competing. The teams are: Tai-Rei, Hun-Kuo, Yu-Long and Hsing-Fu. In addition, there are also foreign players whose different styles of play add more *spice* to the game.

籃球是台灣最風行的運動之一，主要場地常是在學校的運動場，而且男生、女生都喜歡。第一屆瓊斯盃**比賽**於一九七七年七月十三日在台北舉行，從此便成為**一年一度的大事**。瓊斯盃是以威廉‧瓊斯博士為名，他是國際**業餘**籃球聯盟的第一任秘書長，而設立瓊斯盃的目的在於提昇籃球、**奧林匹克**精神及國際**親善**。CBA（**中華職籃聯盟**）在一九九四年十一月**成立**，而現在有四支比賽隊伍，分別是泰瑞、宏國、裕隆和幸福隊。此外，外籍球員打球時不同的風格，更替比賽添加**風味**。

📼 **Dialogue** ➤

外國人：How popular is the CBA in Taiwan?
中華職籃在台灣有多受歡迎？

中國人：Its popularity has increased and is second only to the Baseball league.
受歡迎的程度與日漸增，而僅次於職棒。

外國人：Are foreign players allowed to play in the CBA?
外籍球員也可以加入中華職籃嗎？

中國人：Yes. Each team is allowed a ***maximum*** of five foreign players, including those from mainland China.
可以，每支隊伍**最多**有五個外籍球員的名額，包括來自中國大陸的球員。

外國人：How is the ***level*** of basketball played in the CBA?
中華職籃的**水準**如何？

中國人：We are just starting off, so we are still learning many things. But the players are improving ***constantly*** and the CBA is ***prompting*** more and more people, especially children, to start playing this great game.
我們才剛起步，所以還在學習很多事情，但球員們**不斷地**在進步，而中華職籃也**促使**愈來愈多人，尤其是兒童，開始來從事這項非常好的運動。

Terms and Phrases

- **amateur** 〔'æmə,tʃʊr,-,tʊr 〕 *adj.* 業餘的
- *annual event* 一年一度的大事
- **association** 〔 ə,sosɪ'eʃən,ə,soʃɪ- 〕 *n.* 聯盟
- **compete** 〔 kəm'pit 〕 *v.* 比賽
- **constantly** 〔'kɑnstəntlɪ 〕 *adv.* 不斷地
- **currently** 〔'kɝəntlɪ 〕 *adv.* 最近
- **federation** 〔,fɛdə'reʃən 〕 *n.* 聯盟
- *for the purpose of* 爲了～目的
- **goodwill** 〔'gʊd'wɪl 〕 *n.* 親善
- **inaugurate** 〔 ɪn'ɔgjə,ret 〕 *v.* 就職；落成
- **league** 〔 lig 〕 *n.* 聯盟
- **level** 〔'lɛvl 〕 *n.* 水準；程度
- **maximum** 〔'mæksəməm 〕 *n.* 最大值；最多量
- **Olympic** 〔 o'lɪmpɪk 〕 *adj.* 奧林匹克的
- **playground** 〔'ple,graʊnd 〕 *n.* 運動場
- **promote** 〔 prə'mot 〕 *v.* 提昇；促進
- **prompt** 〔 prɑmpt 〕 *v.* 促使
- *secretary general* 祕書長
- **spice** 〔 spaɪs 〕 *n.* 香料；風味
- **tournament** 〔'tɝnəmənt,'tʊr- 〕 *n.* 比賽

TOPIC 48

郵政服務　Postal Service

Introducing Taiwan

The postal service in Taiwan is one of the best in the world.
There are more than 12,500 post offices around Taiwan pro-
viding fast, efficient service.　In cities *regular deliveries*
are made four times a day and *special deliveries* are made
from early morning till late at night.　It's no problem if letters are addressed in English as our postmen have a lot of
experience in delivering them.　Our postmen are also legendary for locating the *destinations* of incorrectly addressed
letters.　Post offices also provide services that are not post
related.　They sell *life insurance*, issue *money orders*, and
provide banking services.　Postal savings accounts are very
popular because post offices are conveniently located and
have long *operating hours*, Monday through Saturday, 8 a.m.
to 6 p.m.　Postal services are also available on Sunday morning and holidays in some post offices.

台灣的郵政服務是世界上最好的之一。全台灣有一萬兩千五百個以
上的郵局，提供迅速、有效的服務。在都市裏，一天遞四次**平信**，
限時專送由清晨到深夜。假如信件是用英文書寫地址的，也沒有問
題，因爲我們的郵差在遞送這類信件方面，有豐富的經驗。在找出
地址寫錯信件的**目的地**時，我們的郵差也是很傳奇的。郵局也提供
和郵政無關的服務。他們賣**人壽保險**，發行**匯票**，並且提供銀行服
務。郵政儲蓄存款非常普遍，因爲郵局設立的地點很近便，而且**營
業時間**長，從星期一到星期六，早上八點到下午六點。部分郵局在
星期天上午及假日，亦提供服務。

Dialogue

外國人： Who are you writing to? 你寫信給誰？

中國人： My *penpal*, she lives in Thailand.
我的**筆友**，她住在泰國。

外國人： Oh neat! How did you meet?
真棒！你們怎麼碰到的？

中國人： I met her when she visited Taiwan. We *exchanged*
addresses before she left.
她來台灣遊覽時，我碰見她。她離開之前，我們**交換了地址**。

外國人： What do you write about? 你寫些什麼？

中國人： Nothing special. I tell her how I'm doing, what's
happening in Taiwan, and anything interesting I can
think of.
沒什麼特別的。我告訴她我近況如何，台灣發生了什麼事
情，還有任何我可以想到的有趣事情。

外國人： Will you be my penpal when I return to South Africa?
當我回到南非時，你會成為我的筆友嗎？

中國人： Sure. 當然。

** aerogram〔'eərə,græm〕*n*. 航空信；航空郵簡
air/surface mail 航空信／（非航空的）平寄郵件
junk mail 由廠商自動寄來的商業廣告信
letterhead〔'lɛtə,hɛd〕*n*. 印在信紙上的信頭（例如公司行號的名稱及地址）
life insurance 人壽保險　*mail order* 郵購　*money order* 滙票
operating hours 營業時間　philatelist〔fə'lætlɪst〕*n*. 集郵者

TOPIC 49

雜誌　報紙　Magazines and Newspapers

Introducing Taiwan

After the *lifting* of the *ban on newspaper registration* in January 1988, now we have nearly 300 newspapers with a total *circulation* of over 5 million. Two of them are even in English, the China Post and the China News. The major dominating Chinese papers are the United Daily News, the China Times and the Liberty Times. We also have an enormous variety of magazines, almost 5000 in all. They range from *weeklies*, to *monthlies*, to *quarterlies*, and the subjects are as *broad* as world news or as *specific* as fishing. The Journalist（Weekly）, CommonWealth, and Wealth Magazine are among the popular Chinese magazines. English *periodicals* include the Free China Review, Sinorama, and so on. Besides, we also have magazines which teach English and the practice texts are at the same time broadcast on radio stations, such as The Studio Classroom, Let's Talk in English, English Digest, etc.

從一九八八年一月**報禁解除**之後，現在我們有將近三百種報紙，總**發行量**超過五百萬份。其中兩份甚至是英文的，英文中國郵報和英文中國日報。主要領先的中文報紙是聯合報、中國時報和自由時報。我們也有很多不同的雜誌，總共將近五千種。範圍從**週刊**、**月刊**、到**季刊**，主題**廣泛**到像世界新聞，或**特殊**到像釣魚的都有。受歡迎的中文雜誌有新新聞週刊、天下雜誌，和財訊。英文**雜誌**包括自由中國評論和光華雜誌等。此外，我們還有教英文的雜誌，而教學內容同時也由電台廣播，例如空中英語教室、大家說英語、實用空中美語文摘等。

🔲 **Dialogue 1**

外國人： Are the newspapers *censored*? 報紙要經過**審查**嗎？

中國人： Newspapers here practice self-censorship as newspapers
do in America. We don't print news that will harm
our country's well-being.

這裏的報紙就像美國報紙一樣，實行自我審查。我們不會刊
出損害國家福祉的新聞。

外國人： Who owns the newspapers? 誰擁有這些報紙？

中國人： Some are government owned, many are privately owned, and the rest are owned jointly.

有些是政府所有，很多是私人擁有，其餘的則是政府和私人
共有。

外國人： Do people here believe what newspapers say?

這裏的人相信報上所說嗎？

中國人： Yes, but as anywhere, sometimes we have to *read
between the lines*.

是的，但就和任何地方一樣，有時候我們必須**領會字裏行間
的言外之意**。

🔲 **Dialogue 2**

外國人： Where can I find American magazines?

我在哪裏可以找到美國雜誌？

中國人：Many bookstores carry them and you'll also find them at tourist hotels. 很多書店都有，你也可以在觀光飯店裏找到。

外國人：I've looked everywhere but I can't find a single copy of Men's Health magazine. Do you know where I can get a copy？

我到處看遍，却找不到一本健康人雜誌。你知道我要到哪裏才能買到嗎？

中國人：There are probably not enough readers in Taipei to justify most bookshops to sell it. But you can try the larger bookshops, who usually stock a wider selection of foreign magazines.

在台北可能讀者不夠多，所以沒辦法在大部分書店販賣。不過你可以試試大一點的書局，它們通常會多進一點外國雜誌，選擇性較大。

broad〔brɔd〕*adj.* 廣泛的   censorship〔'sɛnsəʃɪp〕*n.* 檢查；檢查制度
circulation〔,sɝkjə'leʃən〕*n.* 發行數；銷售量
classified ads 分類廣告   comic〔'kamɪk〕*n.* 連環圖畫
cover story 雜誌中與封面圖片有關的主題報導；封面故事
daily／weekly／monthly／quarterly／annually 日報／週刊／月刊／季刊／年報
editor〔'ɛdɪtɚ〕*n.* 編輯
editorial〔,ɛdə'torɪəl, -'tɔr-〕*adj.* 編輯的；主筆的   *n.* 社論
headline〔'hɛd,laɪn〕*n.* 大字標出的重要標題
journalism〔'dʒɝnl,ɪzəm〕*n.* 新聞業；報章雜誌
magazine subscription 訂閱雜誌
press〔prɛs〕*n.* 印刷事業，新聞界   publisher〔'pʌblɪʃɚ〕*n.* 發行人
read between the lines 領會言外之意   reporter〔rɪ'portɚ〕*n.* 記者
specific〔spɪ'sɪfɪk〕*adj.* 明確的，特殊的

廣播 電視 **Radio and Television**

🔲 **Question**

Are there many TV and radio stations in Taiwan?

在台灣有很多電視台和無線電台嗎？

🔲 **Reply**

Yes, there are three private *commercial television networks*, namely Taiwan Television Enterprise (TTV), the China Television Company (CTV), and the Chinese Television System (CTS), and the growing *cable TV stations*, *trammitted* all over the island. In addition to the *programs* locally produced, there are also foreign programs shown and important international events which are *broadcast live*. Taiwan has one of the world's highest *concentration* of radio stations, with nearly two hundred radio stations serving Taiwan. The oldest is the *state-run* Broadcasting Corporation of China (BCC), which now operates four *national radio networks*, including ones devoted to news and pop music.

是的，有三家私人的**商業電視網**，也就是台視、中視、華視，和日漸成長的**有線電視台**（**第四台**），**傳送**到全省各地。除了本地製作的**節目**外，也播映外國的節目，以及現場實況轉播的重要國際事件。台灣的廣播電台是全世界最**密集**的之一，有將近二百家電台在服務。歷史最悠久的是**國營的**中國廣播公司，目前有四個**全國廣播網**，包括新聞網和流行音樂網。

Dialogue 1

外國人： What's the most popular program on TV?
電視上最受歡迎的節目是什麼？

中國人： Probably the *variety shows*. Taiwanese viewers all love
to watch variety shows.
大概是**綜藝節目**吧。台灣觀眾都喜歡看綜藝節目。

外國人： Are there any English language programs on TV?
電視上有英語節目嗎？

中國人： Yes, there are. On the three main TV stations, there
are many *foreign films*, and on cable TV, we got HBO,
CNN, ES PN, Star TV, etc.
有的，在三家主要電視台，有許多**外國影集**；而在第四台，
我們也有HBO, CNN, ESPN, 衛星電視等等。

外國人： Kids in the States watch a lot of TV. How about
kids here in Taiwan?
美國小孩電視看很多。台灣此地的孩子呢？

中國人： With the *pressure* of *schoolwork* and being out of house
from very early to very late every day, most young
people in Taiwan don't have much time to watch TV.
由於**課業壓力**，再加上每天早出晚歸，台灣的大部分年輕人
沒有太多時間看電視。

Dialogue 2

外國人： What's ICRT?　ICRT是什麼？

中國人：It's the ***around-the-clock*** English language radio station here. ICRT is an ***acronym*** for International Community Radio Taipei.

它是這裏**二十四小時播放**的英語廣播電台。ICRT 是 International Community Radio Taipei 這幾個字的**開頭字母所組成的字**，也就是台北社區廣播電台。

外國人：How did ICRT come about? ICRT 是怎麼來的？

中國人：It used to be the AFNT or American Forces Network Taiwan. When the U.S. troops pulled out, we decided to continue operating the radio station, because we believed it provided a necessary service.

它曾經是AFNT，台灣美軍電台。當美軍撤離時，我們決定繼續經營這個電台，因為我們認為它提供了必要的服務。

外國人：Does ICRT have a large audience？
ICRT有廣大的聽衆嗎？

中國人：Yes, it's the most popular station among our young people. Its D. J. Tony Taylor has become quite a ***celebrity***.

有，它是在年輕人當中最受歡迎的電台。它的音樂節目主持人湯尼・泰勒已經相當**有名**。

Terms and Phrases

- **acronym**〔'ækrənɪm〕 *n.* 由數個字開頭所組成的字
- **around the clock**〔ə'raʊndðə'klɑk〕 *adj.* 日以繼夜的；
  不休止的
- **broadcast**〔'brɔd,kæst〕 *v.* 廣播
- **cable**〔'kebl〕 *n.* 電纜　　***cable TV*** 有線電視
- **celebrity**〔sə'lɛbrətɪ〕 *n.* 名人
- **commercial**〔kə'mɝʃəl〕 *adj.* 商業的；由廣告資助的
- **concentration**〔,kɑnsn'treʃən, -sɛn-〕 *n.* 集中
- **corporation**〔,kɔrpə'reʃən〕 *n.* 公司
- **devote**〔dɪ'vot〕 *v.* 致力於；奉獻
- **enterprise**〔'ɛntɚ,praɪz〕 *n.* 企業
- **live**〔laɪv〕 *adv.* 現場轉播地
- **namely**〔'nemlɪ〕 *adv.* 也就是
- **network**〔'nɛt,wɝk〕 *n.* 網路；廣播網
- **pressure**〔'prɛʃɚ〕 *n.* 壓力
- **private**〔'praɪvɪt〕 *adj.* 私人的
- **schoolwork**〔'skul,wɝk〕 *n.* 功課；課業
- **state-run**〔'stet'rʌn〕 *adj.* 國營的；州營的
- **transmit**〔træns'mɪt〕 *v.* 傳播；(無線電) 傳送
- ***variety show*** 綜藝節目

✦ The Taipei World Trade Center / 台北世貿中心

Q : There is now a Computer Show going on in *the Taipei World Trade Center*. Where is this place?

現在有一個電腦展在台北世貿中心舉行。世貿中心在哪裏?

A : The Taipei World Trade Center is situated in the eastern part of the city and is the ***centerpiece*** of the Hsinyi Redevelopment Project. It also includes other buildings such as the Grand Hyatt hotel, a convention center, and an administrative building. The Taipei World Trade Center is the largest of its kind in Southeast Asia and is the one-stop-shop center for local as well as foreign businessmen. The Taipei World Trade Center also has the most comprehensive collection of products under one roof in Taiwan.

台北世貿中心在本市東區,是信義計畫區中**最重要的建築**。它包括了其他建築,例如凱悅飯店、會議中心和行政大樓。台北世貿中心的規模,是東南亞地區同類型建築中最大的,它是本地和國外商人的採購中心。台北世貿中心也擁有全台灣包羅最廣的產品。

** centerpiece〔'sɛntɚˌpis〕*n.* 最重要的人或物
comprehensive〔ˌkɑmprɪ'hɛnsɪv〕*adj.* 廣泛的

Chapter 6

ISSUES

問題

INTRODUCING TAIWAN IN ENGLISH • TOPIC 51

住，是民生問題（ *problem of the people's livelihood* ）重要需求之一。台灣由於工商繁榮，人口不斷增加，人民對「住」的需求，無論在質、量方面也相形地愈來愈高。政府為了達成「人人有自宅」的目標，年年都撥下大筆經費興建**國民住宅**（ *public housing; government housing* ），提供一般民眾**貸款**（ *loan* ）置產，頗費一番苦心，然而由於規劃不善、施工不良、售價偏高以及屋數供不應求等問題，經常引起大眾爭相指責與詬病。目前都市中可供建築居住的有限**空間**（ *space* ）愈來愈少，放眼望去，都市如**叢林**（ *jungle* ），一棟棟高樓推攔過來，儼然便是林立的巨樹一般，臨空向人群壓迫而來，頗具威脅感。所謂「台北居，大不易」當可說是最好的寫照。

《 Terms and Phrases 》

- *share an apartment* 分租公寓
- *house to let; house for rent* 房屋出租
- landlord〔'lænd, lɔrd〕*n.* 房東　　　landlady〔'lænd, ledɪ〕*n.* 房東太太
- tenant〔'tɛnənt〕*n.* 房客（不與房東合住）
- lodger〔'lɑdʒə〕*n.* 房客（與房東合住）
- boarder〔'bɔrdə〕*n.* 房客（與房東同膳宿）
- *realtor; real estate agent* 房屋經紀人　　 *house number* 門牌號碼
- *name plate* 門牌　　 sell〔sɛl〕*v.* 賣；售
- location〔lo'keʃən〕*n.* 地點；位置　　 *private property* 私產
- *down payment* 定金　 mortgage〔'mɔrgɪdʒ〕*n., v.* 抵押
- dormitory〔'dɔrmə, tɔrɪ〕*n.* 宿舍
- *raise the rent* 房租上漲　　 *sign a deed* (*or lease*) 過戶

TOPIC 51

臺北的住宅問題　Taipei's Housing Problem

📼 **Dialogue** ▶

外國人： I read in the " China Post " the other day that there
are many empty apartments in Taipei. Why, then, is
there still so much ***construction*** going on everywhere?
我幾天前在「中國郵報」上讀到說，台北有許多空的公寓。
那麼，爲什麼到處還有這麼多**施工**在進行？

中國人： Recently, there has indeed been a ***surplus*** of apartments
in Taipei, though prices are also going up. However,
in general, well-built apartments in a nice location are
usually sold easily.
最近，台北的確公寓**過剩**，雖然房價也在上漲。不過，一般
說來，在好**地點**蓋得好的公寓還是很容易賣的。

　　　　　＊　　　　　＊　　　　　＊

外國人： Does it mean that the empty ones are badly built and
in poor locations?
這麼說，那些空房子是蓋得不好又地點不佳嘍？

中國人： That is often the case. Many builders have just built
apartment ***blocks*** on any available piece of land, without considering the surrounding environment.
經常是這個樣子。很多建築商祇是把公寓**建築物**蓋在任何一
塊可以利用的土地上，而沒考慮到四周的環境。

外國人： If there are so many apartments, why are many people still living in **shacks**?

如果有這麼多的公寓的話，為什麼還有許多人住在**簡陋的小屋**裏？

中國人： They often get used to their surroundings and don't want to move to a new area, **leaving** their friends **behind**. Besides, some of the **public housing** which has been designed for them has not been built very well and so perhaps they are afraid that the building might **collapse**, or something.

他們通常是已經習慣了四周的環境，而且不想**丟下**自己的朋友，搬到新的地方。再說，有些為他們設計的**國民住宅**蓋得並不好。所以呢，可能他們怕房子會**垮掉**，還是什麼的。

*　　　　　　*　　　　　　*

外國人： You mean if there is an **earthquake**?

你是說，如果有**地震**的話？

中國人： Yes, I guess so. 對呀，我想是吧。

外國人： I understand a lot of people are trying to move out to the **suburbs** where the houses are cheaper and the air fresher.

我知道，有許多人設法搬到**郊區**住，那裏房子比較便宜，空氣也比較新鮮。

外國人： Yes. A lot of people have had enough of living in the city with its *pollution* and other *inconveniences*. However, living in the suburbs is not without its problems. People have to spend a great deal more time *commuting* to and from work and some of these new housing complexes don't have an adequate water supply and other facilities.

是的。許多人住在城市裏，已經受夠了**污染**和其他的**不便**。不過，住在郊區也不是就沒問題。要花更多的時間**通勤來回**上下班，而且有些新的綜合住宅沒有足夠的水供應和其他的設備。

construction〔kən'strʌkʃən〕*n.* 建築物

surplus〔'sɝplʌs〕*n.* 過剩　　location〔lo'keʃən〕*n.* 位置

block〔blɑk〕*n.* 接連在一起的一片建築物（如商店、辦公室、公寓等）

shack〔ʃæk〕*n.* 簡陋的小屋（通常為木材架成）

leave behind 遺棄　　collapse〔kə'læps〕*v.* 倒塌

earthquake〔'ɝθ,kwek〕*n.* 地震　　suburb〔'sʌbɝb〕*n.* 城郊；郊區

pollution〔pə'luʃən〕*n.* 污染

inconvenience〔,ɪnkən'vinjəns〕*n.* 不便

commute〔kə'mjut〕*v.* 通勤；每天往返兩地

INTRODUCING ━ TAIWAN IN ENGLISH · TOPIC 52

交通問題

　　台北市嚴重的交通問題一直為人所詬病，尤其在街頭上隨時可見成群擁擠的車輛以及煙霧迷漫的廢氣(*exhaust*)和噪音(*din*)，早晚上下班的尖峰時段（*rush hour*）更不時出現塞車的景象。這些問題多半來自都市裏日益激增的人口與車輛數目，據統計台北每年增加兩萬多輛自用小汽車，可以排滿五條建國南北路，而機車每年的增加率亦相當驚人。因此都市交通問題，如空氣污染（*air pollution*）、噪音、能源浪費、擁擠、停車（*parking*）困難等便一一接踵而至。目前政府正致力於改善台北市的交通問題，地下鐵（*subway*）工程和大眾捷運系統（*Taipei's Mass Rapid Transit System, 或稱MRT system*）逐漸完工之後，將可慢慢解決台北市的交通困境。

《 Terms and Phrases 》

- ***superhighway*** 高速公路　　　***toll station*** 收費站
- ***Mass Rapid Transit System*** 大衆捷運系統（簡稱 *MRT system* ）
- pedestrian〔pə'dɛstrɪən〕*n*. 行人　　subway〔'sʌb,we〕*n*. 地下道
- signpost〔'saɪn,post〕*n*. 交通標誌；路標
- jaywalker〔'dʒe,wɔkə〕*n*.　（不遵守交通規則）任意穿越馬路的人
- ***safety island*** 安全島　　***rear-end collision*** 連環車禍
- ***traffic regulations*** 交通規則　　over-loading〔,ovə'lodɪŋ〕*n*. 超載
- ***excessive speed*** 超速　　***traffic accident*** 車禍
- ***rush hour*** 尖峯時刻　　***highway patrol*** 公路交通警察
- ***violation of the traffic regulations*** 違反交通規則
- ***observance of the traffic regulations*** 遵守交通規則
- hijack〔'haɪ,dʒæk〕*v*. 刼（車、船、飛機）
- congested〔kən'dʒɛstɪd〕*adj*. 擁擠的　　afford〔ə'fɔrd〕*v*. 能堪；力足以
- traffic〔'træfɪk〕*n*. 運輸；交通量　　illegal〔ɪ'ligl〕*adj*. 非法的
- spectator〔spɛk'tetə〕*n*. 旁觀者　　recklessly〔'rɛklɪslɪ〕*adv*. 莽撞地

TOPIC 52

交通 問題   **Traffic Problems**

Dialogue

外國人：Yesterday, when I arrived at my hotel having just come from the airport, I was *appalled* by the traffic. It's *terrible*.

　　　　昨天，在我剛從機場回到我的旅館時，我被這裏的交通**嚇到**了。眞**糟糕**。

中國人：Yes, the traffic problem is a very serious one in Taipei at present. 沒錯，目前台北的交通問題非常嚴重。

外國人：Why is that？I've visited a few other cities and the traffic in those places was never quite that bad.

　　　　爲什麼？我去過一些其他城市，那裏的交通就沒那麼糟糕。

中國人：The problem in Taipei is that besides being a very *congested* city, many more people are now able to *afford* their own cars and motorcycles, and that is why we now see so many vehicles on the road.

　　　　問題是，台北除了是一個非常**擁擠**的都市外，越來越多人現在都有能力**買得起**自己的汽車和摩托車，這也是爲什麼我們在路上看到那麼多車輛的原因。

外國人：Isn't the government building more roads or wider ones for all this extra *traffic*？政府是不是在蓋更多或更寬的道路，來容納這些額外的**交通量**？

** appall〔ə'pɔl〕v. 驚嚇；使驚駭　　　terrible〔'tɛrəbl〕adj. 極壞的

中國人：Yes, there are more elevated roads being built, and inside Taipei city there will be the MRT which should help ease congestion. Between Taipei city and Taipei county, there are also new highways being built, and they should help tackle the traffic problem.

有啊！還有一些高架道路在興建。在台北市區內，捷運系統將可有助於舒解交通阻塞。而在台北市與台北縣間，也要修築新的公路，如此便可幫助解決交通問題。

外國人：It's not just that there are many cars and motorbikes on the road — the pollution is just terrible!

不只是路上有太多汽車和摩托車，污染也很嚴重！

中國人：The authorities are trying to catch those who pollute the air. It is difficult but things should improve as soon as the Mass Rapid Transit System is finished. After that the government intends to limit the number of motor vehicles on the road.

政府正設法在抓那些污染空氣的人。這很困難，但等到捷運系統完成時，事情應該會好轉。在那之後，政府打算限制路上車輛的數量。

外國人：When will that be ready? 什麼時候可以建好？

中國人：It already has one line running, and five more being constructed. It is hoped that the whole system will be running by the year 2000.

已有一條路線開始營運，而其他五條路線仍在修築中。整個系統希望能在西元二千年時全部加入營運。

外國人：I heard recently that **motorcycle races** are held near Taipei on public roads. Could I go to see one?

最近聽說，台北附近的公路上有飆車。我能去看看嗎？

中國人： They are *illegal* and even as a *spectator* you may *get killed* as the riders drive very *recklessly*. So perhaps it would be better not to go.

他們是**非法的**，而且即使你是一個**旁觀者**，也有可能**送命**，因為他們騎得很**莽撞**。所以，也許還是不要去的好。

☆ *Some Important Signposts* （重要路標）

• No thoroughfare ; Street closed 禁止通行

• Keep to the right 靠右通行

• No right (*left*) turn 禁止右（左）轉

• Please watch your step 小心走路

• Under Construction 施工中

• No U turn 禁止廻轉

• No parking 禁止停車

• No passing 禁止超車

Railway Crossing
鐵路平交道

Speed Limit 50 k.p.h.
時速限制五十公里

INTRODUCING TAIWAN IN ENGLISH • TOPIC 53

雛妓問題

　　最近社會上一連串聲援**雛妓**（*child prostitution*）的行動引起了一般大眾的關切。實際上，台灣雛妓問題的產生遠非一日之寒，長久以來由於法律對於人口販子刑罰太輕，警察包庇**老鴇**（*pimp*）和人口販子等現象，導致問題日益嚴重。根據**調查**（*research*），這些雛妓年齡在十一歲到十三歲之間，有些來自**山胞**（*aborigine*）或生活教育水平較低的家庭，其父母為錢財所誘，將這些尚且天真無知的孩童送進了火坑。當然雛妓之中也不乏為歹徒所誘騙，被強迫關在**妓院**（*brothel*），終年不見天日，無法和外界聯繫。在此我們不免自問：一個號稱文明開放進步的社會怎能在警方和大眾的共同漠視之下，容許這種**非人道**（*inhumane*）的人口買賣交易？雛妓問題暴露出社會夾縫中黑暗、原始且醜陋的罪惡面。我們該如何才能幫助這些無辜的孩童走出黑暗，過著正常而平靜的生活？這個問題需要社會當局和大眾共同解決。法官必須加重量刑，嚴懲人口販子；嫖客必須以**強姦**（*rape*）未成年孩童論罪；警察必須加強掃蕩以雛妓拉客的老鴇，如此才有望遏止雛妓問題的罪惡根源。

≪ Terms and Phrases ≫

- prostitution [,prɑstə'tjuʃən] *n.* 賣淫
- attention [ə'tɛnʃən] *n.* 注意
- research ['risɚtʃ] *n.* 研究；調查
- extent [ɪk'stɛnt] *n.* 程度；範圍
- *make money* 賺錢
- uneducated [ʌn'ɛdʒə,ketɪd] *adj.* 未受教育的
- agreed [ə'grid] *adj.* 經過同意的
- frequent [frɪ'kwɛnt] *v.* 常去
- homosexual [,homə'sɛkʃəl] *n.* 同性戀
- profession [prə'fɛʃən] *n.* 職業

- *for that matter* 就那件事而論
- general ['dʒɛnərəl] *adj.* 一般的
- determine [dɪ'tɚmɪn] *v.* 確定；決定
- racket ['rækɪt] *n.* 〔俗〕職業
- aborigine [,æbə'rɪdʒəni] *n.* 原始居民
- hoodlum ['hudləm] *n.* 流氓
- brothel ['brɔθəl] *n.* 妓院
- involve [ɪn'vɑlv] *v.* 參與
- lure [lʊr] *v.* 引誘
- *crack down* 採取嚴厲手段

TOPIC 53

雛妓　問題　**The Child Prostitution Problem**

Dialogue

外國人： I understand that **prostitution** is quite a serious problem in Taipei as in most big cities in the world. However, is child prostitution a serious problem in Taipei, or in Taiwan **for that matter**?

我知道，台北就像全世界大部分的大都市一樣，**賣淫**是一個相當嚴重的問題。不過，**關於這件事**，雛妓在台北，或者在台灣也是個嚴重的問題嗎？

中國人： Prostitution has generally been regarded as a part of the society we live in. However, it is only recently that the problem of child prostitution has caught the **attention** of the **general** public.

賣淫通常被視爲是我們生活社會的一部分。不過，只有最近，雛妓問題才引起**一般**大衆的**注意**。

　　　　*　　　　　　*　　　　　　*

外國人： So what you mean is that child prostitution does exist in Taiwan.

你是說，雛妓問題確實存在台灣。

中國人： Yes, though more **research** still needs to be done to **determine** the **extent** of it.

是的，雖然還要做更多的**研究調查**才能**確定**到什麼**程度**。

外國人：What kind of children *engage in* this prostitution
racket？

　　是什麼樣的小孩**從事**這種賣淫的**職業**？

中國人：The child could have been bought from very poor families or even be the child of a *prostitite*. As a prostitute
gets older, she will *make* less *money* and so she has a
child, and turns the child into a prostitute. This is
not only sad but also a very serious problem.

　　小孩可能是從很窮的人家買來的，或甚至是**妓女**的小孩。當
一個妓女老了，**賺**的**錢**少了，她就讓自己的小孩也成為妓女。
這不但悲哀，而且是個非常嚴重的問題。

外國人：That is really bad. How come？

　　真的很嚴重，怎麼會這樣呢？

中國人：The children are from very poor families who are *uneducated*. The families cannot afford to raise their
child, and *hoodlums exploit* this by offering the families large sums of money for their child. Once the
child is sold she is *condemned* into a life of misery.
It's human *slavery*.

　　這些小孩都來自非常貧窮、**沒有受過教育的**家庭。他們的家
庭養不起孩子，而**流氓**就**利用**這一點，出高價向這些家庭買
走他們的小孩。一旦孩子被賣，她就**註定**陷入悲慘的一生了，
這真是**奴役人類**。

✱✱ exploit〔ɪkˈsplɔɪt〕*v.* 剝削；不正當地利用

condemn〔kənˈdɛm〕*v.* 註定　　slavery〔ˈslevərɪ〕*n.* 奴役

外國人： Why in Taipei?

　　　　爲什麼在台北?

中國人： Taipei is where all the money is. It has the most
people, including tourists. All sorts of people visit
the **brothels**, from locals to foreigners.

　　　　台北是金錢聚集的地方，這兒有最多的人口，包括觀光客。
各式各樣的人都可能去**妓院**，從本地人到外國人都有。

外國人： Are there only girls **involved**? What about boys?

　　　　只**牽涉**到女孩子嗎? 男孩子呢?

中國人： It used to be mostly girls, but now with **homosexuals
on the increase**, it is a sad fact that more boys are
being **lured** into the **profession**. The police are trying
to **crack down** on this child slave labor, and I hope
they succeed.

　　　　以前大部分都是女孩子，但現在**同性戀**在**增加**中，越來越多
男孩子被**誘引**入這個**行業**，是一個可悲的事實。警方正設法
嚴厲取締這種奴役童工，我希望他們成功。

TOPIC 54

整頓臺灣都市　　Cleaning up Taiwan's Cities

🔲 **Question** ▶

Is Taiwan doing anything to clean up her cities?

台灣是否有作任何整頓市容的工作？

🔲 **Reply** ▶

Yes, we are forced to clean up. Pollution in our cities has reached levels that are barely tolerable. Our air is filthy, our rivers are dirty, our land is full of *dumping grounds*, and even the noise level is irritating. Air pollution is caused primarily by car and motorcycle *exhausts*, thus *emission standards* are being *upgraded*. Water pollution is caused chiefly by *untreated sewage* and *industrial wastes*, thus we are building sewage treatment plants and requiring industries to implement pollution control measures. We are also seeking better ways of disposing *rubbish* and implementing noise control laws. Our economic success was steaming ahead with little concern for our *environment*, but we have reached the limit.

是的，我們不得不整頓。在都市裏的污染已經到了令人難以忍受的程度了。空氣骯髒、河流污穢，我們的土地到處都是**垃圾傾倒場**，甚至連噪音的音量都令人生氣。空氣污染主要來自汽車機車**廢氣的排放**，因此已提高排放標準。水污染主要是**未經處理的污水和工業廢料**造成的，因此我們建立了污水處理廠，而且要求各工業執行污染控制措施。我們也尋找更好的**垃圾**處置方法以及實施噪音控制法。我們在經濟上蓬勃發展，却對**環境**賦予極少的關懷，不過我們已到了極限。

** barely 〔ˈbɛrlɪ〕 *adv.* 幾不能　　implement 〔ˈɪmpləˌmɛnt〕 *v.* 實施
steam 〔stim〕 *v.* 藉蒸汽力行駛；不斷進行

Dialogue 1

外國人： Why do so many people here wear surgical masks (*respirators*)? 為什麼這裏有這麼多人戴口罩？

中國人： Have you ever **blown your nose** after you've been out awhile? The air is full of **soot** which the masks help filter out.

在你出去一下之後，你是否曾經**擤鼻涕**？空氣中充滿了**黑煙灰**，口罩有助於濾除。

外國人： This is like Los Angeles. We have a saying there that we don't breathe anything we can't see.

這就和洛杉磯一樣。我們那兒有句俗語說，我們不吸我們看不見的東西。

中國人： Do you wear masks there? 你們在那裏也戴口罩嗎？

外國人： No, we never developed the **practice**.

不，我們沒有養成這樣的**習慣**。

中國人： Why does Los Angeles have an air pollution problem? 為什麼洛杉磯有空氣污染的問題？

外國人： Well, one reason is that Los Angeles, like Taipei, is surrounded by mountains, so **smog** stays over the city, if there's no strong winds.

嗯，一個原因是洛杉磯和台北一樣環繞著山，所以如果沒有強風的話，**煙霧會停留在城市裏面**。

〔□□〕 **Dialogue 2**

外國人： Let's go swimming in Tamsui River. 我們到淡水河去游泳。

中國人： Are you crazy, even fish don't swim in there.
你瘋了，連魚都不在那裏游了。

外國人： Air pollution, water pollution, noise pollution, I've had
it with Taipei. Where can I experience nature again?
空氣污染、水污染、噪音污染，我在台北受夠了。我到哪裏
才能再感受到自然？

中國人： Get out of Taipei and go see the *countryside*. Much of
Taiwan is still *rural*.
離開台北，到**鄉間**看看。台灣的很多地方仍然保有**鄉村特色**。

外國人： Why are the Chinese willing to live in cities and put up
with all this mess？
爲什麼中國人情願住在都市而忍受這種混亂？

中國人： We don't like living alone and being *isolated*. We very
much prefer "je-nao" so we're willing to put up with the
pollution and other *hassles* of *city-life*.
我們不喜歡獨居和**孤立**。我們非常喜歡「熱鬧」，所以我們
情願忍受污染及其他**都市生活**的**困擾**。

外國人： This is different from America where we value *privacy*
and *independence*. 這和美國不同，在那裏我們重視**隱私**和**獨立**。

中國人： Yes, but I also know that more people keep dogs and
cats for *company* in America.
是的。不過，我也知道，在美國很多人養狗和貓來作**伴**。

** *put up with* 忍受

TOPIC 55

Economy

What's the *lowdown* on Taiwan's economy?

台灣經濟的**眞相**究竟是如何?

Reply

Despite its small size, it is amazing how well Taiwan has done economically. She is the world's 20th largest economy, and is the 13th largest trading nation. Taiwan's *per capita income* is US$10,566, the 25th highest in the world. This is not recent, Taiwan's economy has grown steadily in the past forty years and it wasn't until recently that the economic growth rate came down to *single figures*. The economic success of Taiwan is a result of a strict educational system, an *emphasis* on Chinese cultural values and of course, very hard work.

儘管面積很小,台灣在經濟方面表現出色,却是令人驚歎。台灣經濟排名全世界第二十名,同時是第十三大貿易國。台灣**個人平均所得**是10566美元,居全世界第二十五位。這不是最近才發生的,台灣經濟在過去四十年來,一直穩定成長,直到最近,經濟成長率才下降到**個位數**。台灣經濟的成功,是來自於嚴格的教育制度,**重視**中國文化的價值,當然還有非常努力的工作。

** lowdown〔'lo'daʊn〕*n.* 眞相   emphasis〔'ɛmfəsɪs〕*n.* 強調

🎧 **Dialogue 1**

外國人： Taiwan is very rich, isn't it？
台灣非常富有，是嗎？

中國人： Pretty much so. Our **GNP** in 1993 was US＄220.1
billion. But this wasn't easy. We worked very hard
to get to where we are today.
的確是的，我們的**國民生產毛額**在一九九三年，便達到了二
千二百零一億美金。但這並不容易，我們非常努力，才達到
了今日的成就。

外國人： I see that everyone works very hard in Taipei.
我看得出來，在台北人人都很努力工作。

中國人： It's a part of Chinese culture to work very hard.
Hasn't it **paid off** well？
工作努力是中華文化的一部分，而且我們不是很**成功**嗎？

外國人： Oh yes. You guys also have large **foreign exchange
reserves**, if I'm not mistaken.
噢，是的。如果我沒記錯的話，你們也有非常大筆的**外匯
存底**。

中國人： Yes, Taiwan has the largest foreign exchange reserves
in the world, standing at over US＄85 billion.
沒錯，台灣的外滙存底是全世界最高的，超過美金八百五
十億以上。

** **GNP**（＝gross national product）國民生產毛額

Dialogue 2

外國人：I know that one of Taiwan's biggest industries is *semiconductor*. 我知道台灣最大的工業之一是**半導體工業**。

中國人：Right. Taiwan's semiconductor industry is the fifth largest in the world, and is worth US$10 billion. *Monitors*, *notebook computers*, and *motherboards* are the three main items. Taiwan is also the world's third largest producer of *laptop computers*.

是的，台灣的半導體工業居世界第五，價值一百億美金。**電腦螢幕、筆記型電腦和主機板**，是最暢銷的前三名產品，台灣也是全世界第三大的**筆記型電腦**生產國。

外國人：What about other *export* industries？
那其他的**出口**工業呢？

中國人：Traditionally the main industries were those which were *labor intensive*, such as textiles, food processing and garments. Now these are being gradually replaced by *capital* and technology intensive industries such as chemicals, electronics and information.

傳統上，主要工業都是**勞力密集**，例如紡織、食物加工，和服飾。而現在，這些已逐漸被**資金**及技術密集的工業所取代，如化學、電子、資訊等。

** laptop〔'læp,tɑp〕*n*. 膝上型（筆記型）電腦
textile〔'tɛkstl, -taɪl〕*n*. 紡織物
garment〔'gɑrmənt〕*n*. 衣服　　replace〔rɪ'ples〕*v*. 取代
technology〔tɛk'nɑlədʒɪ〕*n*. 技術　　electronics〔ɪ,lɛk'trɑnɪks〕*n*. 電子

TOPIC 56

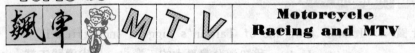

飆車 MTV — **Motorcycle Racing and MTV**

Dialogue 1

外國人： Why are the races so popular? 為什麼飆車這麼流行？

中國人： People today are more affluent than ever, they have more free time than ever, but they also lead more *stressful* lives. The excitement of motorcycle racing is an *outlet* for them.

今天人們比以往更爲富裕,也比以往有更多的時間,不過，也過著比較**有壓力的**生活。飆車的刺激,對他們而言是種**發洩**。

外國人： Americans watch auto racing for similar reasons, but you know a study was done to determine why people like to go to auto races and the *primary* reason, the study revealed, is that people like to watch the cars crash! Do you think the popularity of motorcycle racing is an *indication* of a decline in Chinese society?

美國人看賽車,也是相似的理由,可是你知道嗎,有一項研究測定爲什麼人們喜歡賽車,研究顯示,**主要的**原因在於人們喜歡看車子撞毀！你認爲流行飆車是否也是中國社會衰敗的一種**象徵**？

中國人： Perhaps, the *values* and *attitudes* of Taiwan's young people are changing as our economy grows and as Western influences increase. They're moving away from traditional goals such as *scholarship* and more toward goals such as "having fun while you're still young."

也許,由於經濟成長以及西方影響力增加,台灣年輕人的**價值**及**態度**都在改變。他們逐漸遠離了諸如「**學識**」的傳統目標,而朝向像是「年少及時行樂」的這些目標。

Dialogue 2

外國人： What happens when the police try to stop the races?

當警察試圖阻止飆車時，發生了什麼事？

中國人： Riots have resulted and some of them have gotten pretty **hairy**. They've **torched** police stations, **damaged** police cars, and **injured** policemen.

發生暴動，而且有些人變得相當**令人厭惡**。他們**燒**警察局，**毀壞**警車，並**傷害**警察。

外國人： Has the law always received so much **disrespect**?

法律總是這麼受到**蔑視**嗎？

中國人： Well, some people say after **martial law** was lifted people have become very **bold** against the law.

嗯，有些人說**戒嚴法**解除之後，人們變得非常**大膽的**和法律作對。

外國人： Then do you think lifting martial law was not a good idea?

那麼你認為解除戒嚴法並不是個好主意？

中國人： Of course lifting martial law was a good idea, as it has given the people more **freedom**. But many young people **interpret** it to mean they can do almost anything they want.

當然，解除戒嚴法是一個好主意，它使人們享有更多的**自由**，但是很多年輕人却把它**解釋**成，這表示他們幾乎可以為所欲為。

🔲 **Dialogue 3** ▶

外國人：Why does the law only allow licensed movie houses to
　　　　show videotapes?
　　　　為什麼法律只允許有執照的電影屋放映錄影帶？

中國人：This is to protect the copyrights of movies. *Copyright*
　　　　laws for movies are designed to insure moviemakers
　　　　that *royalties* are paid when their movies are shown.
　　　　MTV centers pay no royalties and even show *pirated*
　　　　films.
　　　　這是在保護電影的版權。電影的**版權法**是設來確保電影業者，
　　　　他們的電影上映時，就付了**版稅**。MTV中心並沒有付版稅，
　　　　甚至放映**盜版**的影片。

外國人：But Taiwan is famous for *ignoring* international copy-
　　　　right laws, so why is there so much concern now?
　　　　但是台灣以**忽視**國際版權法聞名，為什麼現在又這麼關心呢？

中國人：This may have been true in the past, but the situation
　　　　is different now. Because Taiwan's economy is so suc-
　　　　cessful we are becoming more careful in protecting
　　　　international copyrights, so as not to *offend* the
　　　　international community.
　　　　過去，這或許沒錯，但是現在情況不同了。因為台灣經濟非常
　　　　成功，我們越來越小心地保護國際版權，以免**觸犯**到**國際社會**。

外國人：Does this mean that it's harder to find cheap pirated
　　　　English books in Taiwan these days?
　　　　這是不是表示，最近在台灣很難找到便宜的盜版英文書籍？

中國人：Yes, there are fewer cheap copies of English books around, and even if you do find them they will be *confiscated* if you try to take them out of the country.

是的，便宜的盜版英文書，四處已經比較少了，即使你眞的找到了，如果你想帶出國，書也會被**沒收**。

Dialogue 4

外國人：Want to go over to the MTV center？

想不想去MTV中心？

中國人：No thanks, I never go there. I think it's a *waste of time*.

不要了，謝謝，我從不去那裏，我想那是**浪費時間**。

外國人：Why？ 爲什麼？

中國人：I can think of better things to do than *vegetating* in front of a TV screen and *deluding* myself with *fantasies*. 我可以想出更好的事情去作，比**無所事事**耗在電視螢幕前，用**幻想欺騙**自我好得多。

外國人：What do you want to do then？

那麼你想作什麼？

中國人：Let's go *birdwatching* at Yangmingshan.

我們到陽明山去**賞鳥**（研究鳥類的自然生態）。

TOPIC 57

Sun Yat-sen

Question

Who's Sun Yat-sen？I see his picture all over the place.

誰是孫中山？我在每個地方都看到他的照片。

Reply

Sun Yat-sen is the ***Founding Father*** of Modern China. He led
the overthrow of the ***inept Manchu government*** and gave birth
to the Republic of China. Sun Yat-sen was born on November
12, 1866 in Kuangtung Province and graduated from Hong
Kong Medical College in 1892. Medicine, however, was not
where his interests lay. The weakness of the Manchu government against the foreign powers who were carving up China
inspired him with thoughts of ***revolution***. The National Revolution led by Sun Yat-sen ended the 4000 years of ***dynastic***
rule on October 10, 1911, a date we now ***commemorate*** as
Double Tenth National Day. Sun Yat-sen died of cancer in
Peiping on March 12, 1925. He died too soon.

孫中山先生是現代中國的**開國者**。他領導推翻了**無效率的滿清政府**，
並且建立中華民國。孫中山在一八六六年十一月十二日生於廣東省，
一八九二年時，從香港西醫院畢業。然而，醫學並不是他的興趣所
在。滿清政府對抗外來強權割分中國的軟弱，激起了他**革命**的思想。
孫中山所領導的國民革命在一九一一年十月十日，結束了四千年來
的**王朝統治**，這個日子也就是我們現在**慶祝**的雙十節。孫中山在一
九二五年三月十二日因癌症死於北平。他死得太早了。

** carve up 分割（肉等）；劃分（遺產等）

🔲 **Dialogue 1**

外國人： What are the *Three Principles of the People*?
三民主義是什麼？

中國人： They are *nationalism*, *democracy*, and *livelihood*. Our government is based on these principles.
民族主義、民權主義，以及民生主義。我們的政府就是以這些主義為基礎的。

外國人： What does livelihood mean?
民生主義是什麼意思？

中國人： This Principle is concerned with raising our people's standard of living. It draws strong points from both *capitalism* and *socialism*, using capitalistic ideas to *motivate* people and socialistic ideas to stem unequal *distributions of wealth*.
這個主義是關於提昇人民的生活水準。它從資本主義和社會主義抽出重點，用資本主義的觀念激發人民，用社會主義的觀念阻止財富分配不平等。

外國人： Who's the *author* of these Principles?
三民主義的創始者是誰？

中國人： Dr. Sun Yat-sen. He based the Principles on both Chinese and Western political philosophy, from Confucius to Lincoln.
孫中山博士。他以從孔子到林肯的中國及西方政治哲學，作為三民主義的基礎。

🔲 **Dialogue 2** ➤

外國人 : Did Chiang Kai-shek and Sun Yat-sen know each other?

　　　　蔣中正和孫中山認識彼此嗎?

中國人 : Yes, Chiang Kai-shek considered himself a *disciple* of
　　　　Dr. Sun Yat-sen. Sun Yat-sen had appointed him *com-
　　　　mandant* of *Whampoa Military Academy*.

　　　　是的，蔣中正認為他是孫中山的**信徒**。孫中山並指定他為**黃
　　　　埔軍校**的**校長**。

外國人 : Weren't their wives sisters?

　　　　他們的妻子不是姊妹嗎?

中國人 : Yes, the *Soong* sisters were daughters of a powerful
　　　　Shanghai banking family.

　　　　是的，**宋家**姊妹是一個強而有力的上海銀行家族的女兒。

外國人 : Are Chiang Kai-shek and Sun Yat-sen the most import-
　　　　ant figures in modern Chinese history?

　　　　蔣中正和孫中山，是現代中國史上最重要的人物嗎?

中國人 : Yes, as you will notice, only their *portraits* are
　　　　printed on our *currency*.

　　　　是的，就如你注意到的，祇有他們的**肖像**印在我們現在通行
　　　　的**貨幣**上面。

Terms and Phrases

· **author** 〔 'ɔθɚ 〕 *n.* 創始者；作者

· **capitalism** 〔 'kæpətl̩,ɪzəm 〕 *n.* 資本主義

· **commandant** 〔 ,kɑmən'dænt,-'dɑnt 〕 *n.* 指揮
官；軍事學校校長

· **commemorate** 〔 kə'mɛmə,ret 〕 *v.* 紀念；慶祝

· **currency** 〔 'kɝ̩nsɪ 〕 *n.* 通貨（硬幣或紙幣）

· **democracy** 〔 də'mɑkrəsɪ 〕 *n.* 民主主義；民主政治

· **disciple** 〔 dɪ'saɪpl̩ 〕 *n.* 門徒

· ***distribution of wealth*** 財富分配

· ***dynastic rule*** 王朝統治

✄   ✄   ✄

· ***Founding Father*** 開國者；創立人

· **inept** 〔 ɪn'ɛpt 〕 *adj.* 不合適的；無效率的

· **livelihood** 〔 'laɪvlɪ,hʊd 〕 *n.* 生計；民生主義

· **motivate** 〔 'motə,vet 〕 *v.* 引起動機；激發

· **nationalism** 〔 'næʃənl̩,ɪzəm 〕 *n.* 民族主義；國家主義

· **portrait** 〔 'portret, 'pɔr-, -trɪt 〕 *n.* 人像；肖像

· **revolution** 〔 ,rɛvə'luʃən 〕 *n.* 革命

TOPIC 58

 **Cheng Cheng-Kung**

🔲 **Question**

Who is Cheng Cheng-kung？鄭成功是誰？

🔲 **Reply**

Cheng Cheng-kung, a Ming dynasty *loyalist*, *liberated* Taiwan from Dutch rule. On April 29, 1661 Cheng landed on Taiwan with an *armada* of war *junks* and 30,000 soldiers. After six months of fighting he ended the Dutch occupation of Taiwan. On Taiwan, Cheng proved to be a statesman of exceptionally *high caliber*. Our island *prospered* under his wise administration. But perhaps Cheng's greatest contribution to Taiwan was his love for Chinese culture, he sparked a Chinese cultural renaissance. More than a thousand artists, poets, and scholars followed Cheng to Taiwan, many of whom opened schools. Cheng is *venerated* on Taiwan as a "chun wang," or a perfect man.

鄭成功是明朝的**忠臣**，把台灣從荷蘭人統治中**解放**出來。一六六一年四月二十九日，鄭成功和戰**船艦隊**、三萬名士兵登陸台灣。六個月的戰鬥之後，他結束了荷蘭人對台灣的佔據。在台灣，鄭成功表現出是一個罕有的**才能卓越**的政治家。我們的島在他睿智的管理下**繁榮**起來。但是，也許鄭成功對台灣最大的貢獻是，他對中國文化的熱愛，他引燃了中華文化復興。超過一千名的藝術家、詩人、學者跟隨鄭成功到台灣來，其中很多人開辦學校。在台灣鄭成功被**敬**爲「郡王」，或者完美的人。

Dialogue 1

外國人： Do people here regard Cheng Cheng-kung as *divine*?

這裏的人認爲鄭成功是**神**嗎？

中國人： Some do, some believe he was an *incarnation* of *Matsu* the Goddess of the Sea.

有些人是，有些人相信他是海的女神，**媽祖**的**化身**。

外國人： Are there days set aside to honor him?

有沒有節日是紀念他的？

中國人： Yes, impressive ceremonies take place at his *shrine* on April 29 the *anniversary* of his landing on Taiwan, and on his birthday the 14th day of the 7th month on the lunar calender.

有，四月二十九日，他登陸台灣的**週年紀念日**，以及農曆七月十四他生日時，都會在他的**廟**裏舉行予人深刻印象的儀式。

外國人： Where is his shrine? 他的**廟**在哪裏？

中國人： At Tainan, it was built by Emperor Kuang Hsu of the *Ching dynasty* who forgave Cheng for having *opposed* the dynasty.

在台南，是**清朝**的光緒皇帝所建，他原諒鄭成功**反抗**清朝。

Dialogue 2

外國人： Why did the Dutch occupy Taiwan?

荷蘭人爲什麼佔據台灣？

中國人：Because of it's *strategic location* as a base for trade in the Orient.

因爲，台灣正位於東方貿易據點的**戰略位置**。

外國人：What was Taiwan like under Dutch occuption？

在荷蘭人佔領下，台灣是怎麼樣的？

中國人：The Dutch occupation was unpopular. They imposed heavy taxes and labor requirements on the people of Taiwan, and then imported *zealous missionaries* to *convert* us to Christianity.

荷蘭人佔領並不受到歡迎。他們對台灣人民加以重稅，及勞力要求，並使很多**熱心的傳敎士**來台，使我們**皈依**基督敎。

外國人：How else did the Dutch *exploit* Taiwan？

荷蘭人在其他方面，如何**剝削**台灣？

中國人：One notorious role the Dutch played here was introducing and encouraging the people of Taiwan to smoke tobacco by mixing it with *opium*.

荷蘭人在這裏扮演一個聲名狼藉的角色是，介紹並鼓勵台灣人民，吸食摻了**鴉片**的**煙草**。

Terms and Phrases

- **anniversary** 〔͵ænə'vɝsərɪ〕 *n*. 周年紀念
- **armada** 〔ɑr'mɑdə, -'medə〕 *n*. 艦隊
- **caliber** 〔'kæləbɚ〕 *n*.才能;才幹   *Ching dynasty* 清朝
- **convert** 〔kən'vɝt〕 *v*. 使改變信仰;皈依
- **divine** 〔də'vaɪn〕 *adj*. 神的;如神的
- **exploit** 〔ɪk'splɔɪt〕 *v*. 剝削;利用
- **incarnation** 〔͵ɪnkɑr'neʃən〕 *n*. 化身
- **junk** 〔dʒʌŋk〕 *n*. 中國的大帆船(通常爲三桅平底)
- **liberate** 〔'lɪbə͵ret〕 *v*. 解放;使獲自由
- **loyalist** 〔'lɔɪəlɪst〕 *n*. 忠於政府的人;(尤指)暴
  亂時擁護政府元首者;忠臣
- *Matsu* 媽祖   *Ming dynasty* 明朝
- **missionary** 〔'mɪʃən͵ɛrɪ〕 *n*. 傳教士
- **occupation** 〔͵ɑkjə'peʃən〕 *n*. 佔有;據有
- **opium** 〔'opɪəm〕 *n*.鴉片   **oppose** 〔ə'poz〕 *v*.反對
- **prosper** 〔'prɑspɚ〕 *v*. 旺盛;成功
- **shrine** 〔ʃraɪn〕 *n*.廟;祠   *strategic location* 戰略的位置
- **trifle** 〔'traɪfḷ〕 *n*. 無價值或不重要的東西、事件
- **venerate** 〔'vɛnə͵ret〕 *v*. 對…深懷敬意;崇敬
- **zealous** 〔'zɛləs〕 *adj*. 熱心的;熱誠的

TOPIC 59

心境平和　Peace of Mind

▶ Question

Are the Chinese more at peace with themselves？

中國人比較容易保持平靜嗎？

▶ Reply

Yes, if compared with Westerners. An American writer once noted that the mass of men lead lives of quiet *desperation*. Americans do not know *contentment*. On the other hand, one of the outstanding characteristics of the Chinese people is knowing *inner peace*. Throughout the ages Chinese poets have celebrated this state of mind. It's achieved by separating one from oneself through constant *spiritual cultivation*. A person possessing such a mental state is in unity with nature, attaching no more importance to himself than to an ant or a blade of grass. He never *flinches* in the face of *mortal danger* for he knows his soul *transcends* life and death. Peace of mind provides a fertile ground for the growth of wisdom.

是的，如果是和西方人比較的話。一個美國的作家曾經留意到，大多數人的過著相當**拼命**的生活。美國人並不知道**滿足**。在另一方面，中國人突出的性格之一是，知道**內心的平靜**。長久以來，中國的詩人一直頌揚著這種心靈狀態。內心的平靜是藉由不斷的**精神修養**，使一個人和自身分離而達到的。一個擁有如此心境的人，與自然是和諧的，並且認為自身的重要性並不多於一隻螞蟻或一片玻璃。在面對**瀕死的危險**時，他絕不**退縮**，因為他知道他的靈魂已**超脫**生與死。心境平和為智慧的增長提供了一塊沃土。

Dialogue 1

外國人： I don't think contentment is necessarily a good thing.
我不覺得滿足必然是一件好事。

中國人： Why not? 為什麼不?

外國人： If the society stresses "contentment" then people will be hesitant to change and **progress**, and they'll be satisfied with ignorance.
如果社會強調「滿足」，那麼人們就會不願意求改變、求**進步**，他們會無知地滿足。

中國人： Has the **discontentment** of the West helped make **progress**? 西方人的**不滿**對**進步**有幫助嗎?

外國人： Yes, we're always seeking to know the truth to understand the unknown. We have a successful culture based on **logic** and rationality.
是，我們一向尋求對真理的認識來了解未知。我們有以**邏輯**和理性為根據的成功的文化。

中國人： I must admit Chinese culture may appear **illogical** and irrational when compared with Western culture. For us, it's not sufficient for something to be merely logically correct, it must also be in harmony with **human nature**. The result may be less logical but it is more **humanistic**.
我必須承認中國文化和西方文化比較起來，可能會顯得**不合邏輯**而且不理性,對我們而言,某件事情僅僅邏輯上正確是不夠的，必須要和**人性**一致。結果可能比較不合邏輯，但是比較**合乎人性**。

** hesitant〔ˋhɛzətənt〕*adj*. 猶豫的　　rationality〔͵ræʃəˋnælətɪ〕*n*. 理性

🔲 **Dialogue 2** ➤

外國人 : I really like the *laid-back* attitude of Taipei.
我眞的喜歡台北**悠閒**的態度。

中國人 : What do you mean laid-back? I find life very *stressful* in
Taipei. 你說悠閒是什麼意思呢?我覺得台北的生活**壓力很重**。

外國人 : You should go to New York City and experience what *stress*
really means. I couldn't live in New York long term, I'd
burn-out. The *pace of life* in Taipei is relaxed compared
to most major cities of the world.
你該到紐約市去體驗一下,**壓力**的眞正意義。我無法在紐約長
住,我會**完蛋**。台北的**生活步調**和世界多數主要都市比較起來,
是很輕鬆的。

中國人 : What exactly do you mean by " laid back "?
你所謂的「悠閒」究竟是什麼意思?

外國人 : Well, first of all, I feel safe in Taipei. I can *let my*
guard down here, which I could not do back in New York.
Taipei's low crime rate is part of it, it's also the whole
feeling of the city, from the old men doing *tai chi* early in
the morning to the crowded outdoor foodstalls late at
night. People here know to enjoy life.
嗯,第一,在台北我覺得很安全。在這裏我可以**放低警戒心**,
這是我回紐約時不能夠的,台北的犯罪率低是部分原因,同時
也是整個都市的感覺,從大淸早老人打**太極拳**,到深夜外頭擁
擠的飲食攤。這裏的人知道怎麼享受生活。

** foodstall〔ˋfʊd,stɔl〕*n.* 飲食攤

Terms and Phrases

- ***be at peace with*** 與～保持友好、和諧；平靜
- ***burn out*** 竭盡；熄火
- **contentment** 〔 kən'tɛntmənt 〕 *n.* 滿意；滿足
- **discontentment** 〔,dɪ skən'tɛntmənt 〕 *n.* 不滿
- **desperation** 〔,dɛspə'reʃən〕 *n.* 不顧一切的冒險；拼命
- **flinch** 〔 flɪntʃ 〕 *v.* 退縮；畏縮
- **humanistic** 〔,hjumən'ɪstɪk 〕 *adj.* 人性的；人道的
- **ignorance** 〔'ɪgnərəns〕 *n.* 無知
- ***inner peace*** 內心的平靜   ***laid-back*** 悠閒
- ***let my guard down*** 降低警戒心
- **logic** 〔 'lɑdʒɪk 〕 *n.* 邏輯
- **logical** 〔 'lɑdʒɪkl̩ 〕 *adj.* 合邏輯的
- **illogical** 〔 ɪ'lɑdʒɪkl̩ 〕 *adj.* 不合邏輯的
- ***mortal danger*** 瀕死的危險
- ***pace of life*** 生活步調
- **rational** 〔 'ræʃənl̩ 〕 *adj.* 理性的
- **irrational** 〔 ɪ'ræʃənl̩ 〕 *adj.* 無理性的
- ***spiritual cultivation*** 精神修養
- **stressful** 〔 'strɛsfəl 〕 *adj.* 充滿著壓力、緊張的
- **transcend** 〔 træn'sɛnd 〕 *v.* 超越；超脫

TOPIC 60

公共衛生　Public Health

🔲 **Question** ▶

How's the public health of Taiwan?
台灣的公共衛生怎麼樣？

🔲 **Reply** ▶

Excellent, Taiwan is one of the healthiest places in Asia.
Malaria, for instance, has been completely *eradicated*, and
no cases of *cholera* or *smallpox* have been reported for years.
Physicians in Taiwan are among the world's best as only the
best students are permitted into *medical schools*. Besides,
there is a scheme called *National Health Insurance* which
most of the locals are under now. By paying some money re-
gularly, you get some of your medical bills paid for you by
the government when you become ill. It's a good way of se-
curing the health of the nation.

　　好極了，台灣是亞洲最衛生的地方之一。例如瘧疾，已完全被消滅，
而據報，已有許多年沒有霍亂或天花的病例。台灣的醫生是全世界
的佼佼者，因為只有最優秀的學生，才能獲准進入醫學院。此外，
目前的全民健保，大部分人民都已納入，藉著定期繳納一點錢，當
你生病時，你的醫藥費用就有部分由政府負擔。這是一個確保全民
健康的好方法。

Dialogue 1

外國人： Oh no, I forgot to get *vaccinations* before coming to Taiwan. Am I gonna catch a horrible disease here?

喔！糟了！我來台灣之前忘了**接種疫苗**。我會在這裏得可怕的疾病嗎？

中國人： No, don't worry. You don't need vaccinations for Taiwan unless you've been in a cholera-*infected* area, then you must be *inoculated* before coming.

不會，別擔心。你不必因爲來台灣就去接種疫苗，除非你曾到過霍亂**傳染**區，那麼你來之前，就要**接受預防注射**。

外國人： How about AIDS? Do I have to worry about AIDS here?

愛滋病怎麼樣呢？我在這裏要擔心愛滋病嗎？

中國人： The number of people *infected* with AIDS in Taiwan is increasing, but the numbers are still small compared to the West. Of course, it is always wise to be careful.

在台灣，**感染**愛滋病的病患數目逐漸增加，不過和西方比起來，數量還算少。當然，小心點總是明智的。

Dialogue 2

外國人： I've been suffering from mental problems. Are there any good *psychiatrists* here?

我一直爲心理問題所苦。這裏有沒有不錯的**精神病醫師**呢？

** cholera 〔'kɑlərə〕 *n.* 霍亂

中國人 : Going to see the psychiatrists isn't popular here, there's a *stigma* attached to it. Wanna see a *fortune teller* instead? 去看精神病醫師在這裏並不普遍，那被認爲是個**恥辱**。想去找算命的人嗎？

外國人 : What can a fortune teller do？算命的人能作什麼？

中國人 : Chinese fortune tellers are very *insightful*. They can tell you a lot about yourself.
中國的算命的人非常**富有洞察力**。他們可以告訴你很多關於你自己的事。

外國人 : But what I need is someone to tell me I'm a good person. Will the fortune teller tell me good things about myself?
但是我要的是，有人告訴我說我是個好人。算命的人會告訴我關於我自己的好事嗎？

中國人 : That's not hard to arrange. 那倒不難安排。

** psychiatrist〔saɪˈkarətrɪst〕*n.* 精神病醫師

台灣的衛生保健工作實施經年以來成效卓越，在**衛生單位**（*Health Bureau*）極力推廣**預防接種**（*vaccination*）與防疫措施嚴密之下，11 項**法定傳染病**（*notifiable communicable diseases*）早已根絕或被控制。近年來更由於社會形態的演變，公共衛生推行重點已由急性傳染病的防治，轉為側重社會醫學的推展，例如全民醫療保險、復健、公害防治、食品衛生、社會福利等項目。

Terms and Phrases

- **AIDS** 〔edz〕 *n.* 愛滋病（ Acquired Immune Deficiency Syndrome 後天免疫不全症候群的縮寫）
- **attach** 〔ə'tætʃ〕 *v.* 附加；認爲有
- **cholera** 〔'kɑlərə〕 *n.* 霍亂
- **eradicate** 〔ɪ'rædɪ,ket〕 *v.* 撲滅；消滅
- *fortune teller* 算命的人
- **infect** 〔ɪn'fɛkt〕 *v.* 傳染
- **inoculate** 〔ɪn'ɑkjə,let〕 *v.* 接種
- **insightful** 〔'ɪn,saɪtfʊl〕 *adj.* 富於洞察力的
- **insurance** 〔ɪn'ʃʊrəns〕 *n.* 保險
- **malaria** 〔mə'lɛrɪə〕 *n.* 瘧疾
- *medical school* 醫學院
- **mental** 〔'mɛntḷ〕 *adj.* 心理的；精神的
- **physician** 〔fə'zɪʃən〕 *n.* 醫生；內科醫生
- **psychiatrist** 〔saɪ'kaɪətrɪst〕 *n.* 精神科醫生
- **scheme** 〔skim〕 *n.* 計畫；方案
- **secure** 〔sɪ'kjʊr〕 *v.* 確保；使安全
- **smallpox** 〔'smɔl,pɑks〕 *n.* 天花
- **stigma** 〔'stɪgmə〕 *n.* 恥辱
- **vaccination** 〔,væksṇ'eʃən〕 *n.* 接種疫苗；種痘

TOPIC 61

Learning Mandarin Chinese

🔊 Question ▶

Where can I study Mandarin in Taipei?

我可以在台北的哪裏學國語？

🔊 Reply ▶

The three best known programs are the "Stanford Program" at National Taiwan University, the Mandarin Training Center at National Taiwan Normal University, and the Mandarin Daily News. Of the three the Mandarin Daily News is the easiest to enter and new classes begin every month. Getting into the Mandarin Training Center is more difficult as it requires *college transcripts* and *health certificates*. The Stanford Program is the most difficult to get in as it requires *entrance examinations*. It's also the most *rigorous* program of the three. There are, in addition, numerous private language schools, the best known is the *Taipei Language Institute*.

三個最有名的課程計劃是國立台灣大學的「史丹福計劃」，國立師範大學的國語教學中心，和國語日報。三個當中，國語日報是最容易進去的，而且每個月開始新課程。進入國語教學中心比較難，因為它要**大學成績單**和**健康證明書**。史丹佛計劃是最難進的，因為它要**入學考試**，同時也是三個之中最**嚴格**的課程。除此之外，有很多私立語文學校，最有名的是**台北語言中心**。

Dialogue 1

外國人： I don't like learning Mandarin at private *language schools*. They don't take teaching very seriously.

我不喜歡在私立的**語文學校**學國語。他們並沒有教的很認眞。

中國人： Yes, many of these are set up to allow *foreigners* to extend their *visas*. Otherwise they have to leave Taiwan after two months.

是啊，很多是設來讓**外國人護照**延期，否則他們就要在兩個月之後離開台灣。

外國人： Is there any other way to learn Mandarin without enrolling in a university?

不在大學註冊，有沒有其他方法可學國語？

中國人： Yes, do a *language exchange*. 有，作**語言交換**。

外國人： How do I find a good language partner?

我如何找到一個不錯的語言夥伴？

中國人： Put ads on college *bulletin boards*. There are many qualified students who would be willing.

在大學的**佈告欄**上登廣告。很多合格的學生會願意的。

Dialogue 2

外國人： Is there a difference between the *Chinese characters* here and on the mainland?

這裏和大陸的**中國字**有不同之處嗎？

中國人： Yes, in an attempt to make learning Chinese characters easier, the mainland has *simplified* them, we still
use the *traditional forms* on Taiwan.

有，爲了使學中國字更容易，大陸已經把中國字**簡化**了。我
們在台灣仍舊用**傳統的形式**。

外國人： Have the simplified characters been successful ?

簡體字已經成功了嗎？

中國人： No, they're encountering many problems with them.
For example when the simplified characters are put in a
computer many of them become *indistinguishable*. The
mainland is coming back to traditional forms.

不，他們遭遇了很多問題。舉例來說，簡體字輸入電腦時，
很多變得**無法分辨**。大陸又回到傳統的形式。

外國人： Which form does Hong Kong use ?

香港用的是哪一種形式？

中國人： They also use the traditional forms.

他們也用傳統的形式。

Terms and Phrases

- *bulletin board* 佈告欄　*Chinese character* 中國字
- *college transcript* 大學成績單
- **colloquial** 〔kə'lokwɪəl〕*adj.* 俗語的；會話的
- **conversation** 〔,kɑnvə'seʃən〕*n.* 談話；會談
- *entrance examination* 大學考試
- **grammar** 〔'græmə〕*n.* 文法；措辭
- *health certificate* 健康證明書
- **indistinguishable** 〔,ɪndɪs'tɪŋgwɪʃəbl̩〕*adj.* 不能辨別的
- *language exchange* 語言交換

- *language school* 語文學校
- **linguistic** 〔lɪŋ'gwɪstɪk〕*adj.* 語言上的；語言學上的
- **multilingual** 〔,mʌltɪ'lɪŋgwəl〕*adj.* 通曉多國語言的
- **rigorous** 〔'rɪgərəs〕*adj.* 嚴格的；確實的
- **simplify** 〔'sɪmplə,faɪ〕*v.* 使單純；簡化
- *talk is cheap* 作不到卻說得出口
- *traditional form* 傳統的形式
- **visa** 〔'vizə〕*v.,n.* 簽證

✦ Folk Crafts / 民俗手工藝品

Q : I would like to buy some native *folk crafts*. Where can I buy them in Taipei？我要買一些本地的**民俗手工藝品**。在台北，哪裏我可以買到？

A : You could buy them almost anywhere here, but the best place you can go to is *the Taiwan Crafts Center*. It started business in 1984 and is located in downtown Taipei. All the products you'll see there have passed through a committee of experts, who check for quality and design. They even have an ***international delivery service***. The products displayed there include lanterns, stone carvings, bronzes, sculptures, crystalware, jade, wood carvings, furniture, dolls and other toys, embroidery, bambooware, assorted jewelry and handbags made of horsehair. You can go there every day except on Monday.

在這裏幾乎任何地方，你都可以買到，不過你最好是到**台灣手工藝中心**去買。它在一九八四年，開始營業，座落在台北的商業區。你在那裏所看到的所有產品，都經過專家所組成的委員會，來加以品質檢查和設計。他們甚至有**國際送貨服務**。那裏展示的產品包括有燈籠、石刻、青銅器、雕塑品、水晶器皿、玉器、木刻、傢俱、洋娃娃和其他玩具、刺繡、竹器，各式各樣的珠寶和馬鬃製的手提袋。每天你都可以去那裏買，星期一除外。

Chapter 7
BASIC
CONVERSATION

接待外賓基礎會話

At the Airport
接　機

Dialog 1

A : Excuse me. Are you Mr. Crown?

B : Yes, I am.

A : I am Lin from Taiwan Travel Agency. *I am your tour guide.*

B : Oh, I see.

A : 恕我冒昧。你是克勞恩先生嗎？

B : 是的。

A : 我是臺灣旅行社的林。**你的導遊。**

B : 喔，我知道了。

≪ Exercise ≫

1. Are you | Mr. Crown? / Miss Coxhead? / Mrs. Wegner?　　你是 | 克勞恩先生嗎？ / 卡克斯海德小姐？ / 偉格納太太？

2. I am | Lin / Cheng / Wang | from | Taiwan Travel Agency. / World Travel Agency. / Taipei.　　我是 | 臺灣旅行社的林。 / 世界旅行社的陳。 / 從台北來的王。

Dialog 2

A : Are you from World Travel Agency?

B : Yes.

A : I am the head of this tour group. My name is Kenny Wegner.

A : 你是世界旅行社的人嗎？

B : 是的。

A : 我是這個旅行團的領隊。我叫肯尼・偉格納。

B : Oh, are you? *How do you do*? My name is Johnson Ho. *I'm glad to meet you.*

B：哦，是你啊？**你好**，我是何強生。**很高興認識你。**

A : I'm glad to meet you, too.

A：彼此，彼此。

≪ Exercise ≫ ────────────

1. I am
| a head of this group. |
| a captain of the team. |
| a leader of the party. |

我是
| 這個團的領隊。 |
| 這個隊的隊長。 |
| 這個團體的領袖。 |

2. I am
| glad to |
| happy |
| pleased |
meet you.

我很
| 高興 |
| 高興 |
| 榮幸 |
認識你。

Dialog 3

A : Hi, Jack. Welcome to Taiwan.

A：嗨，傑克。歡迎到臺灣來。

B : Hello, John. *How have you been*?

B：嗨，約翰。**近來如何？**

A : I've been fine. *How about you*?

A：我很好。**你呢？**

B : I've been fine, too.

B：我也很好。

≪ Exercise ≫ ────────────

1. How
| have you been? |
| are you? |
| are you doing? |

你
| 近來如何？ |
| 好嗎？ |
| 好嗎？ |

2. I've been fine.
| How about you? |
| And you? |

我很好。
| 你呢？ |
| 你呢？ |

TAIWAN TALK 63 Getting Transportation to the Hotel
找交通工具到旅館

Dialog 1

A : How do we go to the hotel ?　　A：我們怎麼去旅館？

B : Let's go by *limousine*.　　B：我們搭**大型豪華巴士**去吧。

A : O.K.　How much does it cost ?　A：好的。多少錢？

B : $ 400.　　B：四百元。

≪ Exercise ≫

1. How do we 　go to the hotel ?　　我們怎麼　去旅館？
　　　　　　　get to the hotel?　　　　　　　到旅館？

What do we take to go to the hotel ? 我們搭什麼到旅館？

2. Let's go 　by limousine.　　我們搭　大型豪華巴士　去吧。
　　　　　　by bus.　　　　　　　巴士
　　　　　　by taxi.　　　　　　　計程車

Dialog 2

A : Where can I get a taxi ?　　A：我可以在哪兒搭計程車？

B : *Right over there*.　　B：**就在那兒**。

A : How long does it take to get　A：到希爾頓飯店要花多久時
　　to the Hilton Hotel ?　　　　間？

B : It takes about one hour.　　B：大約一小時。

** limousine〔,lımə'zin〕*n.*（接送旅客於機場、市區間的）大型豪華巴士

≪ Exercise ≫────────────

1. Where can I get | a taxi ?
                   | a bus ?
                   | a limousine ?

我可以在哪兒搭 | 計程車 ?
             | 巴士 ?
             | 大型豪華巴士 ?

2. How long does it take to get | to the King Hotel ?
                                | the Queen Hotel ?
                                | from the airport to the hotel ?

到國王飯店 | 要花多久時間 ?
到皇后飯店 |
從機場到旅館 |

Dialog 3

A : How do we get to the hotel ?　　A：我們怎麼去旅館 ?

B : *A bus is waiting for all of you.*　　B：一輛巴士正等候諸位呢!

A : That's good. We are 35 people　　A：那很好。我們總共有三十
　　 (persons) all together.　　　　　　五人。

B : The bus is big enough.　　　　B：巴士夠大的。

≪ Exercise ≫────────────

1. A bus is waiting for all of you. 一輛巴士正等候諸位了。
   A taxi has been waiting for all of you. 一輛計程車已經在等候諸位了。

2. The bus | is big enough.
           | has enough seats for everyone.
           | room for everyone.

巴士 | 夠大
     | 有足夠的座位容納每個人。
     | 有足夠的空間容納每個人。

 **64** *On the Way to the Hotel*

去旅館途中

Dialog 1

A : Is this your first time to visit Taiwan ?

B : Yes, I'm so excited.

A : *You look so.*

B : This will be a good trip.

A : 這是你第一次來臺灣觀光嗎？

B : 是的，我好興奮。

A : 看樣子也是。

B : 這將是一次美好的旅行。

≪ Exercise ≫

1. Is this your first time to visit Taiwan？這是你第一次來臺灣觀光嗎？
   Have you been to Taiwan before？你以前到過臺灣嗎？
   Have you visited Taiwan before？你以前來臺灣觀光過嗎？

2. This will be a | good / nice | trip.　　這將是一次 | 美好 / 愉快 | 的旅行

   I will have a good time.　　我會玩得很愉快。

Dialog 2

A : *How was your flight* ?

B : Not bad, but I couldn't sleep well.

A : I understand that. I had the same experience, too.

B : Now, shall we go ?

A : 旅途愉快嗎？

B : 不壞，但我卻睡不好。

A : 我了解那種滋味。我也有過同樣的經驗。

B : 現在，我們可以走了嗎？

≪ **Exercise** ≫————————

1. How was your | flight ? / trip? / guide ? |　旅途 / 旅行 / 導遊 | 如何？

2. Now, shall we | go ? / leave ? / take off ? |　現在，我們能 | 走了 / 動身 / 出發 | 吧？

Dialog 3

A : What is our hotel ?　　A：我們住哪家旅館？

B : Paradise.　　B：樂園。

A : I've never heard of it before. Where is it ?　　A：我從未聽說過。是在哪兒？

B : It's a ***brand-new*** hotel in Taipei.　　B：那是台北一家**全新的**旅館。

A : That sounds good.　　A：聽起來不錯。

≪ **Exercise** ≫————————

1. Where | is it ? / is it located ? |　是 | 在哪兒？ / 位於哪兒？ |
How far is it ?　　有多遠？

2. It's | a brand-new / a very old / a beautiful | hotel.　　它是 | 最新的 / 非常老舊的 / 很美的 | 旅館。

 **Checking in at the Hotel**

辦住旅館手續

Dialog 1

A： May I help you？

B： Yes. My name is Kenny Wegner. World Travel Agency *made a reservation for* me from Chicago.

A： Wait a minute, please. Yes. We have your reservation.

B： That's good.

A： 我能爲你效勞嗎？

B： 是的。我是肯尼・偉格納。 世界旅行社從芝加哥替我 **預訂**了房間。

A： 請稍待。是的，我們有你 的預訂。

B： 那很好。

≪**Exercise**≫

1. May I help you？ 我能爲你效勞嗎？
2. Can I help you？ 我能爲你效勞嗎？
   What can I do for you？ 有什麼可以效勞的？

2. World Travel Agency

| made a reservation for me. |
| booked a room for me. |
| got a room for me. |

世界旅行社替我 | 預訂 / 預訂了 / 訂了 | 房間。

Dialog 2

A： Excuse me. I am the tour conductor of this tour. Would you *check the reservation of* this tour？

A： 恕我冒昧，我是這次旅行 的導遊。請你**查對**一下這 次旅行的**預約**好嗎？

B： What is the name of the tour?　B： 旅行名稱是什麼？

A： Oriental Tour.　A： 東方之旅。

B： Oh, Yes. We surely have the reservation. You are supposed to stay here for five days. Is that right?　B： 哦，是的。我們的確有這個預約。你們預計在此停留五天。對嗎？

A： Yes.　A： 對。

≪ **Exercise** ≫────────────

1. Would you | check our reservation?
 it for me, please?
 look it up for me, please? | 請你 | 查對一下我們的預約
 替我查對一下
 替我查查看 | 好嗎？

2. You are supposed to stay here for | five days.
 six days.
 a week. | 你們預計在此停留 | 五天。
 六天。
 一周。

Getting Information for Sightseeing
詢問觀光資料

66

Dialog 1

A: Excuse me. I'd like to go *sightseeing*. Where can I get information for that?

B: Oh, you'd better talk to that gentleman sitting over there.

A: O.K.

A: 恕我冒昧。我想去**觀光**。我可以在哪兒獲得這類資料？

B: 喔，你最好和坐在那兒的先生談談。

A: 好的。

≪ Exercise ≫

1. I'd like to

| go sightseeing. |
| take a trip. |
| go on a tour. |

我想去

| 觀光。 |
| 旅行。 |
| 遊覽。 |

2. You'd better

| talk to that gentleman. |
| ask that gentleman. |
| consult with that lady. |

你最好

| 和那位先生談談。 |
| 問那位先生。 |
| 請敎那位女士。 |

Dialog 2

A: I want to take a tour tonight. Which one do you suggest?

B: Well, we have three different night tours. I would recommend you to take this " Imperial Tour. "

A: 我今晚想去遊覽。你建議哪一項？

B: 嗯，我們有三種不同的夜遊。我推薦你這項「帝王之旅」。

A： How much does it cost？　　A： 多少錢呢？

B： ＄800 dollars, sir, including
　　 dinner.

B： 八百元，先生，包括晚餐。

A： *That sounds good*. I'll take it.　　A： **聽起來不錯**。就這項吧！

≪ **Exercise** ≫────────────

1. I would │ recommend you to │ take this "Imperial Tour."
　　　　　│ advise
　　　　　│ suggest（that）you

　　我 │ 推薦 │ 你這項「帝王之旅」。
　　　 │ 建議
　　　 │ 建議

2. That │ sounds good.　　　　│ 聽起來不錯。
　　　　│ 　　　interesting.　│ 聽起來很有趣。
　　　　│ looks interesting.　│ 看起來很有趣。

Dialog 3

A： Do you have a sightseeing
　　 tour tonight?

A： 你們今晚有觀光旅行嗎？

B： Sure, we do. What kind of
　　 tour would you like, sir?

B： 當然有。先生，你喜歡哪
　　 一種旅行？

A： I want to see Taiwan tradi-
　　 tional things.

A： 我想看看臺灣傳統的事物。

B： Oh, then this tour must be
　　 good. You can see *folk arts
　　 and skills*.

B： 哦，那麼，這個旅行一定
　　 很棒。你會看到**民俗技藝**。

A : That's good. How much is it?

A : 那很好。多少錢呢?

B : 3,000 NT. Please be back here at 6:00 p.m. Your guide will come to pick you up then.

B : 台幣三千元。請在六點時回到這兒。你的導遊會在那時來接你。

≪ Exercise ≫

1. What kind of | tour / food / movie | do you like, sir? 先生,你喜歡哪一種 | 旅行? / 食物? / 電影? |

2. This | tour / idea / plan | must be | good. / nice. | 這個 | 旅行 / 主意 / 計畫 | 一定 | 很棒。|

TAIWAN TALK 67 *Going out for Shopping*
外出逛街購物

Dialog 1

A : Excuse me. *Where is the nearest department store?*

A : 恕我冒昧。最近的百貨公司在哪裏?

B : Turn left after going out the door. Turn left again at the first corner and walk straight five blocks. You can see the Far East Department Store on your left side.

B : 走出門後左轉。在第一個轉角處再左轉,並直走過五條街。在你左側就是遠東百貨公司。

A : Thank you.

A : 謝謝。

≪ **Exercise** ≫ ─────────────────

1. Turn | left | after going out the door. | 走出門後左轉。
　　　　| right | | 走出門後右轉。
　　　　| left | at the corner of Main Street. | 在大街轉角處左轉。

2. Walk | straight | five blocks. | 直 | 走五條街。
　　　　| up | | 往上 |
　　　　| down | | 往下 |

Dialog 2

A : Is there any ***duty free shop*** around here?

A : 附近有任何**免稅店嗎**？

B : Yes, just three blocks away down there, next to a Chinese restaurant.

B : 有的，就在從那兒走下去三條街的地方，在中國餐館隔壁。

A : What is the name of the shop?

A : 店名是什麼？

B : It's called "The International Shopping Center."

B : 叫做「國際購物中心」。

≪ **Exercise** ≫ ─────────────────

1. Is there | any duty free shop around here?
　　　　　| any second hand shop
　　　　　| any pawnshop

附近有任何 | 免稅商店 | 嗎？
　　　　　| 舊貨店 |
　　　　　| 當舖 |

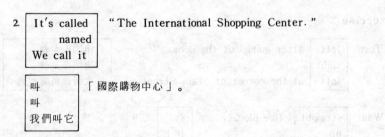

2. It's called
   named
   We call it
   "The International Shopping Center."

叫
叫
我們叫它
「國際購物中心」。

Dialog 3

A: *Could you tell me how to get to* the Far East Department Store?

A: 請問到遠東百貨公司怎麼走？

B: I think you'd better take a subway.

B: 我想你最好搭地下鐵。

A: Which line should I take?

A: 應搭乘哪條路線呢？

B: You should take the Taipei line, the blue train.

B: 你應搭臺北線，藍色的火車身。

≪ Exercise ≫

1. Could   you tell me   how to get to   the Far East Department Store?
   Will   the way to get to

請問到遠東百貨公司怎麼走？

2. You should take   the Taipei line.   你應該搭   台北線。
                      a bus.   公車。
                      a taxi.   計程車。

Changing the Itinerary
變更行程

Dialog 1

A : *Can I request to change our itinerary?*

B : Yes, you can if you want to. How do you want to change it?

A : Well, I want to change Monday's schedule, from shopping to free time. Because we have shopping another day.

B : O.K. It's all right with us.

A：我能要求變更行程嗎？

B：可以的，如果你想的話。你想如何變更呢？

A：嗯，我想把星期一的時間表改掉，把購物改成自由活動。因為，我們另一天也有購物。

B：好的。對我們來說，沒問題。

≪ Exercise ≫

1. Yes, you | can if you want to. / may / could |

可以的，如果你想的話。

2. It's | all right with us. / O.K. / fine. |

對我們來說，沒問題。

Dialog 2

A : Do you mind changing your itinerary?

A：你介意變更行程嗎？

B： Well, *it depends on how you change it*.

B：嗯，**看你如何變更而定。**

A： We want you to go to see Chinese opera instead of puppetry. We have some tickets available.

A：我們想請你去看國劇，而不是去看布袋戲。因為我們有些票，可以利用。

B： That's fine.

B：好的。

≪ **Exercise** ≫────────

1. It depends on

| how you change it. |
| how it is changed. |
| what is changed. |

視

| 你如何變更 |
| 如何變更 |
| 改成什麼 |

而定。

2. We have some

| tickets |
| rooms |
| seats |

available.

我們有些

| 票 |
| 空房間 |
| 空座位 |

可以利用。

Dialog 3

A： How do you suggest to change our itinerary?

A：你建議我們的行程如何變?

B： We want to switch the schedule for Monday and Tuesday. *Do you mind that*?

B：我們想要將星期一和星期二的時間表互換。**你介意嗎?**

A： Not at all. I think it's better.

A：一點也不。我想這樣會更好。

≪ Exercise ≫────────────────

1. Do you mind | that ?
changing it ?
doing so ? | 你介意 | 嗎 ?
變更它嗎 ?
如此做嗎 ?

2. | Not at all.
Of course not.
No, I don't. | I think it's better. | 一點兒也不,
當然不啦 !
不,我不介意, | 我想這樣更好。

 **TAIWAN TALK 69** *Confirmation of the Schedule*
確認預定計劃

Dialog 1

A : Hello. I want to make sure
of tomorrow's *schedule*.

A : 嗨 ,我想確定一下明天的
預定計劃。

B : Yes.

B : 好的 。

A : What time does our bus come
to pick us up?

A : 我們的巴士幾點來接我們
呢 ?

B : It's supposed to be there at
7:30 a.m..

B : 應該是在早上七點半時 ,
抵達那兒 。

≪ Exercise ≫────────────────

1. I want to | make sure of tomorrow's schedule.
confirm
confirm the changed schedule.

我想 | 確定一下明天的預定計劃表 。
確認一下
確認一下變更的預定計劃表 。

2. What time does our bus

come to pick us up？
leave the hotel？
arrive at the hotel？

我們的巴士幾點

來接我們呢？
離開旅館？
抵達旅館？

Dialog 2

A： Do we have any changes in our schedule？

B： Yes. Your bus won't arrive at the hotel at 7:30, because traffic might be heavy tomorrow.

A： So, what time will it be here？

B： *We made it later*. It'll be there by 8:00 a.m.

A： 我們的預定計劃表有任何更動嗎？

B： 有的。你們的巴士在七點半時不會抵達旅館，因為明天的交通可能會很繁重。

A： 那麼，巴士幾點會到這兒來呢？

B： **會稍後到**。它將在早上八點前到那兒。

≪ Exercise ≫————————

1. Traffic might be

heavy.
busy.
tied up.

交通可能會很

繁重。
繁忙。
阻塞。

2. We made it

later.
earlier.
on time.

令

稍後	到。
提早	
準時	

Dialog 3

A : Hello. I heard our schedule changed.

B : 喂 。聽說我們的預定計劃表改變了 。

B : Yes. Tomorrow, you are supposed to go to eat beef noodles, but it has been canceled. Instead, you are going to eat steak.

B : 是的 。你們明天本來應該去嚐嚐牛肉麵 ，但已經被取消了 。你們反而是要去吃牛排 。

A : That's fine. I'm sure everybody will *enjoy it*.

A : 那很好 。我確信每個人都會**喜歡**的 。

B : I think so, too.

B : 我也是這麼想 。

≪ Exercise ≫

1. It has been
canceled.	已經	取消了 。
called off.		取消了 。
postponed.		延期了 。

2. I'm sure everybody will enjoy it. 我確信每個人都會喜歡 。
   I hope everybody will enjoy it. 我希望每個人都會喜歡 。
   I'm sure everybody will have a good time. 我確信每個人都會玩得很愉快 。

 **70** *Seeing off at the Airport*

機場送行

Dialog 1

A: Have you got a ticket for the flight?

A: 你買好機票嗎？

B: Yes. Thank you for everything you have done for me.

B: 是的。謝謝你爲我所做的一切事情。

A: That's all right. It's my pleasure.

A: 不要客氣。這是我的榮幸。

B: I had a very good time.

B: 我玩得很愉快。

A: *I'm glad to hear that*.

A: **我很高興聽到你這麼説。**

≪ Exercise ≫

1. Thank you for

| everything you have done for me. |
| your warm hospitality. |
| the nice time. |

謝謝你

| 爲我所做的一切事情。 |
| 熱誠的招待。 |
| 這段愉快的時光。 |

2.

| I had a very good time. |
| stay. |
| I enjoyed it myself very much. |

| 我玩得很愉快。 |
| 我這次停留很愉快。 |
| 我玩得十分愉快。 |

Dialog 2

A： Have you bought *souvenirs* for your wife and son?

A： 你替太太和兒子買**紀念品**了嗎？

B： Sure. I've bought a dress for my wife, and a sword for my boy.

B： 當然。我替太太買了件衣服，替兒子買了把劍。

A： You must be a good husband and daddy for them.

A： 對他們來說，你一定是好丈夫、好爸爸。

B： I hope I am.

B： 我希望是。

A： Now, are you ready?

A： 現在，你準備好了嗎？

≪ Exercise ≫

1. I've bought

| a dress for my wife. |
| a doll for my daughter. |
| a pipe for myself. |

我替

太太	買了	件衣服。
女兒		個洋娃娃。
自己		根煙斗。

2. I hope I am a good

| husband. |
| teacher. |
| student. |

我希望我是個好

| 丈夫。 |
| 老師。 |
| 學生。 |

Dialog 3

A： Which flight will you take?

A： 你搭哪班飛機？

B： CAL 001. Everybody looks to have had a good time and we thank you.

B： 中華航空公司的○○一號班機。每個人似乎都玩得很愉快，謝謝你。

A： I hope you've had a memorable trip.

A： 我希望你有個值得回憶的旅行。

B：Taiwan was beautiful and the people are nice. I want to come back here again.

B：臺灣很美，人民也都很好。 我想再來一趟。

A：*Take care*

A：保重（再見）。

B：Good bye.

B：再見。

≪ Exercise ≫

1. Which flight

will you take?
are you going to take?
is yours?

你搭　哪班飛機？
要搭
你搭哪一個班次？

2.

Take care.
Be careful.
Watch out for yourself.

保重。
小心。
你自己要保重。

心得筆記欄

全國最完整的文法書 ☆☆☆

文 法 寶 典

▶ **劉 毅 編著**

　　這是一套想學好英文的人必備的工具書，作者積多年豐富的教學經驗，針對大家所不了解和最容易犯錯的地方，編寫成一套完整的文法書。

　　本書編排方式與眾不同，首先給讀者整體的概念，再詳述文法中的細節部分，內容十分完整。文法說明以圖表為中心，一目了然，並且務求深入淺出。無論您在考試中或其他書中所遇到的任何不了解的問題，或是您感到最煩惱的文法問題，查閱**文法寶典**均可迎刃而解。例如：哪些副詞可修飾名詞或代名詞？(P.228)；什麼是介副詞？(P.543)；那些名詞可以當副詞用？(P.100)；倒裝句(P.629)、省略句(P.644)等特殊構句，為什麼倒裝？為什麼省略？原來的句子是什麼樣子？在**文法寶典**裏都有詳盡的說明。

　　例如，有人學了**觀念錯誤的**「假設法現在式」的公式，

> If＋現在式動詞……，主詞＋shall（will, may, can）＋原形動詞

只會造：If it rains, I will stay at home.

而不敢造：If you *are* right, I *am* wrong.

　　　　　If I *said* that, I *was* mistaken.

　　　　（If 子句不一定用在假設法，也可表示條件子句的直說法。）

可見如果學文法不求徹底了解，反而成為學習英文的絆腳石，對於這些易出錯的地方，我們都特別加以說明（詳見 P.356）。

　　文法寶典每冊均附有練習，只要讀完本書、做完練習，您必定信心十足，大幅提高對英文的興趣與實力。

◉ **全套五冊，售價900元。市面不售，請直接向本公司購買。**

東海書局
大新書局
奇奇書局
全國優良圖
書展藍源德
好學生書局
●中壢●
立德書局
文明書局
文化書局
貞德書局
建宏書局
博士書局
奇奇書局
大學書局
●新竹●
大學書局
昇大書局
六藝出版社
竹一書局
仁文書局
學府書局
文華書局
黎明書局
文國書局
金鼎獎書局
大新書局
文山書局
弘文書局
德興書局
學風書局
泰昌書局
滋朗書局
排行榜書局
光南書局
大華書報社
●苗栗●
益文書局
芙華書局
建國書局
文華書局
●基隆●
文粹書局
育德書局

自立書局
明德書局
中興書局
文隆書局
建國書局
文豐書局
●台中市●
宏明書局
曉園出版社
台中門市
滄海書局
大學圖書
供應社
逢甲書局
聯經出版社
中央書局
大眾書局
新大方書局
中華書局
文軒書局
柏林書局
亞勝補習班
文化書城
三民書局
台一書局
興大書局
興大書齋
興文書局
正文書局
新能書局
新學友學局
全文書局
國鼎書局
國寶書局
華文書局
建國書局
汗牛書屋
享聲唱片行
華中書局
逢甲大學
諾貝爾書局
中部書報社
中一書局
明道書局

振文書局
中台一專
盛文書局
●台中縣●
三民書局
建成書局
欣欣唱片行
大千書局
中一書局
明道書局
●彰化●
復文書局
東門書局
新新書局
台聯書局
時代書局
成功書局
世界書局
來來書局
翰林書局
一新書局
中山書局
文明書局
●雲林●
建中書局
大山書局
文芳書局
國光書局
良昌書局
三民書局
●嘉義市●
文豐書局
慶隆盛書局
義豐書局
志成書局
大漢書局
書苑庭書局
學英公司
天才書局
學英書局
光南書局
嘉聯書報社
●嘉義縣●
建成書局

●台南縣●
全勝書局
博大書局
第一書局
南一書局
柳營書局
●台南市●
欣欣文化社
光南唱片行
嘉南書社
第一書局
東華書局
成功大學
書　局　部
成大書城
文山書局
孟子書局
大友書局
松文書局
盛文書局
台南書局
日勝書局
旭日書局
南台圖書
公　　司
金寶書局
船塢書坊
南一書局
大統唱片行
國正書局
源文書局
永茂書報社
天才書局
●高雄縣●
延平書局
欣良書局
大岡山書城
時代書局
鳳山大書城
遠東大書城
天下書局
杏綱書局
統一書局
百科書局

志成書局
光遠書局
●高雄市●
高雄書報社
宏昇書局
理想書局
高文堂書局
松柏書局
三民書局
光南書局
國鼎書局
文英書局
黎明書局
光明書局
前程書局
労行書局
登文書局
青山外語
補　習　班
六合書局
美新書局
朝代書局
意文書局
地　下　街
文化廣場
大立百貨公
司圖書部
大統百貨公
司圖書部
黎明文化
有前書局
建工書局
鐘樓書局
青年書局
瓊林書局
大學城書局
引想力書局
永大書局
杏莊書局
儒林書局
雄大書局
復文書局
致遠書局
明仁書局

宏亞書局
瀚文書局
天祥書局
廣文書局
楊氏書局
慈珊書局
盛文書局
光　　統
圖書百貨
愛偉書局
●屏東●
復文書局
建利書局
百成書局
新星書局
百科書局
屏東書城
屏東唱片行
英格文教社
賢明書局
大古今書局
屏東農專
圖　書　部
順時書局
百順書局

Editorial Staff

- 企劃・編著 / 葉淑霞
- 英文撰稿
  Bruce S. Stewart・Thomas Chung
  Edward C. Yulo・John C. Didier
- 校訂
  劉　毅・陳淑靜・謝靜慧・武藍蕙・湯碧秋
  王慈嫻・林美伶・陸　妙・王怡華・蔡琇瑩
- 校閱
  Larry J. Marx・Lois M. Findler
  John H. Voelker・Keith Gaunt
- 封面設計 / 張鳳儀
- 攝影・版面設計 / 張鳳儀・唐　旻
- 完稿 / 黃新家・黃春蓮・吳正順
- 打字
  黃淑貞・倪秀梅・蘇淑玲・吳秋香
  洪桂美・徐湘君・
- 校對
  王慶銘・林韶慧・葉美利・陳瑠琍・陳佳麗
  李南施・謝靜芳・吳濱伶・莊心怡

國立中央圖書館出版品預行編目資料

英文介紹台灣 / 葉淑霞編著　　　--二版一刷--

　〔台北市〕：學習發行；

　〔台北市〕：紅螞蟻總經銷，1994〔民 83〕

　　面；公分

　　ISBN 957-519-009-2（平裝）

　1. 英國語言—讀本　　　2. 臺灣—描述與遊記

805.18　　　　　　　　　　　　　　83011137

英語介紹台灣

編　　　著／葉　淑　霞

發　行　所／學習出版有限公司　　　☎ (02) 2704-5525

郵　撥　帳　號／0512727-2 學習出版社帳戶

登　記　證／局版台業 2179 號

印　刷　所／裕強彩色印刷有限公司

台 北 門 市／台北市許昌街 10 號 2 F　　☎ (02) 2331-4060・2331-9209

台 中 門 市／台中市綠川東街 32 號 8 F 23 室　　☎ (04) 2223-2838

台灣總經銷／紅螞蟻圖書有限公司　　☎ (02) 2795-3656

美國總經銷／Evergreen Book Store　　☎ (818) 2813622

本公司網址　www.learnbook.com.tw

電 子 郵 件　learnbook@learnbook.com.tw

售價：新台幣一百八十元正

2003 年 11 月 1 日二版三刷

ISBN 957-519-009-2